Grandmother's
SEWING BOX

by
Carol Ann Tardiff

ISBN 0-7414-4117-9

Cover credit: Katie Tardiff

Editing credit: Eleanor Burley

Scripture quotations contained herein are from the New Revised Standard Version Bible. Copyright © 1989, by the Division of Christian Education of the National Council of the Churches of Christ in the U.S.A., and are used by permission. All rights reserved.

Published by:

PUBLISHING.COM

1094 New DeHaven Street, Suite 100
West Conshohocken, PA 19428-2713
Info@buybooksontheweb.com
www.buybooksontheweb.com
Toll-free (877) BUY BOOK
Local Phone (610) 941-9999
Fax (610) 941-9959

Printed in the United States of America

Printed on Recycled Paper

Published July 2007

Consecration:
To Jesus Christ
– my Lord, my God and my all –
and to Mother Mary

Dedication:
To my sisters – Ev, Ele and Barb –
who are my best friends,

and to Ed Sheerin (1927-2007)
who will always be, for me and many others,
the perfect example of the Legion spirit

Note: In order not to disrupt the continuity of the story,
there are no footnotes;
however, additional information is given at the end of the book.

The joy born of love of God enables us to see the world
from an entirely different point of view.
Before, when shackled to the ego, we were cooped up
within the narrow walls of space and time.

But once the chains are broken,
one falls heir to immensities beyond all telling.

Then we find our greatest joys
not in the things we cling to, but in what we surrender;
not in the asking for anything, but in the giving of something;
not in what others can do for us,
but in what we can do for others.

Archbishop Fulton J. Sheen
(1895 – 1979)

1

It all began with a knock at the door.

It was the end of May, shortly before my seventeenth birthday. I remember it was May because of the awful odor drifting through the window from the large ailanthus tree in the alley. Some people call the ailanthus the "tree of heaven" due to its ability to grow where no other self-respecting tree would. I ended up owing my life to that tree, so maybe heaven really did have something to do with it. But there was nothing heavenly about its scent when it bloomed and, that year, the hot weather had caused it to bloom early. It was a sure sign that summer with all its heat had arrived to stay.

Our apartment had no air conditioning, so I was sprawled on the old sofa trying to catch a breeze from a fan rotating on the floor. With headphones on, I leafed listlessly through a fashion magazine with one hand while waving the other with its freshly-applied nail polish in the muggy air.

"TONY!" I heard my name yelled when the music in my ears paused a few seconds between songs. "Would you get your lazy—"

The expletive following was muffled by another blast of music in my ears. I glanced over at my older sister where she was slumped in a living room chair. With its stuffing poking through rips in the stained fabric, the chair had seen better days. Then again, so had my sister. Jen was wearing a jogging suit—although that particular outfit's jogging days were long past—and her own stuffing was bursting through the seams. Face puffy, a can of beer in hand, she stared blearily at the TV.

I didn't bother removing my headphones to ask her to repeat what she said. It was probably the same mantra I heard with wearisome regularity—"Tony, do the dishes!" "Tony, pick up your junk!" A person didn't need to look very far to realize it would take more than washing a sinkful of dishes or straightening my things to make our place look presentable. Why should I bother? After a few more beers she would never remember what she wanted me to do anyway.

I blew on my fingernails, punched up the volume on my CD player and reached for the bottle of polish. Out of the corner of my eye, I saw Jen haul herself out of the chair. Her lips were flapping but I didn't hear a word of what she said. She wasn't coming my way. That was all I cared about.

She made her way unsteadily to the door and yanked it open. I expected to see Melvin, who lived in the apartment directly across from us. His mouth pursed like a shriveled prune, he would probably poke a bony finger at my sister and scold her to turn down the TV, grumbling that he couldn't sleep a wink with all the noise. A fussy old man, that Melvin. Too bad he had the misfortune of living in that run-down building with its run-down tenants, including us.

But it wasn't Melvin or anyone else I recognized. When Jen flung the door open, the two people standing there looked surprised. Maybe they thought no one had heard them knocking with the TV blaring so loudly. The man, dressed nicely but casually on that steamy day, was silver-haired and slender. He towered over his female companion who wore a flowered dress with a bright blue scarf knotted around her head.

They looked rather odd together—the old, white guy and the much younger black woman. They probably weren't husband and wife. And why were they at our door? For a minute I had the silly thought that they were lost and needed directions. But that really *was* silly, since who would come all the way up to the third floor of an apartment building, especially one as inhospitable as ours, simply to ask directions?

Although I watched them curiously as they spoke with my sister, I wasn't curious enough to turn off my music. Jen had propped herself against the doorway like she couldn't stand on her own. Maybe she couldn't. I wasn't sure just how many beers she had already put away.

As she closed the door and stumbled back to her chair, I pulled a headphone away from my ear long enough to ask, "Who were those people?"

2

"They're from a churr…ch."

"What'd they want?"

"They wanna come back—"

"What for?"

She picked up the remote and flipped the channel. "Dunno. Told 'em I didn't care."

Letting the headphone snap back, I concentrated on the task of finishing my nails. I didn't have the slightest interest in anyone from any church. I was merely surprised my sister hadn't told them where to get off.

The next day was Memorial Day and there was no school. On most days, Jen would pick up a sub or pizza on her way home from work. She expected me to do my homework weekdays after school, and I was pretty good at pretending to do it so she wouldn't ask me to make dinner. But since I wasn't in class that day, dinner would be my job. I needed to see what I could dig up in our kitchen.

Although we called the room with the fridge and stove "the kitchen," only in your worst nightmares could you imagine anything like that one. The chipped, Formica-topped counter, piled high with outdated newspapers and crumpled receipts, also sported stale donuts in crushed cartons, burnt pieces of toast and half-empty glasses with cigarette ashes floating in them. Empty beer cans and pop bottles littered every available horizontal surface. Just trying to navigate your way through the overflowing wastebaskets and rubbish on the floor could turn into your big accomplishment for the day.

The lone upper cabinet was stuffed with a conglomeration of threadbare towels and multiple jars of instant coffee. The lower one contained dishwasher detergent for the dishwasher we didn't have, dusty collections of outdated canned goods and contorted plastic containers without lids. It wasn't long before I abandoned the quest to find anything edible in the kitchen and, instead, went searching for the shopping bags I knew were scattered around the living room. In one of the bags I came upon a box of macaroni and cheese, purchased sometime in the past year and never seen again.

"A pan, a pan…my kingdom for a pan," I muttered dramatically. I eyed a stack of old, dented pots, but realized every one of them was either too small or its handle in danger of coming

3

off. I was pointedly ignoring the saucepan sitting on the stove. It had been there at least a week and contained the mummified remains of chili. Finally, though, I had to resign myself to using that very pan since it was the only one large enough. I blazed a trail through the garbage on the floor, ran lukewarm water into the pan and tried to scrape it clean.

"Not too bad," Jen said that evening as we polished off the mac and cheese. Perhaps the chili I had been unable to scrape out of the pan added a subtle nuance of flavor. I decided not to mention it, though, as Jen was never in a good mood when she got home from work.

My sister hated her job and couldn't stand most of her co-workers. There were only a few—like Irene, an older woman who was pleasant to everyone—whom she regarded as tolerable. I couldn't see what was so bad about the supermarket where she worked, but I knew better than to tell her how lucky she was to have the job. I would have loved to have a job—any job. I was sick of school and bored with hanging around the apartment. But Jen wouldn't hear of me looking for work until summer. She said that it would take too much of my time, that I needed to concentrate on my schoolwork to keep my grades up. I wondered what she would say when she saw my next report card.

After supper, Jen announced she had a date and told me to do the dishes. I removed them from the table but didn't bother washing them. What were a few more dirty dishes lying around? Besides, the kitchen was too dark in the evening to try to do anything. The antiquated light fixtures flickered off whenever they felt like it—which was often. The entire building had a multitude of problems, but the electrical ones were what you tended to notice the most.

A familiar staccato knocking came at the door and I opened it.

"Jen!" I yelled to my sister in the bedroom getting changed. "Killer's here!"

Of course, his name wasn't really Killer. It was Max Keller, but I thought the nickname fit. I never could figure out what my sister saw in the hulking brute. He had to be at least forty, much too old for Jen who was twenty-three at the time. His graying hair was buzzed close to his head, and his belly cascaded over a gold-buckled belt which barely held up dangerously low-riding jeans. His T-shirt sleeves were rolled high on his shoulders.

If he was trying to show off his muscles or tattoos, or both, I wasn't impressed. If there was a good thing to be said about Killer, it was that the sheer size and meanness of him kept the other deadbeats away.

Holding a six-pack in one hand, Killer removed the cigarette from his lips and ground it into an overflowing ashtray on the endtable. Then he spit into the same ashtray. I grimaced and turned away in disgust. But I was grateful, at least, he wasn't shadowed that evening by his cousin, Gordy. *Him* I called "Weasel," as he was always slinking around, never saying much, his beady eyes darting over everything—most particularly over me. I tried to make myself scarce whenever he came over.

"Hey, kid, whatsup?" Killer grunted without as much as a glance in my direction.

My sister waltzed out of her room and flung her arms around his neck. "Hiya, Maxie!" she gushed. "Whaddya want to watch tonight?"

"You!"

Laughing uproariously at his wit, they tumbled onto the sofa and popped open their beers. Annoyed, I yanked my pillow out from behind them. It was bad enough they had commandeered the sofa, which was where I slept, but I knew they would spend half the night guzzling and nuzzling in front of the TV and the other half in Jen's bedroom.

"I'm going to Lee's," I yelled over the TV. Jen paid me little attention.

"Watch those hallways," was all she said.

2

Watch those hallways. I already knew that. Although it wasn't that late, the hall, with its ceiling lights broken, was already dark. I picked my way through the trash strewn about, but the kind of trash I worried most about wasn't the stuff on the floor. Luckily the only signs of life were several blaring radios and loud shouting coming from apartment 3F. Pretty typical night.

I hoisted my pillow like a shield and hurried down the stairs. When I reached the first landing, I heard a scream. It was followed by a crash—but I didn't wait around to dwell on it. In a place like ours, you learned quickly to mind your own business. I flew down the second flight, rounded a corner and pounded on the nearest door. It was opened by a tall, huskily-built woman with an upsweep of graying hair and a welcoming smile.

"Well, lookee who's here, Mama!" she called behind her. "We have a guest—Antonia's come to see us!"

The affectionate way she said "Antonia," with a broad inflection, almost made me despise my name a little less. I say *almost*, because I didn't care much for my given name, preferring the masculine-sounding "Tony." My sister called me Antonia only when she was mad at me.

"Hi, Lee," I said with a long, put-upon sigh, "can I spend the night?"

She ushered me inside without another word, knowing the query meant Jen was entertaining her boyfriend again. It wasn't the first time I had been an overnight guest at Leona's.

"Hello, Mama Lucy," I greeted the elderly lady seated at the kitchen table. When she grinned at me, her face became a wreath of mahogany wrinkles topped with a halo of white hair. She nodded vigorously and said how lovely it was to see me again.

Whether she remembered my name, though, or even knew who I was, was a matter for speculation.

"Mama and I were jes' fixin' to go to bed," Leona said. "You go right ahead and get the couch set for yourself."

In the linen closet I found a faded, flowered sheet. I didn't bother with a blanket, as the heat of the day still stalked the apartment. The overhead fan on the high ceiling stirred the air as I whipped the sheet onto the couch and collapsed onto it. I could hear Leona in the bedroom murmuring prayers with her mother.

She returned to the living room, switched off most of the lights and dropped into an easy chair. Rubbing her tired eyes, she inquired kindly how things were going with me and Jen. I said I was fine, school was all right and, no, Jen hadn't gotten rid of that loser of a boyfriend yet.

Leona shook her head. "I know your sister can do better for herself. That guy's trouble and he's jes' usin' her."

"I think it's mutual," I said.

"Wasn't her last boyfriend even older than this fella?"

Frowning at the unpleasant memory, I nodded. There was silence as she pondered for a time. At last she asked, "Antonia, how old was Jennifer when she lost her daddy?"

I had to think hard. "I don't know. Maybe about three."

Silent again, Leona dabbed perspiration from her face with a lace-edged handkerchief while the fan whirred valiantly in its mission to provide relief. When nothing else was forthcoming, I said, "You don't think *that* has anything to do with her choice of boyfriends, do you? Jen's just stupid, that's all. Besides, I lost my father, too, but you don't see me running after boys—or old men."

"You and your sister are very different," Leona replied. "You got a good head on your shoulders, Antonia. But don't be too hard on her. As the sayin' goes, you haven't walked in her shoes."

With a prolonged sigh, she heaved herself out of the chair.

"Jes' remember, Antonia, God has a better plan for you and Jennifer. Why don't you pray and ask him for help?"

For a long moment, I stared at her. I didn't know much about God, but it was obvious he wasn't doing a whole lot to help Leona. Lee worked part-time as an aide at a nursing home and sometimes helped another woman clean office buildings. It couldn't have been easy at her age, and it was even more difficult when she had to find someone to keep an eye on Mama. Usually she took her mother to the nursing home with her, where Mama could play bingo or watch TV with the residents. But sometimes she'd bring Mama up to our place and pay Jen or me to watch her for the day.

Leona's faith in God was obvious. So why was she stuck living there in that hellhole of a building, working her fingers to the bone every day? Yet I didn't want to point that out to the one person on earth who would take me in on a moment's notice.

"Well," I answered lightly, "God would have a lot of work to do to help *us*!"

She smiled. "G' night, Antonia."

As she disappeared into her bedroom, I punched my pillow and flipped it over in search of a cool spot. I had only stated the obvious. God would have an *awful* lot of work to do.

"Be home by seven!"

My sister swayed on her feet. She was hung over, but it didn't stop her from sniping at me the next morning. Glaring at her, I shot back a snide reply.

"I will if I want to!"

"You'd better! Or I'll beat your—"

"Shut up! You can't tell me what to do! You're not my mother!"

I was livid. I had tossed and turned through the sweltering night and then, when I got back home, I couldn't find anything. Jen had swept all my clothes off the end of the sofa—the only place I had to keep them—and thrown them onto the piles of junk lying everywhere.

Anyway, it was true. She wasn't my mother. She wasn't even my sister, really. Jen and I were only half-sisters. Same mother, different fathers. Since we had only each other after my father died in an accident and our mother from cancer, you'd think we would treat each other a little better.

The argument began when I informed her I was going to Amanda's after school. I thought it was stupid of Jen to keep reminding me to be home by seven, as I was well aware that staying out later in our part of the city would be the dumbest thing to do. Her bossiness that morning bugged me and I wasn't in any mood to continue our argument, so I grabbed my backpack, ran down the stairs and out the front door.

Once outside, I stopped to take a few calming breaths. My empty stomach felt a bit queasy. Even at that time of morning, the sidewalk already sizzled in the hot sun. The smell of the city—car exhaust, rotting garbage and the stench left from nightly visits of derelicts to the alleys—was nauseating.

Our three-story apartment building had probably been considered quite elegant when it was built back in the 1920's. It had even had a grand ballroom on the ground floor. Long before we arrived, though, the ballroom had been divided into smaller apartments. The exterior of the building, once solid and respectable, was now missing bricks by the truckload. Paint peeled from aging window frames in long, curling strips of grey. Many of the glass panes were cracked, with duct tape the only thing holding them together. On summer nights, one could hear the high-pitched chittering of bats as they glided to and from the roof on silent wings.

In spite of the heat that morning, I shivered a little as I glanced up at the façade. If there had been cement gargoyles, grinning sardonically down at me from the heights, the building couldn't have seemed any more menacing. It was so different from the nice apartment Jen and I had moved to after our mother died. In those days, before my sister started drinking, we had managed quite well. Then the money started to run out and we moved several times, finally ending up in that awful place.

We knew hardly any of the other residents, but it seemed like all had fallen through society's cracks in one way or another. Every so often, one or another of them would get fed up with the crotchety plumbing or some other thing and would call the city offices. Maybe the inspector would come and maybe he wouldn't, depending on how busy he was and whether his office happened to be a hot-button issue in an election year. Perhaps a citation would even be issued and a few minor repairs made. Yet it hardly made a dent in the building's problems.

If a resident got desperate enough, he or she might get up the nerve to tap timidly on the door of the irascible manager. Mona the Monarch ruled her shabby little kingdom with a pipe wrench as a scepter. Most of us didn't willingly interact with her. Consequently, the majority of the troubles were simply endured by the majority of the residents. Perhaps there was a lingering suspicion that, if things were really fixed up the way they should be, the rent would be raised beyond what any of us could afford.

That afternoon after school, I went over to Amanda's. Although she and I weren't exactly friends, we had been assigned a science project together. It didn't take us long to finish. As soon as I could, I left to catch a bus to my favorite hangout.

Disembarking in front, I barely glanced at the imposing granite edifice as I pushed through the revolving glass door and stepped into a brightly lit, cavernous lobby. Hurrying through the crowds in the different rooms, I finally found an empty chair and dropped into it. With great anticipation, I looked around and contemplated all the shelves upon shelves of adventures.

Of course, most people knew them as *books*. There was no place I'd rather be than in the library, surrounded by exciting ideas and places beyond imagining. From the time I was little, reading took me far away from whatever I didn't want to be present to at the moment. I loved to read, and I devoured book upon book.

That was another way I was different from my sister. Jen's idea of a good time was to throw a party for dozens of her closest friends. Not that she *had* dozens of friends any more. Lately, she seemed to have only a few losers like Killer to hang around with. No way did she understand me or my passion for reading, and I wasn't about to tell her how often I traveled to the downtown public library by myself.

However, on that day she almost found me out. I read and read and got lost in my reading, and left the library way past the time I had originally planned. I was sure Jen was going to kill me—assuming, of course, I made it home in one piece.

It wasn't dark yet, as it was almost summer and daylight hadn't yet faded from the sky. Still, I knew it was too late to be out alone on the streets. By evening, gangs of unsavory characters began to hang around buildings, most notably buildings like ours.

I got off the bus to walk home and had barely turned our corner when I knew I was in trouble. A rough-looking crowd in baggy pants, chunky jewelry and black T-shirts was milling around on the front sidewalk. Radios blasted rap music and bottles were being passed around. I watched a car glide up to the curb and an arm reach through the open window. I took a quick step backward and tried to shrink into a shadowed doorway. Several heads swiveled in my direction.

I'd been noticed.

3

Fearing my books would be scattered or my purse stolen—or something worse—I doubled back down the sidewalk. Hoots and curses, mocking laughter and running footsteps followed me. I ran and didn't look back. Fortunately, I was skinny and was able to slip into a barely-foot-wide corridor between two buildings. My heart pounded wildly as I scooted sideways, dragging my pack behind me and snagging my clothes on the uneven brick walls. After what seemed an eternity, I burst out the back and raced down the alley toward the rear of the apartment building. I knew it would be only a matter of minutes before those creeps found their way around to the alley. I had no intention of waiting around to see if I was right.

Arriving at my building, I jumped up on a wall projection and grabbed the weathered metal railing just above my head. It wobbled a bit, but I was able to haul myself onto the second-floor balcony. From there, I climbed onto a cracked concrete planter where I could reach the rail of our own balcony. My shoe found a toehold in the pockmarked wall and, within seconds, I was pounding on our back door.

It opened with a *bang!* My sister, framed in the doorway, glowered at me.

"You're late!"

Not, "Are you all right?" or "I was worried." Not even, "Why were you climbing up the balconies?"

I pushed past her and slammed and locked the door. I was winded and panting, but rather proud of myself for my quick thinking and safe, though unusual, arrival home. What I didn't stop to think about at the time was, if it was so easy for *me* to get up to our third-floor apartment, wouldn't it be just as easy for someone else?

My only concern at that moment was my sister's anger. Since she wasn't drunk, I could find myself in hot water. I dropped my backpack, trying to appear casual while catching my breath.

"So?" I asked.

"Look at your clothes!" she screeched. "They're torn! Don't I work hard enough without throwing away money on clothes? What kind of idiot are you, anyway, coming home this time of night?"

Exhausted, I sank onto the sofa. My arms and legs felt like rubber. It suddenly hit me how sick I was of everything. Sick of the city, sick of that horrible place we lived. And sick of my sister harping at me. Whatever happened to the life we once had?

Without warning, I burst into tears. At least she left me alone after that.

I liked it better on days when Jen was scheduled to work, as she didn't drink then. But the following Sunday she was at home and on a trajectory to getting drunk once more. There was again a knock at the door, and there stood the same odd couple I had nearly forgotten about. I couldn't believe it when my sister invited them in. What would possess her to want to talk to people from some church? At the time, it never occurred to me my sister might be lonely. I just chalked up what I thought was her poor judgment to the booze.

Jen amiably waved them to the sofa, where they perched precariously on its sunken edge. If they noticed the disastrous state of the apartment, they didn't let on. Unlike Melvin. The only time Melvin had come in, he acted like he would catch the cooties if he touched anything. Maybe he would have. It was hard to know what might be growing in the garbage lying around. Then there was Leona. When she had first come to our place with Lucy in tow, she glanced around, blinked several times and swallowed hard, probably wondering if she should leave her beloved Mama or if Mama might disappear under an avalanche of junk. If Leona had had any other choice where to leave her mother that day, she likely would have left and never come back.

The woman visitor, dressed in a bright yellow tunic, introduced herself as Beatrice and the man as Frank. Beatrice asked my sister her name. Her voice slurring a bit, she answered, "Jennifer." Frank nodded and smiled widely, claiming that that was one of his favorite names.

I listened to the small talk from the kitchen, where I was trying to wash the scum out of several glasses. Jen had insisted our guests have something to drink, for the day was every bit as hot as it had been the first time they had appeared. I returned with two almost-clean glasses filled with tepid water and interrupted them.

"What are you people, anyway?" I asked. "Jehovah's Witnesses?"

Jen looked appalled at my abruptness. As she tried to figure out what she should yell at me about, the man's eyes crinkled in amusement.

"No, no," he said pointing to his nametag which read *St. Therese Catholic Church,* with *Frank* written underneath. "Do you know where St. Therese's is located?"

I nodded, having passed the church often on the bus to and from the library. *Oops!* I glanced worriedly at my sister. I hadn't meant to let it slip that I was familiar with that part of town. But a few beers saved me. Jen was shaking her head in confusion. She turned her attention back to them.

"What brings you here to see ush t'day?"

"We're visiting all the people in the neighborhood," replied Beatrice. "We've already met many of the people in your building."

I was a bit taken aback. Were they crazy? Who would go door-to-door in our neighborhood, with crack houses and dope dealers on every corner? We ourselves knew hardly anyone in our own building. Beatrice must have noticed my look of unbelief, because a grin split her face and a laugh bubbled out.

"Honey, don't worry about us! We only go around in broad daylight—and always in pairs. We haven't had any trouble."

Yet, I thought to myself. I knew from experience that broad daylight was no guarantee there wouldn't be trouble. The elderly man and petite woman looked to be no match for the slime which always hung around there.

For awhile they listened politely to Jen ramble on about nothing before they asked about her family.

"It's jush Tony 'n me," she said slowly, trying to find the words. "When our mom died, I was eighteen and my sis-shter twelve. I think." She furrowed her brow. "Tony, weren't you about twelve?"

"Yes!" I snapped. Was she going to tell strangers our whole life story? Frowning in disapproval, I turned to the visitors and asked, "How'd you get into our building?"

"Oh, we just pushed a couple of doorbells."

That didn't surprise me. While the security door system was about the only thing in the building which still worked, anyone could get in by simply buzzing randomly. *Someone* would let them in.

Frank said to Jen, "May I ask—do you have a church you go to?"

My sister pursed her lips. "Umm, I don't think so. Do we, Tony?"

"No!"

My irritation didn't seem to faze Jen, as she continued, "But I think we used to. We went with Mom to church sh...some...times. Remember, Tony?"

Frank and Beatrice looked at me and I stared back in chilly silence. They glanced at each other and then at Jen whose eyes were starting to close. Beatrice cleared her throat loudly. When that didn't get a response, she and Frank stood up, saying they'd return at a better time. I'm surprised they ever came back at all, considering what happened next.

The air exploded suddenly with the sound of gunshots. The three of us jumped up and spun around to look wildly at the door to the hallway. Jen's eyelids never even fluttered.

We heard angry yelling and loud commotion and then the wail of sirens. I was too frightened to move, but Frank hurried to me and grabbed my arm while Beatrice shook Jen and got her onto her feet. We all piled into the bedroom and slammed the door.

There wasn't much room in there, as it was a disaster like the rest of the apartment. With a moan, Jen crashed onto the bed and the rest of us huddled together behind the door. My breathing sounded awfully loud in my ears. Frank put a hand on my shoulder while Beatrice prayed softly under her breath.

There was nothing to do but nervously wait it out. After some time, I noticed the worst of the chaos seemed to be coming from the front part of the building.

"Oh, no!" I cried. "Lee!" I started opening the door to use the phone. Frank stopped me.

"Stay here," he ordered. "A stray gunshot could easily pierce that old door!"

"But Lee—I need to know if she's all right!"

"Where does she live?"

"In 1F. First floor, right next to the stairs."

"We went there. No one was home."

I sighed in relief. I remembered Leona and Lucy spent most Sundays at church services and visiting with friends. They seldom returned home before dinnertime.

It got pretty stuffy in that room before things finally quieted down. We cautiously poked our heads out. Flashing blue lights from the alley reflected off the dingy walls and the sound of knocking was coming down the hallway. When a knock came at our door, along with the words, "Police! Open up," Frank was the one who spoke to the officer.

After closing the door, Frank told us the police had cleaned out "a nest of vipers" in several of the apartments. And since the cops were still milling around, he thought it might be a good time for Beatrice and him to go. They warned me to lock the door behind them—not that I would forget—and left with a promise of prayer for us.

I leaned against the door, eyes closed, and tried to pull myself together. Then I decided to use my pent-up energy to wash dishes. Before long, though, hearing a snore issuing from the bedroom, I quit my self-appointed task and picked up a book to lose myself in a nicer, safer world.

4

I was more than a little surprised when our intrepid visitors did, in fact, return. Or rather, Frank did. Instead of Beatrice, a young man named Carlos was with him. At home by myself that day, I didn't really care to invite them in. Whatever would we talk about? However, in light of what had happened the previous time, I figured I owed them that small courtesy.

After we discussed the excitement of his last visit, Frank asked what I was doing with school out for the summer.

"My birthday was this week," I replied. "My sister brought home a cake for me."

I didn't mention that the cake had been half-price because the writing on top said, "Congratulations to the Graduate." With a sharp knife, Jen scraped off the last three words. I had been hoping for a birthday present, but was disappointed as usual. My sister declared that she bought me clothes when I needed them—even though the clothes were the cheapest she could find on sale and I had to wear them until they were reduced to rags.

Of course, looking back at it now, I realize I should have been grateful Jen took care of me at all. How many sisters, still young themselves, would take on the responsibility of a sibling?

I didn't tell any of that to the visitors, afraid that if I thought too much about how it used to be—with a mother and a home of our own—I might fall apart. So I changed the subject.

"I've been applying for work at different places," I said, "but the jobs are already taken by college kids home for the summer. There's nothing left."

"Put applications in anyway," Carlos advised. "Especially at fast-food joints. Someone's always quitting or getting fired."

He smiled at me and his straight teeth shone white against his olive complexion. I blushed, feeling suddenly awkward. I wondered why a young, good-looking guy like him would be hanging around with an old guy like Frank.

Carlos told me that he attended youth group at their church and asked if I would like to come sometime. I said I wouldn't. If I was going to go to any church at all—which I wasn't—I would go with Leona and Lucy to their Baptist church where at least I knew someone. But Carlos wasn't easily put off. He took out a brochure for his church and a pen and circled the day and time for the youth group meeting.

"And your sister is...how old?" he asked.

"Uh...twenty-three."

"Wonderful!" Frank exclaimed. "The group is for high school through early twenties. Why don't you both come?"

Although I took the brochure politely, I was relieved when they left. Tossing it onto the trash heap in the kitchen, I didn't think any more about it. Therefore, I was totally surprised when Jen picked it up the next day.

"Where'd this come from?" she asked.

"Oh, people from that church came yesterday."

She scanned the brochure. "What'd they say?"

"They want us to go to a youth meeting at their church. Oh, Jen!" I said, as a new idea hit me. "It's too bad you weren't here! The old man brought this really hot guy with him. About your age," I added wickedly. "Maybe you should go to that thing and you'll get to meet him."

Jen didn't even look up at my teasing. "Maybe I will," she said.

I rolled my eyes. Sure, I thought. She'll forget all about it with her next beer.

But Jen surprised me. She didn't forget, even though Killer spent Saturday night at our place and they both got stone drunk. By Sunday evening, though, she managed to pull herself together and asked if I wanted to go.

"Go where?"

"To that church."

"Are you crazy? *Holy* people go there. What makes you think they'd be happy to see us?" I thought I detected a faint scent of alcohol still clinging to her.

Jen shrugged. "Whatever. I want to see what it's like. You coming?"

I rubbed my nose, thinking it might be something different from hanging around the apartment all the time, but finally said, "No, I don't think so."

I wasn't as nervy as my sister. I had no desire to find out what would happen if people like us showed up at a church meeting. Even if it *would* have been nice to see Carlos again.

It was still early when Jen arrived home from the youth meeting. She tossed her purse, hitting the ashtray which spun off the endtable and dumped ashes and butts all over the floor. She ignored the mess as she kicked her shoes onto the closest heap.

I was watching TV in the dark, trying to muster enough energy to take a cool shower. "So, how'd it go?" I asked.

She went to rummage in the fridge and I heard the *pop* of a can opening. Returning to the living room, she slumped into a chair and was silent.

"Well, that's that," she finally said.

"What d'ya mean?"

"I'm not going there again." She took a long swig of beer.

I looked smugly at her. "I told you. They don't want people like us there."

She stared, unseeing, at a yawning hole in the wall plaster. I asked impatiently, "Was Carlos there?"

"I don't remember any Carlos. Actually, I hardly met anyone at all. There was a girl named Maria who came up to me when I first got there and asked if I was new. Then she got a funny look on her face and went to talk to some guy, and before I knew it he came over and said if I was drinking, I couldn't stay. I tried to tell him I hadn't had anything to drink all day, but he walked me to the door and told me I could come back anytime as long as I was sober."

Jen stopped and ran her fingers through her hair. For the first time I noticed how tired and sad she seemed. Maybe I just wasn't paying attention other times.

"Was the guy mean?"

She shook her head. "No, but he meant business. I was so embarrassed, I just left."

I couldn't believe my sister felt embarrassed about her drinking. I learned something new all the time.

"So, anyway, like I said, that's that."

Saying she had to go to work in the morning, she finished her beer and went to the bedroom. Eventually, though, I realized that that *wasn't* that.

A few days later, I was on my way home after spending the morning looking for work at local stores and restaurants. Place after place had either rudely brushed me off, told me to come back in a couple of weeks or laughed outright in my face. Discouraged, I wandered the city streets, looking into store windows and daydreaming about all the things I couldn't afford—and would *never* be able to afford without a job.

I felt his presence behind me before I saw his reflection in the window into which I'd been staring. I spun around and a slow grin, which I found enormously attractive, slid across his face. His poker-straight brown hair, tousled by the breeze, blew into his eyes and he brushed it back nonchalantly.

"Hey, Tony! How ya doin'?"

"Hiya, Kenny," I answered with an uncertain smile.

Kenny was in one of my classes at school but he had never spoken to me before. Self-consciously, I tried to smooth down my hair which always sprung into frizz as soon as the weather got humid. I was envious that my sister could hop out of the shower, run a comb through her hair and be out the door while I was still trying to get my hair to stay where I wanted it. I hoped Kenny wouldn't notice the unruly curl I tucked behind my ear.

He fell into step beside me and we continued up the street together, laughing over something which had happened in class that day. He had such a dry sense of humor, I soon forgot my initial shyness. We walked and talked, and talked and walked. But as time passed, I began to get anxious. I did *not* want to arrive back at the apartment with Kenny at my side. If anyone saw us together, it would surely get back to my sister and I'd never hear the end of it. Besides, what teenage girl would want a boy like Kenny to find out she lived in such a dump?

So at the next corner I turned down a different street, pretending I had an errand in that direction. After a few more blocks, laughing and talking all the way, we found ourselves in front of a drugstore. I told Kenny I needed to buy some makeup.

"Okay," he said, "I got to get going anyway. But hey! I'll see you around!"

I grinned, saying I hoped so, and meant it with all my heart. I never had a boy as cute as Kenny pay me any attention before. Actually, I never had *any* boy talk to me at school, if you didn't count the scumbags who would sidle up in the hallways and ask if I'd like to score some weed or coke. A long time ago, I learned to spot them coming and I'd go the other way.

Upon my arrival home, I groaned to myself when I saw Frank and Beatrice standing outside our door talking to Leona and Lucy. Omigosh! I had completely forgotten I promised to watch Mama! Watching Leona's mother was the easiest job in the world, and the ten dollars I'd be paid wasn't hard to take, either.

There was nothing to do but invite them all in.

"Gosh, Lee, I'm sorry. I was out looking for a job and completely forgot about you and Mama coming." I didn't mention about Kenny and me yakking up one street and down another.

"That's okay, Antonia. I was gettin' a little worried, but I knew that something important musta held you up."

I nodded guiltily and Leona rushed out. The church people, unfortunately, were not in the same hurry to leave. I cleared a place for everyone to sit.

As I sat awkwardly looking at them, I noticed for the first time that Frank's eyes were the color of a clear sky on a summer day. Jen had blue eyes, too, whereas I had inherited my father's nondescript brown ones. If my sister would only stop bleaching her hair to death and drop a few pounds, I reflected, she might get a boyfriend better than Killer. Maybe I wasn't as attractive as Jen, but there was no way I was going to drink my life away like she was doing. I had things I wanted to do and places I wanted to go— even if I didn't know how I would accomplish it.

I brought my attention back to Frank. Beaming, he asked, "Did you or your sister have a chance to go to the youth meeting Carlos mentioned?"

"Yeah," I answered. "Jen went."

Neither mentioned anything more about it. Maybe they already knew. Maybe Carlos had been the guy who had kicked my sister out. At any rate, I wasn't volunteering any further information.

Frank leaned toward me. "Tony, do you have any idea how much God loves you?"

I was trying to come up with a smart-aleck answer when there came a soft voice at my elbow.

"God heals the broken-headed."

Mama had a way of popping out with the darndest things. The three of us stared at her and she nodded amiably back at us.

"Well, Mama Lucy," I said, glad for the interruption, "if anyone has a broken head, it's Jen, not me." I giggled nervously and the visitors smiled.

"But seriously, Tony," Beatrice said, "God loves you and has a wonderful plan for you."

Wasn't that something like what Leona had said to me weeks earlier? Were they conspiring with her to convert me? I frowned suspiciously at them.

"So? He hasn't said anything to *me* about any plans." Besides, I thought, I had plans of my own. Maybe if God could get me a job and get us out of that awful apartment, I might start to believe in all that stuff.

"Have you asked him?" Frank's blue eyes were fastened on mine.

"No, and I don't intend to."

The conversation was getting really strange. I stood, hoping they would get the hint to leave.

Just at that moment, Mama said loudly, "ASK AND YOU SHALL PERCEIVE; KNOCK AND THE STORE SHALL BE OPENED UNTO YOU!"

I hurriedly ushered the visitors out. I didn't have any idea what Mama was talking about. And I certainly didn't have any idea what her words would mean to Jen and me many months down the road.

5

That night, Jen came home from work with a bulging garbage bag. She dumped the contents unceremoniously onto the sofa.

"From Irene again," she said. "I don't know why she thinks I want these old clothes she's throwing out."

She pawed through them, tossing aside a frayed coat, some pants which had seen better days, a worn denim jumper and other things. She selected a sweatshirt which was passable, then stuffed the rest back into the bag and tossed the whole thing onto a mountain of similar bags. It was my opinion she should drop all of them into the nearest dumpster, but she said she didn't want to hurt Irene's feelings. So there they remained, overstuffed bags with squatter's rights in the corner of our overstuffed living room.

On her way into the kitchen, something new atop the pile on the end table caught her eye.

"What's this?"

"Oh, those church people came by again! It's from them."

She picked up the small, gold-colored medal threaded onto a narrow ribbon long enough to go around a person's neck. The medal was made of cheap plastic, but Jen examined it like it was the finest of gems.

I pointed. "There's a booklet that goes with it."

Putting the ribbon around her neck, she opened the booklet. I was surprised. Even though I had dutifully left the things there for her, I figured she would probably just throw them away. She didn't tell me until later—until much, *much* later—that she vaguely remembered her father wearing a similar medal.

"It's called a 'Miraculous Medal,'" she said, reading from the booklet. "It's supposed to have been designed by the Blessed Mother, Mary herself. Think of that!"

I looked at her in amazement. She may have had some background in that Catholic stuff—after all, we knew her dad had been Catholic—but still, why would she care about it?

"Back in 1830," she read aloud, "there was this nun in France named Sister Catherine La...uh...Laboure. In the convent chapel, she saw a vision of the Blessed Mother who told her she had a special mission for her. The next time Sister Catherine saw the Blessed Mother, Mary was standing on what seemed to be a globe, and there were rays of light streaming from rings on her fingers. Mary explained that the rays symbolized the *graces* she obtains for those who ask for them."

"Uhh...yeah. Sure. What are graces?"

She shrugged and continued reading the story. "When Sister Catherine saw the vision again, Mary was framed with the inscription, *'O Mary, conceived without sin, pray for us who have recourse to thee.'*" Jen paused. "Hmm... 'recourse' must mean we can turn to her when we need something."

"What's the rest mean?" I don't know why I bothered asking. Jen looked as confused as I was.

She ignored the interruption. "This sister was asked by Mary to have a medal made with the image on it. On the reverse side was to be a circle of twelve stars around a cross, for Jesus, and an 'M,' for Mary. It says the twelve stars are mentioned in the book of Revelation, in the Bible." She flipped over the medal to look at the other side. "And on the back there's two hearts below the cross, representing the love of Jesus and his mother for us.

"Well, I really don't get it," she continued, sliding the booklet into her shirt pocket. "Are those people coming back? I'd like to ask them some questions."

"I don't know," I said, "and I don't care."

After my sister went to bed that evening, I switched off all the lights in the apartment and sprawled on the sofa. I liked to lie there and think, with no illumination except from the streetlight in the alley. The darkness concealed the ugly evidence of our depressing lives. During those late-night thinking sessions, all sorts of dreams seemed possibilities—before the harsh light of day turned them into impossibilities.

I suddenly remembered I had hidden my own beribboned medal, given to me by the visitors, under a sofa cushion. I wouldn't be caught dead wearing it, but, for some reason, hadn't thrown it away, either. After pulling it from its hiding place, I lay on my back holding it high over my head, watching it swing back and forth and glint golden in the faint light. I briefly considered twirling the loop of ribbon on my finger and slinging it. Maybe I could hit that hole in the wall. I could imagine the medal disappearing into it, descending like a balm into the building's nether regions where surely the devil lived.

But I never did fling the medal, that night or any other. I simply turned over and tucked it back under the cushion before falling asleep.

Nearly a month passed before our visitors came again. Jen continued to wear the medal, and read—and reread—the little booklet that came with it.

"Hey, listen to this," she said one day. "Great graces are promised to those who wear this medal. I wonder what that means?"

There was that word, *graces,* again.

Another time, she said, "For heaven's sakes." *For heaven's sakes?* I guess she didn't use swear words when talking about religious stuff. "It says here there's been thousands of miracles connected with the medal. That's why everyone calls it the 'Miraculous Medal.' I wonder what kind of miracles? Just think of it!" Her eyes were shining. "Hey, Tony, that's what we need—a miracle!"

I ignored her enthusiasm.

The next time she brought up the subject, she took pains to explain to me that there was no superstition or magic connected with the medal.

"Rather," she read from the booklet, "the medal is a sign of a person's trust and faith that God will hear their prayers through the intercession of the Blessed Mother."

I peered at her over the top of the book I was immersed in. Whatever had come over my sister lately?

"And," she continued, "it says that a *storehouse* of graces is available to those who ask with a humble heart."

At that, I put down my book. Hadn't Mama Lucy said something along those same lines? *Knock and the store shall be opened unto you.* Knock? Just how was one supposed to knock on that heavenly storehouse?

Just then there came a knock—not in heaven, but at our door. I was almost relieved to see our visitors again. Maybe they could answer the questions with which Jen was driving me crazy. When I saw the handsome Carlos with Frank, I grinned slyly, waiting to see my sister's reaction. After introductions, though, she barely paid any attention to him, merely begging Frank to explain more about the Miraculous Medal.

Patiently, Frank explained that *graces* are God's special gifts to us, spiritual and temporal gifts which help us grow in faith, hope and charity.

Jen looked intrigued. "What does that mean?"

"It means God knows what will ultimately give us the most peace and joy in our lives," said Carlos, "and his grace helps us achieve that goal. But grace isn't anything we can merit on our own."

"So how do you get it?"

"You can start by praying. God hears our prayers and grants our requests, if what we ask for is good for our souls. Of course, only he knows that, because he can see the past and future. There's nothing hidden from God. If it seems sometimes like God doesn't answer our prayers, maybe it's because he has a better answer somewhere down the line."

Jen thought for a moment in silence and then glanced down at the booklet in her hand.

"I don't get it. You're talking about God, but this says to ask Mary for those graces."

Our guests settled back on the sofa. It was looking to be a *long* conversation. I wasn't following it all that well—and can't say I was particularly interested—but there was no other place to go in our small apartment.

"Yes," Carlos said, "God is the One to whom *every* prayer is ultimately directed. He's the only one who can answer, as he alone is God. But when we need something, can't we ask others to pray *for* us?"

Strangely, Jen didn't respond right away to his question. She had leaned towards Frank and was staring intently at him.

"What's the matter?" Carlos asked.

With a sigh, Jen straightened and shook her head before answering. "It's nothing. For some reason, a memory of my father came to me. But never mind. It doesn't matter. My dad died a long time ago." She turned back to Carlos. "I'm sorry. Go on. You were saying?"

"I was asking if you think others can pray for us?"

"Well, sure. Leona is always asking her mama to pray for her. And that's not hard to understand, because sometimes Lucy seems to have a direct line to God."

Carlos laughed. "Mothers are like that. I know *my* mother is. Did you know that the Blessed Mother is not only the mother of Jesus, but our mother too?"

"She is?"

"Of course," Frank answered. "The Bible says we are all children of God, and that makes Jesus our brother. So doesn't that make Mary our mother, at least spiritually? Therefore, we can ask our Mother Mary to pray for us that we might obtain the graces we need from God."

At long last our visitors left, and in the following days I didn't have much time to dwell on anything they had said. My life had become very busy. I got a job, just the way Carlos predicted. An employee at the nearby Burger Barn was fired for opening the back door one night to take out the garbage—which was against company rules. Two men waiting outside had forced their way in and robbed the restaurant at gunpoint. Luckily no one was hurt, and lucky me as I got her position. I never did tell my sister about the robbery.

I still hadn't told her about Kenny, either. He often came by the Barn when I was finished working and we'd have a hamburger and fries while we talked. Kenny was cute and fun, and it sure was great having a boyfriend like the other girls.

Yes, things were starting to look up for me. My senior year was fast approaching, and I couldn't wait until I was finally out of school and getting on with my life—even if I didn't have any idea of what that life would entail. My grades weren't so good and I didn't have money for college, so my prospects were really rather bleak.

But as I smiled into Kenny's eyes over chocolate milkshakes, I felt I didn't have a care in the world. At least until I got home.

6

Water was spraying the bathroom walls as I regarded the broken shower knob in my hand with consternation. We eventually managed to stem the fountain with towels, plastic bags and rubber bands, but it was obvious the solution was only temporary. Although the sight of our dripping hair and sodden shirts almost gave me the giggles, my sister's glowering visage sobered me in a hurry.

"Well..." she said, her teeth gritted in exasperation, "maybe I can get Max to take a look at it."

Right. Like Killer knew how to fix plumbing just because he worked on motorcycles. But Jen thought it was worth a try before having to face Mona. Killer arrived that evening with a pipe wrench in his hand and Weasel on his tail. With the three of them crowded into the bathroom, there was no way I was getting anywhere near it. I could listen in on their progress well enough from the living room.

"And what will you give me if I fix it?" I heard Killer ask my sister. I hoped she would give him the boot, but I wouldn't hold my breath waiting.

It was a long evening. They swore at the plumbing, swore at each other and then swore some more for good measure. I ignored them as best I could. When they finally emerged from the bathroom, they were soaked—with perspiration or bath water, I couldn't tell. And the problem was worse than when they had started.

Bossy old Jen tried ordering me to go down and tell Mona. "*I'm* not talking to her!" I barked. "You do it!"

Jen glared at me, took a gulp from the beer can Killer handed her and marched into her room to change. Killer dropped into a chair and flipped on the TV while Weasel prowled the apartment. Relieved when they finally left, I threw myself on the sofa, switched the channel and made myself comfortable. Since they were headed to a party, I figured Jen wouldn't be home until morning.

A banging came at the door and I sprang up to peer through the peephole. It was Mona. With trepidation I opened the door and she strode in like she owned the place. I guess she did, sort of.

Mona was something else. Although perhaps only about fifty, the hard lines around her eyes and mouth made her seem older. The effect was heightened by graying hair pulled back severely from her face. She was short and wiry and slightly stooped from wearing a leather work belt hung with tools. I often wondered if she carried the heavy wrenches everywhere to keep the tenants in line. But with a temper like hers, who needed any other weapon?

Despite her small size, there was nothing delicate about Mona. She was dressed in camouflage overalls with work boots on her feet, ready for combat with the plumbing.

"Blast!" she spit at me. "Your sister stopped at my place! What's the problem?"

I showed her the broken knob. I wondered if I should ask her to look at the lighting problem while she was there, and maybe do something with the broken blinds, but she turned on me in such fury I thought better of it.

"What did you do to the blasted knob that it came off?!"

Like I purposely broke the plumbing? Or like I was dying for her to visit us?

"Well…uh, nothing, actually," I stammered. "I was just taking a shower…"

She wasn't listening. Her gaze shot around the bathroom and my eyes followed. On the edge of the sink I saw brushes and combs with so much tangled hair in them that mice could be nesting there and we would never notice. The back of the toilet and a rickety old shelving unit held curling irons and straightening irons, blow dryers, hairspray and a dozen or more bottles of gel and mousse. Also scissors, old razors, cologne and deodorant and an open bag of potato chips. *Potato chips?* Dust and dirt were everywhere, not to mention empty toilet paper tubes and tons of wadded-up tissues.

"What is the *matter* with you people?" hissed Mona. "This place is a pigsty! Why don't you *clean...it...up?*"

I don't know. Why didn't we? Somehow it seemed our living space had taken on the same hopelessness which permeated the rest of Jen's and my life. We had gotten so used to living day to day that nothing seemed to matter any more.

Anyway, the hallways were Mona's business—and they were filthy, too. So who was she to talk?

Her Majesty finally swept out of the apartment, saying she would return the next day with plumbing parts. I was just happy to see her leave. I had survived the ordeal and hoped Jen would be home when she came again.

As I locked the door after Mona, I heard shouts coming from Melvin's apartment. His daughter must be visiting again. She dropped in every so often to bring a few groceries and his medication. More often than not, her presence resulted in a loud argument. It was hard to figure out why she would let her father live in a place unsafe for anyone, much less a frail, elderly man— even if he never seemed to go anywhere except across the hall to pound on our door.

Accustomed to the racket from Melvin's place, I switched off the lights and TV and lay down. Then I sat up again, turned on a lamp and watched a cockroach scurry away in the sudden brightness. From beneath the sofa cushion, I pulled out the hidden Miraculous Medal on its ribbon. Yes, I thought bleakly, looking at it, we sure could use a miracle. Any kind would do.

Miracles come in all sorts of disguises, and they are not always what they appear to be at first. Sometimes what seems like a miracle is not one at all. And sometimes a miracle creeps in, as I was to find out, when you least expect it.

As I started my senior year that fall, I talked my sister into letting me keep my job part-time. It was lucky I did. We needed the money when Jen's hours at the supermarket were unexpectedly cut. She talked about looking for another job, but her talk was larger than her motivation. Maybe the beer, which she was drinking with increased frequency, had something to do with that.

It had been awhile since we had seen our visitors from the church. I didn't much care, but sometimes Jen would wonder out loud if they were coming back.

"Do you think," she asked me once, "they might have gotten discouraged?"

"Maybe they got mugged," I answered.

And another time, "Why would Frank, who you'd think would want to take it easy at his age, go around talking to people like those around here?"

People like us, I muttered under my breath.

"And then there's Beatrice," she went on, unheeding. "Didn't she say she has children? You'd think she'd be worried about her safety. And Carlos—he's young and not married. Can't he find anything better to do with his time?"

Apparently not, because Carlos returned with Frank one day in mid-September. First they spoke to me, asking how school was going. I said I hated it, that I was just trying to scrape up high enough grades so I wouldn't flunk out. I complained that every hour spent in school was a trial in endurance. Truth be told, just getting through the day without using the *bathroom* took endurance, because no one went in the bathrooms at that school unless they were desperate—or planning to shoot up.

Carlos sat listening politely to me, but I saw him glance occasionally over at Jen. Sober for once and freshly-showered, with her hair pulled high into a ponytail, she looked halfway decent for a change. I wondered if Carlos would notice.

"I want to know," Jen blurted out as soon as she had a chance to talk, "if God hears everyone's prayers?"

"Yes," said Carlos. "Everyone's. God makes no distinctions. If you pray, God will listen. Period."

"But will he answer?"

Frank chuckled lightly. "Why don't you try it and see?"

"Uh…I don't really know how."

"Prayer isn't so much about what words to say," Frank said. "Prayer is talking in a personal way with God. If you don't have an intimate relationship with him, it wouldn't matter if you said dozens of prayers. They'd just be empty words."

"How do you develop that kind of relationship?"

Carlos smiled. "Well, most people want to start at the top of the ladder."

"The ladder? What are you talking about?"

He explained, "As you know, our church is named St. Therese, for St. Therese of Lisieux." He pronounced it *Lissew,* which was not at all what I would have gleaned from the assortment of letters on the church sign. "St. Therese spoke about a 'ladder of holiness' which represents our journey towards God. It's my observation that most people want to get on that ladder somewhere near the top. Don't we all know people who seem to be high up on that ladder, close to God—"

I thought immediately of Mama Lucy.

"—and we think how wonderful it would be to be like them? To have that kind of faith and trust? But what we *don't* see is how much effort they spent climbing that ladder. It can only be done one rung at a time—little by little, day after day, year after year. Most of us want to bypass all the work and jump on somewhere near the top."

Hmm, I thought. If the spiritual life was a ladder, I could imagine my sister and me in a hole far beneath it, not even close enough to grab the bottom rung.

"So, how do you get on this ladder?" Jen persisted. "Even at the bottom?"

"What do *you* think?"

"Umm...saying prayers before bed? Going to church?"

"Not bad, but that's not it."

After a prolonged silence, Carlos answered the question himself. "First, we need to ask God to give us the *desire* to pray. Otherwise, in spite of our best intentions, we'll find everything else—job, school, entertainment, friends and, especially, the *telephone*—gets in the way. Without the desire to pray, we'll soon get discouraged and stop trying."

He leaned forward. "Scripture tells us 'we don't know how to pray as we ought.' That is so true. Prayer is a gift and we have to be humble enough to ask for it." His voice rose in fervor. "Our very desire to take a step towards God comes from him. Remember, *he wants us more than we want him!*"

Whoa! That was *way* more than I ever wanted to know about prayer!

Frank broke in then, a soft counterpoint to the intensity of the younger man. "You know, the youth group at our church is meeting again tonight. Why don't the two of you come?"

"And I'll pick you up at seven so you don't have to take the bus," Carlos added quickly.

I easily saw through his ruse to make sure Jen didn't show up smelling like beer. I figured my sister would get on her high horse and refuse, so perhaps it *was* a bit of a miracle when she agreed to go with him.

I claimed I had homework to do and didn't have time. However, the real reason I didn't want to go was because I was nursing a fantasy about Carlos—sweet-looking Carlos—and my sister. I pictured him owning a classy sports car. Red, preferably. And when he'd tool up to our place in it, heads would turn with envy as the two of them took off into the sunset.

A rusty old Honda wasn't exactly what I had in mind. Unfortunately, that's what Carlos and a friend of his arrived in to pick up Jen that evening. The only looks they got were ones of annoyance as the car backfired.

At least, I comforted myself, Jen was sober. That may have been another miracle.

The following day was one of those times when Leona couldn't take her mother to the nursing home with her. So Lucy sat contentedly at our kitchen table while Jen ironed her way through a pile of clothes and told the old lady about all the problems with her supermarket job.

"Mama, I just don't know why I stay there. Cashel, that's the boss—weird name, huh?—can't seem to get his act together. He asks for something and then changes his mind a million times. Like we're supposed to know what he's thinking? Even Irene is ready to quit, but I know she won't 'cuz she doesn't want to look for another job at her age."

Mama nodded her head like she understood everything. "That's quite a conflubberance, isn't it?" she said.

"And then there's Marcy, who thinks she's better than everyone else. She points out every little thing, like if I'm a few minutes late getting back from break or don't have my vest buttoned or my name tag's crooked. Stupid things like that. And she makes a point of mentioning it just when Cashel happens to be close by."

Mama shook her head slowly. "Ah, well," she said. "Such is life. You needn't tell me all the perpendiculars."

Jen, who had the uncanny knack of knowing what Lucy was talking about, chuckled.

"You're probably right, Mama. Even though I wish I had a better job, this one is so handy. It's right on the bus route and I can get mark-downs on food. And they did promise to restore my hours soon. Maybe I just have to hold tight."

"Hold tight," Mama repeated. "Tight as a drumstick."

Jen scooped up the freshly-ironed clothes and deposited them on a chair in the bedroom where they could garner more wrinkles before being worn again. Returning to the living room, she shoved a pile of magazines off the easy chair and collapsed into it, picking up the conversation with hardly a pause.

"You wanna hear about the meeting at church last night?"

Was she talking to Mama—or to me? I had been asleep when she came home the night before, so I listened more closely.

"Luckily the bouncer guy wasn't there," she was saying. "I wasn't looking forward to seeing *him* again. Carlos introduced me to some of the others, then we sat down to watch a skit. It didn't make a whole lot of sense to me. It began with singing—"

When Jen mentioned *singing,* Mama began to croon softly, "In the sweet bye and bye—"

Jen talked over her, so I guess she was speaking to me after all. "Then some kid dressed like a mad scientist…I'm not kidding!…goes over to a whiteboard and gives a lecture. He was talking in a funny voice and waving around a ruler. It was something about God's 'electricity' powering our lives. He writes the letters *P-W-R* on the board and tells us how the *power* of God is available to us. He went on for quite awhile and everyone was laughing at his jokes. I didn't understand most of them. Maybe you have to be Catholic."

Her brow wrinkled in thought. "I'm trying to remember what the letters stood for. I know the *'P'* was for *prayer.* He said that prayer isn't all about *us,* how we feel when we pray or what words we use. Didn't Frank say something along those same lines? The guy said it's God who calls us first and prayer is our response to God."

"Prayer is responsible to God," said Mama, echoing Jen— more or less.

"Then there's the *'W,'* which stands for the *Word of God,* or Scripture. He said that ignorance of Scripture is ignorance of Christ. And finally there was the *'R'*…umm…let me think…it was about *receiving* something or other. I have *no* idea what he was talking about. After that, we got some snacks and broke into smaller groups. I stuck with Carlos because I was really out of my element. But I did want to find out more."

33

"Didn't you feel kind of stupid?" I asked.

"Yeah, at first. But once we were in a small group, it didn't bother me to ask questions." That was my sister, I figured, too dumb to realize how dumb she would sound. "They asked me if I owned a Bible. When I said no, someone got me one and said I could keep it."

I glanced around the apartment but didn't see a Bible anywhere—not that I'd be able to spot it, anyway, amidst the junk.

"It's on my bed," Jen said. "I was reading it last night before I went to sleep."

"Now I lay me down to sleep—" broke in Mama Lucy, "—and if I die before I wake, I pray the Lord my tole will stake."

I paid no attention to Mama. *"You're reading the Bible now?"*

Jen shrugged. "The mad scientist said if we want to pray better, we should read the Bible. He suggested starting with the book of Psalms, which contains every kind of prayer there is. I'm already up to Psalm number three."

I never expected to hear *that* from my sister! Shaking my head, I began getting ready for work.

Jen continued, "On the way home, Carlos said I might want to read the parts of the Bible about Jesus, to start with the Gospel of Mark because it's fairly short. I'll do that next."

"So…what do you think of Carlos?" I asked. "Cute, huh?"

Ignoring me, Jen bent over Lucy. "Hey, Mama, what do you say I get my Bible and we read the next psalm together? Maybe you can explain what I can't understand."

That would be interesting. Too bad I couldn't stick around to hear it. As I went out the door, I heard Mama's tremulous voice.

"You can complain but I understand."

7

As September passed, my sister continued to attend Sunday evening youth group. I was always a little disappointed when Carlos couldn't pick her up, but Jen didn't seem to care one way or another. She'd simply take the bus. One time, she even managed to drag me along.

Earlier that day I had been in a foul mood. Kenny and I had had another argument the night before. Our relationship seemed to be falling apart. I was beginning to notice that everything was about him and never about what I wanted. He always expected me to go places and do things with his friends, none of whom I liked very much. They talked about stuff I knew little about and cared about even less, and I got the distinct impression they weren't so keen on me, either.

Another thing about Kenny was his attitude that I could pay for everything myself. Whatever happened to guys paying for a date? A meal here, a movie there—and my money was flowing out almost faster than it came in. My sister and I needed to pool our paychecks just to get by. I couldn't understand why Kenny didn't pick up the tab sometimes. It was only much later I realized he was saving his money for *other* things.

Jen still didn't know about Kenny, so I couldn't exactly tell her why I was so grumpy. Maybe it was the guilt of hiding our relationship which made me agree to go to the youth group with her that night.

At the youth meeting, there was absolutely no one I recognized. Jen introduced me to a Sandy, a Mackenna, a Maria, a Jules, and an older guy named Milo. Several others said hello but I didn't catch their names. They all seemed friendly enough. We were handed cans of pop and cups of popcorn and asked to take a seat to watch a little play they were putting on. Then the basement plunged into darkness.

After a moment, the stage lit up and on the left side a baby appeared. A very big baby. A baby with a moustache and dark hair pulled back into a ponytail. It was Jules, wearing a striped sleeper with an extra-large diaper over it. He had a pacifier in his mouth and was hugging an oversized pink bunny.

All the kids laughed and hooted at Jules. Jen did, too. I thought it was the stupidest thing in the world.

A girl trotted out onto the stage.

"In the beginning," she announced after it quieted a bit, "God created—" She paused, then said with a dramatic flourish, "—a baby!"

The audience hollered, "Hey, baby! *Jules baby!*"

The overgrown baby popped the pacifier from his mouth, smiled a toothy grin and bowed deeply. Then a girl in a flowered apron—was it Sandy or Mackenna?—bounded out and tapped Jules on the shoulder from behind. He spun around, crying, "Mommy!"

He laid his head on her shoulder, leaning down to do so because, as I said, he was a *very big* baby. She wrapped her arms around him and patted him on the back.

"BURRRP!" said Jules, and everyone roared.

The narrator continued. "Whenever a little baby comes into the world, he is the most unselfish creature ever created. Is that right, Mommy?" she turned to ask the mother.

The other girl put her hands on her hips. "Yeah, right!"

The "baby" sank down into a seated position, legs crossed, and began rocking back and forth. "Hey, Mommy!" he said in his deep voice. "I think I need my diaper changed."

"Mommy" started to reach towards him but he put up a hand to stop her.

"Oh, that's all right, Mommy, I can see you're busy right now getting dinner ready, so I can wait." He looked at her with an angelic smile. "Or, maybe I can learn to change it myself. That way I won't have to bother you." Snickers came from the audience.

His mother picked up a plate and spoon from a table and pretended to eat.

"Mommy?" the baby said. "I'm a little hungry, but that's okay. I'll wait till you're finished.

36

"And, Mommy?" he went on. "You know, this sleeper is getting kind of small." He tugged on the sleeper toe at the end of his humungous foot. "But I know money is tight right now, and you need a new dress so you'll look pretty for church on Sunday. So never mind, I'll just cut the feet off—"

"Off the sleeper...or *you?*" yelled someone in the audience. Jules waggled his eyebrows and grinned.

When it was quiet, the narrator turned again to us. "Of course, we all know that isn't the way it really is. A *real* baby comes into the world never thinking about what's good for others, only what's good for him. Totally self-centered, he cries when he's hungry, he cries when he needs his diaper changed, he cries when he's tired, he even cries when he's bored!"

Jules, still seated on the stage, began to whimper and rub his eyes.

"Are you bored, baby?" she asked.

I nearly shouted, "Yes!" The point about being self-centered was totally lost on me.

Then a short kid in cut-offs and a striped polo shirt came out on stage bouncing a large ball. The narrator said, "As the child begins to grow, he learns more every day about not always getting his own way. He learns to put others first by taking turns, listening when others talk, waiting for what he needs and sharing his toys."

Jules reached over and tried to snag the ball. The boy bonked him on the head with it.

"Well, some of the time, anyway," the girl said. "A child is more unselfish than a baby, but he still has a long way to go."

Onto the stage next came a young man in a business suit. The narrator explained that adults should exhibit more and more unselfishness as the years go by, as they learn to give generously of themselves to their spouses, children, friends, neighbors and others.

Lastly, a stooped-over old man hobbled out and stood leaning unsteadily on a cane. A boy next to me yelled out, "Hey, Milo, don't we always tell you how ancient you are?"

Hearing that, Milo twirled his cane and performed a little jig. Then he stumbled "accidentally" and acted as if he could barely get his balance again.

"And so," said the narrator in a serious voice, "here we have the whole continuum of a person's life. From infancy to childhood to adulthood. From total self-absorption as a baby—

and, of course, that's the way it has to be so a helpless baby can get his needs met—to childhood, where we learn we don't always come first, to adulthood where we're supposed to keep growing in unselfishness in order to make the world a better place. Of course, we know that unselfish people, those who put others first, are a lot happier in this life than those who are selfish. And when we reach the end of our life—"

Suddenly, Milo collapsed and the wooden stage echoed loudly with his supposed demise.

"—and we stand before God—"

"Or lay on the stage!" someone shouted. The narrator ignored the heckler.

"—God isn't going to ask us how much money we made or what kind of a car we drove or whether we had a nice career. He'll want to know how much we loved others. So why do *you* think it's important that we learn to be unselfish—to love?"

The lights in the basement flickered on and a dark-haired boy jumped up.

"I know! Because God *is* love! We can't spend eternity with God unless we get rid of our selfishness. Scripture says that nothing unworthy shall enter heaven!"

"Raoul!" the narrator pouted. "You cheated! You must've seen the script."

"Nah," said the boy, "I've just got a good memory! Milo told us that a long time ago."

As the other kids high-fived Raoul and began talking, the corpse on the stage raised his hand and waved at the audience. I hoped that the skit, also, had come to the end of its life. No such luck. As the characters ambled off the stage, two girls rolled out what looked like white doghouses.

Giant babies, dead bodies and now—dogs? What next?

However, the things weren't doghouses. They were supposed to represent the decision each person would ultimately make about his or her life. Which house, we were asked, would we decide to dwell in? A stagehand darted out and hung a sign on each. Written in large block letters on one sign was the word "SELF" and on the other, "LOVE."

"It's our decision to make," declared the narrator. "The opposite of love isn't hate. It's selfishness. We can choose to dwell in the house of *self*—" At that, a guy with a sledgehammer ran out and loudly demolished the first house, "—and at the end of our life we will have nothing but a lot of hurtful memories. Or we can choose to dwell in the house of love, which is where God dwells, and our lives will be filled with his joy." A light bulb went on inside the house and a glow emanated forth.

As the audience broke up into small discussion groups, I still could not believe how corny the whole thing was.

Eight of us crowded around a table in a smaller room. While Jen introduced me to those I hadn't yet met, Milo, a slight man with salt-and-pepper hair, came in and took a seat. I wondered if he was the bouncer from Jen's first night. He didn't seem very intimidating.

He turned to me with an easy grin. "So, what did you think of our little skit tonight?"

I answered honestly and Jen gave me a swift kick under the table. I guess I hadn't hurt anyone's feelings, though, because a boy named Connor said, "You're right, but you haven't seen the worst! Too bad you weren't here the night we did the onion!"

Everyone laughed.

"The onion?"

"Yeah, Milo was dressed up like an onion! The idea was we have to let God peel away the layers of selfishness and sin—"

"And sometimes it makes us cry!" chimed in Maria. "Get it? Onion…cry?"

I nodded politely like I got it. The next half-hour was spent reading aloud from the Bible and discussing it. Eventually the conversation drifted back to the skit.

"I don't know if I'm right," said Connor, "but I've been thinking maybe every sin there ever was stems from selfishness."

"Why do you say that?" asked Milo.

"Because it seems to be behind every bad thing we do. Isn't sin really about *me*, rather than about loving God and others the way God wants us to?"

I stared at Connor. He sure talked on a different plane than Kenny or other kids I knew!

Milo looked around. "What do the rest of you think?"

The group began to analyze every sin they could think of. From stealing to dealing drugs, from lying to getting drunk—did Milo's eyes flash briefly at Jen?—they came to the conclusion that selfishness was indeed the root cause.

Jen, who hadn't said much up until then, interjected quietly, "Well, what if a person does something because he can't help himself?"

That kicked off a lively debate about whether there are times when a person's actions are beyond his or her control. Most thought there could definitely be mitigating circumstances where a person might feel compelled to do what was clearly wrong.

When they ran out of steam, Milo threw out, "And yet—what about God?"

"What do you mean?" Maria asked.

"Aren't you leaving God out of the equation? Don't you believe God can do anything?"

They all said "Yes!" with no hesitation.

"Well, then, can't God help if a person asks him? Even if that person *does* feel a compulsion to sin?"

That led to yet another prolonged discussion. I was relieved when the meeting finally broke up and one of the participants gave us a ride home. Back in our apartment, Jen was quiet, not even responding when I criticized everything that had gone on that evening.

She simply said, "Good night, Tony," and firmly shut her bedroom door.

At breakfast the next morning, Jen was crunching her way through a bowl of sugar-dowsed cornflakes when she suddenly burst out, "I just can't get out of my mind what Milo said last night!"

"He said a lot of things," I responded. "Most of which I couldn't figure out what he was talking about."

"Don't you remember when he said the only way to bring order into our world is to love properly? And the only way to love properly is to understand how much God loves us, and the only way to understand how much God loves us is to pray?"

I shook my head. If those were gems of insight for my sister, they were buried in a whole lot of mud for me.

She persisted, "It was while we were reading the Bible. You know, the part about Christ loving us while we were still sinners?"

I snickered. "They must have picked that verse because they knew you were coming."

Jen's spoon slammed down on the table and her eyes shot daggers at me as she jumped to her feet.

"Antonia!" she screamed, "you're being a real—" Interrupted by the loud ring of the telephone, she stomped off to answer it.

Looking back at it now, I realize I *was* being a real pain in the you-know-what. I don't really know when or how I had developed such an attitude of superiority when it came to my sister. On the one hand, it may be what saved me from falling into her particular sins. But on the other, if I had been more honest with myself, I would have noticed the speck in my own eye resembled an awfully large log.

As I headed out for school that morning, my only thought was, if Jen was getting religion, it didn't seem to be doing her much good.

8

The next time Jen came home from youth group she didn't head to her bedroom like usual, but threw herself into the easy chair. I was watching television in the dark. After some time had passed she still hadn't said anything, so I clicked the remote to lower the volume.

"Hey, Jen, everything okay?"

She simply stared at the TV. I tried again.

"Was there another stupid skit tonight?"

She shook her head but remained silent. Since the conversation was going nowhere, I turned the volume up again and ignored her while she sat like a solemn ghost in the flickering glow from the screen.

After a few more minutes she stood, turned on a lamp and punched the OFF button on the TV.

"Hey!" I protested. "I was watching that!"

"Too bad." She folded her arms and looked around the apartment. "You know what? We're going to clean up this place."

"Clean up!" I squawked. "Tonight?"

She began turning on every light in the apartment and I saw more than a few cockroaches scurry away. In a kitchen cupboard, Jen found a box of super-size trash bags.

"No way!" I protested loudly. "It's late and I've got school tomorrow!"

She paid no attention to me, but simply stood in the middle of the muddle shaking her head. "Where to start?" she muttered. "Where to start?"

"Why don't you start in your bedroom? That way I can go to sleep!"

"Nope," she replied calmly but firmly. "First thing we're going to do is get rid of the trash in this place."

I groaned. However, it looked like if I ever wanted to get to bed, I had better pitch in. For the next several hours we tossed potato chip bags, fast-food containers and tons of old newspapers and magazines. We collected empty beer and pop cans and dumped overflowing ashtrays and wastebaskets. I swept up food wrappers and shriveled French fries from the kitchen floor while Jen hand-picked bits of trash off the worn carpet.

When we were finally done, a bevy of garbage bags sat fat and satiated by our back door. I opened the door, intending to heave them over the balcony railing into the dumpster in the alley. Whenever the cover of the dumpster was open, that was my usual way of disposing of things. If a bag missed its mark and burst open on the ground, what difference did it make? A little more trash in the alley was no big deal.

"Antonia," Jen warned me, "if you miss, you're going to go down and pick it up!"

I sighed. Anyway, the dumpster lid was closed, so I promised to haul the bags down before school in the morning—if she would just let me get to bed. Surprisingly, she agreed.

Jen had the next day off, yet she was already up when Leona came by with Lucy in tow.

"I know it's earlier than I said," Leona explained, "but the nursin' home phoned and asked me to come in early today. And since I have to go with one of the residents to the social security office, I can't take Mama with me."

Jen waved off the apology. "No problem. I've got a lot to do around here today and I'll be glad to have Mama's company."

My sister invited them to have a seat while she made coffee and dropped bread into the toaster. She asked, "Lee, you pray, don't you?"

"Of course! Why do you ask?"

"Do you ever hear God speaking to you while you're praying?"

"For heaven's sake!" laughed Leona. "What a strange question when I barely got m' eyelids open! But, yes, sometimes I feel God is speakin' to me."

"How do you know? Do you hear words?"

"Well, it's hard to describe. I mean, you *can* hear words, I suppose. But most of the time it's more like a thought that comes to you that won't go away. Why do you ask?"

I bit into a piece of jellied toast, fascinated by the conversation. Maybe I would even find out what caused Jen's odd behavior the night before.

"Well, it's kinda strange." My sister stared down at her uneaten toast for a moment before looking up again at Leona. "I went to a youth meeting last night at St. Therese's. But instead of the stuff they usually do, they said we were to go into the church and spend a whole hour praying silently, and then we'd get back together for a discussion. When I heard that, I almost left because I didn't know how to go about praying for so long."

Leona laughed again. "Why, Jennifer, prayin' isn't difficult! It's jes' talkin' to God! He created you and he loves you. He's not lookin' for something to hit you over the head with. You know what? God is on your side!"

Jen chewed her lip, thinking, before continuing, "Well, anyway, what happened was Milo—that's the youth minister— must have seen the look on my face, so he sat me down to talk. He asked if I'd ever spent any amount of time praying before. I said no, that I wouldn't know what to pray about for a whole hour, so I might as well go home. But he encouraged me to go 'sit with the Lord,' as he put it, even if just for a few minutes. He told me to take my Bible and read it wherever it opened up. Also, he said, I could think of things to thank God for."

I wondered if I myself could find anything to thank God for. There was so much bad stuff.

Jen went on, "Then he said to try to be silent inside my head, because maybe God had something to tell me."

I almost laughed out loud. Jen was never silent in her head, especially the mouth part. I wasn't surprised in the least she was telling all this personal stuff to our neighbor.

"And *did* God have something to tell you?" Leona asked.

Jen looked sheepish. "I was kind of afraid to find out, so after a few minutes I got up to leave. That's when a thought popped into my head and wouldn't go away. So how do you know when an idea is from God and when it isn't?"

Leona glanced at her watch and jumped up. "Gotta go," she said, giving Mama a peck on the cheek. "Jennifer, if it's something good, jes' do it! If it's a bad thought, it didn't come from God!" She hurried out.

I also had to run or I'd be late for school, so it wasn't until later that day I found out what was going on with Jen.

When I came in after school, I heard Mama Lucy snoring softly—asleep in the armchair—so I tiptoed to the kitchen to get something to drink. At the doorway, I stopped short.

The dishes were done. All of them. Not only washed, but put away. I had almost forgotten what the sink looked like. Its enamel was chipped and yellowed from decades of hard use, but it was clean. The counter had been cleared and the floor was washed. The old linoleum still curled up at the edges, but at least my shoes didn't stick with every step.

In the dim light, I peered more closely at the stove. The drip pans were black with age but had none of the usual burnt macaroni or sticky drips. Even the burner coils had been scoured. I couldn't believe my eyes. Whatever had gotten into Jen?

I found her in the bathroom on her knees.

"Hey," she said, her voice echoing up from the canyon of the bathtub, "I'm almost done with the tub here. I'll do the sink next while you start on the toilet."

I looked over at the commode and cringed. Grunge and grime had built up inside and out. Just how long was it since it was last cleaned? Shuddering, I shook my head.

"Not on your life!" I said. "I am not touching that thing!"

"Well, you use it, too, don't you?" Jen frowned and sat back on her heels.

"Yes, but—"

"Then grab a rag and get going! I'm not the only one that's left such a mess around here!"

I thought fast. "Tell you what. I'll do the sink and clear off those shelves and wash our brushes and clean the mirror. And I'll pick up the magazines in the corner and sweep the floor and wash the dirt off the wall. I'll even take down the shower curtain and scrub off the mildew. That way when you're done with the toilet, you won't have to do anything else."

Without waiting for an answer, I headed to the kitchen to find a rag and a bottle of cleanser. She didn't say anything else, but hummed to herself as she finished the bathtub. It was only

45

after an hour of hard labor I realized I had been suckered into doing more work than I ever intended. But a deal's a deal, so I kept plugging away long after Jen was done. Lucy had awakened, and I heard Jen sigh loudly before dropping onto the sofa.

"I'm pooped!" she declared.

"Too pooped to particulate," agreed Mama.

"That's right. But it sure feels good to have gotten so much done today. I wonder if Leona will notice when she comes?"

"She'll be coming 'round the mountain when she comes," sang Mama, off-key as usual.

Jen chuckled. "Well, there's fewer mountains to be coming around—around here—now that we've gotten rid of so much junk." Then her voice dropped in discouragement. "Gosh, there's still so much left. What are we going to do with it all?"

"You can throw out those bags of old clothes," I hollered from the bathroom.

"Oh, I don't know," Jen answered. "I was going to toss them, but changed my mind. I just hate to throw out clothes. Maybe I can find someone to use them."

Fat chance, I thought.

She went back to talking things over with Lucy. You could always count on Lucy to be a good listener, even if you didn't understand half of what she said.

"Mama, maybe I just need to sit a minute and think about what I need to do, so everything can be done in the right order."

"Everything should be done decently and in order, first Corinthians fourteen forty," declared Mama.

There was a prolonged silence in the living room. I chuckled to myself. Not even Jen had a clue what the old lady was talking about that time.

Then I heard Jen speak again. "Well, anyway, I need to prioritize my cleaning. What should I take care of first? My stuff, which is mostly in the bedroom, or Tony's clothes which are all over the place?"

"Don't you touch my clothes!" I yelled. "It's not my fault I have nowhere to put them." I trudged wearily out to the living room. "I'm done! Finally!"

There was a knock and Jen let Leona in.

"Hello, Mama." Lee gave Lucy a hug. "Has Jennifer been taking good care of you?"

"She'll be driving six white horses when she comes," her mother replied, and Leona gave us a puzzled look.

Jen tried to explain how "coming 'round a mountain" pertained to our apartment, and that made Leona look around for the first time and exclaim, "Oh, you've gone and done some cleanin'!" Then she looked embarrassed and apologized.

"Don't worry about it," said Jen. "I know it's been an awful mess around here. But we're cleaning up now. I just don't know where to put all Tony's clothes."

"Clothes should be hung in a closet," Leona said quite reasonably.

"But there's only one closet—in my bedroom—and it's already stuffed."

"I know what you mean. These old buildings have tiny closets! I don't think people in the old days had as much stuff as we do nowadays. Even Mama and I have trouble getting everything in. But I'm sure if you put your mind to it, you'll come up with something without lots of trouble."

"Boxes of trouble," Mama said.

Jen stared at her for a moment, then said, "Thank you, Mama."

Leona paid Jen, helped her mother out of the chair and headed to the door. Suddenly she stopped and turned back to Jen.

"You know, you never did say what it was God told you."

"He told me…well…at least I think he did," Jen said, "to 'clean up!'"

9

The next afternoon, Jen hauled home several good-sized boxes. She dropped them in the middle of the floor and removed the smaller ones inside.

"If there's one thing a grocery store has lots of, it's boxes!" she exclaimed. "I could have brought more if I didn't have to come home on the bus."

I folded my jeans and stacked them in a large box, with sweatshirts in another one. Into the smaller boxes went underwear and shirts. There were not enough for me to put *all* my clothes away, but at least there were fewer lying around. After the filled cartons were stacked in a corner, I had to admit our place looked much better.

When Killer came over later that evening, Jen was anxious to see what his reaction would be.

"Hi, Max," she said, stepping back to allow a better view of the room.

"Hey, babe." He moved in for a big smack on the lips. Jen waited for him to say more. When nothing was forthcoming, she asked, "Notice anything different?"

He looked her up and down, then winked. "Gal, you look great!"

She swept her arm through the air. "But how does our place look?"

"Okay." He plunked the beer on the end table and plunked himself down on the sofa. "Come on, let's cuddle."

A look of annoyance crossed Jen's face, but she picked up the TV remote and settled in next to him. I grabbed my pillow and headed to Leona's. When I returned home the next morning, my sister was nursing a hangover. I stayed out of her way. She wasn't scheduled to work, so if she wanted to stay drunk all day, that was her business.

When my shift at work was nearly over that afternoon, I noticed Kenny come in and slide into a booth. I dawdled over my final tasks, not exactly anxious to talk to him. Our arguments had gotten to the point where I didn't even acknowledge him when we passed in the school hallways. Several times I had seen him talking to other girls and I felt insanely jealous. Yet, when he tried speaking to me, I snubbed him.

When it looked like he was planted in the Burger Barn booth to stay, I had no other choice but to finally join him.

"Hey, Tony, how've you been?"

"Not too bad."

"We haven't talked for a while."

I shrugged. "I've been busy."

"Too busy to even talk to me?"

"Why should we talk? All we do is argue."

He pushed the hair out of his eyes. "Well, I was hoping we could try again. You know, there's no one in the world I like as much as you." He reached across the table and touched my hand.

I found my resolve starting to melt. After all, I didn't have any close friends. I didn't get together with other girls or even talk on the phone with them like most kids my age.

I sighed. "Yeah, I know. I miss you, too."

"Some of us are going to the roller rink Friday night. You wanna go?" He smiled at me with that smile I found so irresistible. I was a little annoyed it could affect me so much. But when he added, "I'll pay," I smiled back at him.

"Well, if that's the case, I'd love to."

When we went roller-skating that weekend, I had a blast. There were lots of people I knew at the rink. Amanda and Haley were there with their boyfriends, and Annalisa came with Darnelle from my history class. The eight of us hung around together during breaks, chowing down on nachos and playing video games. The best part of the evening was when Kenny and I held hands and skated around together during the couples' numbers. The evening was so much fun that, when Kenny asked me to go out again the next week, I readily agreed.

In her free time, Jen continued to work on the apartment. She talked Killer into hauling up the stairs a large refrigerator box she spied sitting at the curb. He found an old broom handle which he suspended between two holes in the sides of the box, and then he cut a door in the front according to Jen's specifications.

I was startled when I saw it in a corner of the living room, the last of my clothes on hangers and hanging neatly from the rod.

"Well…" I said slowly, "…I guess that works okay. Looks kind of funny, though, just a big box sitting there."

"Maybe I can paint it so it doesn't stick out so much. What do you think?"

"Fine with me. Just don't get paint on my clothes."

Another day, Jen organized the kitchen. No more jumble in the cabinets, only neat rows of cans and boxes, pots and pans. The table was also cleared off, and we no longer had to shuffle stuff around just to find some eating space. I found the transformation of our apartment rather amazing. I did everything possible not to get sucked into the work, but Jen didn't seem to care if I helped or not. She was on a mission and, once she set her mind to anything, it was best to make oneself scarce.

She was still regularly attending the Sunday evening youth group, so I was surprised one day in October when she announced she wasn't going back.

"Finally had enough of that church business?" I asked.

"No, that's not it. It's just that I'm older than most of the others. They're around your age, Tony. You should go."

I shook my head and she continued, "I'll be going to RCIA classes at the church instead."

"Our what?"

"Not 'our' anything. R-C-I-A. It stands for 'Rite of Christian Initiation for Adults.'"

"What's that? Are you going to become a Catholic?"

"I'm not sure yet. I'm just going to the classes to find out more about it. Carlos suggested it."

"Isn't Carlos in the youth group?"

"Not really. He goes sometimes, but he's older than the others, too. He's taking classes and working. But he said he'd go with me to RCIA on Monday evenings."

"Better watch out. Killer will be jealous!"

She laughed. "Carlos isn't interested in me. And Jules said he might go to RCIA with me, too."

50

"Good grief! Now you've got *two* guys fawning over you! Isn't Jules a little old for youth group, too?"

"Actually, he's twenty-two. I think he's in it because he enjoys working with the younger kids."

"Well," I said, "whatever you do at the church, you better show up sober."

Jen's eyes narrowed. "Well, Missy Good Advice! I have some advice for you, too! You'd better behave yourself with that guy you're seeing!"

"His name's Kenny," I said sullenly. "How'd you find out about him?"

"Doesn't matter. Why didn't you tell me yourself?"

"Didn't want any hassle. Besides, I can take care of myself!"

"Yeah, sure. Well, anyway, I guess you're old enough. Just stay out of trouble."

That was the extent of Jen's big-sisterly advice. *Stay out of trouble.* Even though I didn't need her advice, I probably should have listened anyway. Before I knew it, I was almost in more trouble than I ever could have imagined.

10

Jen stormed through our apartment door. "I can't believe it! Someone stole my coat!"

I was in the kitchen, with Mama Lucy keeping me company as I hunted through old newspapers for an article for science class.

"Don't you have a locker at work?" I asked.

My sister hurled a plastic grocery sack onto the counter. I caught it just before it skidded off the edge, although a can of soup went flying and left a large dent in the wall.

"Yes, I have a locker! I had already taken my coat out to go home, when I remembered I had to pick up a few things, like this darn soup." Of course, she didn't say *darn*. "So I left it on a chair...and when I came back it was gone!" She probably meant the coat, not the soup.

"Well, maybe you didn't leave it where you thought you did." That seemed like a reasonable explanation to me.

She glared at me irritably. "I looked *everywhere* for it! Someone took it!"

"Did you tell Cashel?"

"Don't be an idiot! Of course I did! He said I should have known things which aren't locked up tend to walk away."

"They tend to walk away," repeated Mama, and Jen noticed her for the first time.

"Sorry, Mama," she said, "but I'm ticked off."

If she had really said *ticked off*, Mama would not have replied in all innocence, "Did you say *pistols*? I thought it was your goat that walked away!"

I laughed and Jen heaved a big sigh. It was no use explaining it to Mama. Anyway, I could understand Jen being upset. There wasn't any money to buy another coat.

"What are you going to do?" I asked.

Jen shook her head. "Guess I'll have to wear two sweatshirts and hope I can afford a new coat before it gets really cold."

"What about those bags of clothes Irene gave you? Isn't there a coat in there?"

Jen said, no, she didn't think so, but I suggested she take a look while I warmed the soup for supper. She grabbed the top bag and upended it on the sofa. Out tumbled the old clothes, including the coat I thought I remembered seeing.

"There, I told you!" I said triumphantly.

Jen held up the coat to look at it. It was about her size, but that was really the only positive thing to say about it. The knee-length coat was made of outdated tweedy material, with a row of large plastic buttons down the front. The edges of the sleeves were frayed and the fabric was ripped around the pockets. It was topped off with a tired-looking brown collar.

"This is really ugly!" Jen exclaimed.

Mama Lucy evidently agreed. "Beauty is only skin deep," she said, "but ugly is to the bone!"

"Try it on," I urged. "Maybe it won't be so bad."

But it was. There was no way Jen would let anyone see her in that old thing. She'd freeze to death first.

She shrugged the coat off and ran her hand over the soft pile lining. "Too bad," she said. "The lining is in great shape. If only the outside looked better."

She pouted in silence while we ate our soup, sandwiches, potato chips and Twinkies. Mama and I carried on our own conversation—sort of.

As we finished eating I heard Jen murmur, "I wonder—?"

I said, "What?" as she went to examine the coat again.

She said, "I've got an idea!" and dashed to her bedroom. I heard her pawing through the closet and wondered if it was a way to get out of doing the dishes. As I brushed off the crumbs trailing down the front of Mama's dress, Jen came back and set something down on the table with a heavy *clunk*. I turned to see a large, old-fashioned wooden box. Jen was wiping away dust and cobwebs from its surface.

53

"Is that what I think it is?" I asked. "I haven't seen that for years!"

"Look at this, Mama!" Jen said to Lucy. "This was my grandmother's sewing box. It's been buried at the bottom of my closet all this time."

The rectangular box was made of polished dark wood. The wooden handle arched from one side to the other, and underneath it were two knobs. Jen lifted the knobs upwards and outwards, pulling out trays cleverly hinged to each other. Fully splayed open in staggered tiers, the trays showed off their contents.

When Mama saw the neat rows of pastel and jewel-toned thread in the uppermost tray, her eyes sparkled.

"Oh, my! Look at all the pretty pools of thread—and bobbins!" she said, although it sounded more like *bobbies*. The tray under the *pools* and *bobbies* held snaps and zippers, hooks and eyes, and seam tape and rickrack. If some of the items weren't still in their original wrappers, I never would have known what they were.

Jen hefted a pair of sewing shears. "Boy, these are heavy. Nothing like those cheap things we have today."

There were also smaller, sharp-pointed scissors with worn golden handles, and a whole jumble of things apparently employed at one time in the fine art of sewing. In the last tray, balls of yarn in a rainbow of colors were packed together. Underneath them, at the very bottom, was a dog-eared instruction book for a long-gone sewing machine.

When I realized Jen was no longer beside me, I looked around for her. She was seated on the sofa, wielding the sewing shears over the old coat on her lap.

"What are you doing?" I asked.

Deep in concentration, she didn't answer.

By the time Leona arrived to pick up her mother, my sister had cut away the entire top layer of the coat, leaving only little squares of the tweed around the buttons and buttonholes. Basically, all that was left was the lining.

Lee glanced at the scraps on the floor. "Have you taken up sewing?"

Jen explained, "I happened to think of my grandmother's sewing box I had stored away. I remember how much I loved it when I was little. I was fascinated by all the colors of thread and other neat stuff. Sometimes she'd even let me try sewing on a small piece of fabric. I'm going to make a coat for myself."

She noticed me shoving the pile of scraps into a garbage bag. "Hey, don't throw that away! I might use it some time."

It would be fascinating to see what Jen planned to do with the coat. Though she had done a little mending for our mother years ago, she hadn't employed such domestic skills in a long time.

Leona left with Mama after making Jen promise she'd show them the finished coat. The phone rang and I answered it.

"Jen, it's Killer."

"Ask him what he wants."

"Max, she's busy right now. What do you want?" I listened and turned back to my sister.

"He has to take his aunt to the doctor and can't come over."

That got her attention. She looked up at me from under her long bangs, her eyes skeptical. "To the doctor? On a Saturday night?"

"That's what he said."

Jen shrugged and turned back to her sewing. "Whatever."

"Uh...she said she'll see you next week," I said into the receiver and hung up. "No Maxie on a Saturday night? Whatever are you going to do?"

She ignored my jibe. "Get me a beer, wouldja, Tony? I might sew all night!"

"Have fun," I said. "Kenny's picking me up. We're going to the library." By that time, Kenny knew where I lived. After our apartment was cleaned up, I had invited him up a few times.

Jen looked at me in surprise. "The library? What is there to do at the library?"

"Just hang out."

I didn't bother to mention how long it took me to talk Kenny into a library date. I was only able to accomplish it by agreeing to go with him to a party at his friend's house the following weekend. *That* was certainly one of the dumber things I ever did.

"So how was your library date?" Jen said, sticking pins between her lips.

It was morning and I was getting ready for work. My sister had already been up sewing for hours. While I was gone the previous night, she had used colored thread to sew decorative stitches around each of the button patches still fastened to the coat lining. She had also removed the collar and whip-stitched the raw top edge of the coat with yarn. It almost looked like it was meant to be that way. She did the same with the sleeves and now was working on the rest of the coat. Thinking it still looked a little plain, she had cut long strips of fabric from old shirts she found in the clothes bags, twisted them into thin ropes and was sewing them on in a pattern of flowers sprouting from the bottom hem.

I watched her work for a moment before saying, "Okay, I guess. I showed him all the different rooms, but the only thing he really liked was the tech room. We signed up for a computer and played games until it closed."

"Well," mumbled Jen through the pins, "guess you can't get into trouble at a library."

I decided not to mention the upcoming party.

By the time I got home later that day, she had finished the coat and proudly modeled it for me. I had to admit it certainly was unique, in a funky-looking sort of way.

"I already showed it to Leona and Lucy," she said, "and I'm gonna wear it to work tomorrow."

After work the next day, Jen was jubilant.

"Sasha loved it!" she said, referring to a co-worker. "She wants me to make one as a gift for her sister!" Jen dumped out all the other clothes bags, searching for another coat. She was disappointed not to find any.

"Why don't you just ask her to bring you an old coat?" I suggested. "And is she going to pay you for your time?"

"I hadn't thought about it."

"Well, I think you should. It's a lot of work." And, I figured, we could use the money.

After supper, Jen looked at the huge pile of second-hand clothes on the sofa.

"You know what, Tony?" Her eyes sparkled with excitement. "I think there are a lot of possibilities in this old stuff! Look here." She showed me a faded pair of blue jeans, too big for either of us. "If I cut off the bottom of the legs where they're not so worn, sew together the bottom cuffs, hem the top and add a strap cut from the top of the jeans, I could make one-of-a-kind denim purses. And I could decorate them with yarn.

"And all these old sweatshirts! What if I was to cut out the good parts from the front and back, sew up the edges and stuff them to make pillows?"

"This one here says 'Michigan State.'" I held it up for her to see.

"That's right! Don't you think someone might like a handmade pillow with their favorite college on it?"

"What would you use for stuffing?"

She looked around. "I can cut up all the pieces of coat and sweatshirts and everything else I can't use, and that would make pretty good stuffing."

Smiling, I shook my head. I hadn't seen my sister so enthused about anything in a long time. She probably would have started immediately if she hadn't looked at the clock and realized that Carlos would be picking her up shortly for class.

11

The following Saturday evening, even though I told Jen I was going roller-skating, I actually planned to go with Kenny to his friend's party. As Kenny jockeyed for a parking spot in the lineup of cars outside his friend's house, I asked if I'd know anyone at the party. He assured me there would be kids from school there.

"And wait till you see the nice set-up in the basement, with stereo and video games. There's ping-pong and a pool table, too."

There was also a bar in the basement, I found out. And no adults anywhere.

The house was already crowded by the time we arrived. I recognized Annalisa and Darnelle and several others, but the rest of the guests were strangers to me. At first, the party was fun. I discovered I had a knack for ping-pong, and Kenny and I took on team after team and beat them all. His friend, John, played the amiable host—until later in the evening when the locked liquor cabinet was broken into and he began drinking with the rest.

After finishing ping-pong, Kenny and I went upstairs where the party was noisier and the music louder. People were packed into the small living room. Some were trying to dance, others were draped on chairs, the floor and each other's laps. The air was gradually becoming thick with cigarette smoke and with a sweeter smell I couldn't at first identify.

When I saw a reefer pass from hand to hand and noticed Kenny taking a drag, I pulled at his sleeve.

"Hey, I think we should go."

"It's okay," he said, "I'm not gonna get stoned. Come on, Tony, try it."

I shook my head. "I'm going to use the bathroom. Watch my can of pop so no one puts anything into it."

I wonder now why I never got caught up in the usual things so many other young people fall prey to. Maybe it was all my reading which gave me dreams of something better. Or maybe the prayers of others were protecting me, even though I didn't realize it then. At the time, I only knew I couldn't be talked into doing something I didn't want to do. I liked to be *different,* unlike the losers I saw around me.

And there were plenty of losers at that party. I fought my way through them, only to find a line-up outside the bathroom door. Figuring there would be another john on the second floor, I pushed upwards through the bodies on the stairs. But there was a wait there, too. I had no choice but to get in line. It was quite some time before I had a chance to look for Kenny again. I discovered him on the floor in the kitchen, propped against the wall.

"Hiya, Ton-eee!" He grinned up at me.

"Kenny!" I hollered through the noise, shaking him hard by the shoulders. "Have you taken something?"

"Lynx brought some really goo....d stuff." He swung an arm towards the boy sprawled next to him. That must have been Lynx.

"Kenny, let's go!" My voice hit the higher decibels, but still I was nearly drowned out by a blaring CD player.

"Ton-eee," said Kenny, staring at me. "You have ants crawling all over yee-ou."

Instinctively, I brushed a hand over my face, then tried to pull Kenny up. He was heavy and was not cooperating in the least.

"Forget it," came a loud voice behind me. A tall blond boy I didn't recognize was watching the scene between Kenny and me. "He's wasted. Do you really want him driving you home?" He grabbed my hand. "Come with me. I'll get my coat and give you a ride home."

Before I had a chance to even think, he hauled me up the crowded steps and past the second-floor bathroom line. Further down the hallway, he opened a door.

"My coat's in here." He pulled me into a dark bedroom and kicked the door closed. Then he turned, grasped both my wrists and began kissing me hard.

I tried squirming away. "Stop it! What are you doing?"

He yanked me closer and wrapped an arm around my neck. His hot breath in my face smelled of liquor as I struggled to push him away. I was scared. I knew even if I managed to scream, there was little chance anyone would hear me. And if they did, would they even care? I tried desperately to figure out a way to extricate myself from his grasp.

All of a sudden, brilliant blue lights were flashing across the ceiling. That got my captor's attention.

"What's that about?" Releasing me, he jerked up the window blinds. "It's the cops! Holy sh—" He yanked open the door and made a beeline for the stairs.

I took several long, steadying breaths before I, too, headed for the stairway. But there was a crunch of kids trying to cram their way down and I was behind them all. I knew I wasn't going to make it.

I looked wildly about me and then ran into the empty bathroom. There I stopped and tried desperately to think. I had been saved from one dilemma, but now the cops were outside. What was I going to do?

Loud shouting and sounds of banging doors erupted from downstairs and the ever-increasing wail of sirens filled the air. I was scared. Would I be arrested? True, I hadn't been drinking or messing with drugs, but I'd probably be hauled off to jail with everyone else. What if I couldn't graduate? Jen was going to skin me alive!

All sorts of escape plans ran through my mind, including the thought of jumping from a second-story window and running as fast as I could. But I knew that was ridiculous. I discarded that idea immediately.

What was I going to do?

Suddenly the word *"Hide!"* popped into my mind. That seemed to make more sense than anything, but the question was—*where?*

Under a bed? In a closet? Any of those places seemed too obvious.

Trying not to succumb to panic, I slumped against the bathroom wall. Wait a minute—the bottom of the wall moved! I pushed on it and it swung inward. There I saw a cubbyhole with an old laundry chute cut into the floor. It was well-hidden by the top-hinged door, framed with molding and painted to match the walls.

I squirmed my way under the door into the tight spot. By sitting against the back of the space, I could prop my feet against the door to keep it from moving. Just in time, too. Someone pounded up the stairs and into the bathroom. I heard the shower curtain being pulled back and the linen closet opened. Then footsteps came close to where I was hidden and stopped. Knuckles rapped sharply on the laundry chute door.

When the door didn't move, the footsteps receded into the hallway and joined others as the house was apparently searched thoroughly. After an interminable length of time, the commotion stopped and the sirens died away. In the dark, airless space, beads of sweat trickled down my face. I took quick but light breaths and steeled myself to remain still.

Eventually, though, I had to consider how I was going to get out. I wondered if I'd be able to drop through the laundry chute, which was only a few inches from my backside, to the basement. However, I didn't know how wide the chute was. What if I ended up like a character in a TV sitcom, stuck fast in that chute? What if the owners of the house came back home to find me helplessly dangling?

In the end, I decided there was only one sensible way to get out—the same way I got in. By shifting my feet, which had fallen asleep and tingled like crazy, I was able to pull up the swinging door and peer out. Except for the moonlight shimmering around the edges of the bathroom window shade, the house seemed to be dark. Stifling a sneeze, I cautiously slithered out of the hole. I listened for the least sound while tiptoeing to the steps and starting down. When a stair creaked under my footstep, I froze. But everything remained quiet, so I crept down to the front door and cracked it open. The front yard and street were deserted. I stepped outside and gratefully gulped the fresh night air.

Then I was struck with a new reality. How in the world was I going to get home? I sprinted down to the corner and stopped under a streetlight to look at my watch. It was after two! And even worse, I hadn't paid any attention to where Kenny was driving. Now I didn't know where I was.

I had to do something, so I started walking. The night was terribly chilly. I had left my sweater at the party house and there was no way I was going back for it. Wrapping my arms around me for warmth, I kept glancing nervously about me at the dark houses and yards.

All of a sudden there came a rustling from behind a line of thick shrubbery. I gasped and was preparing to run, when a black cat streaked out and loped across the street. Trembling a little, I forced myself to continue on. I tried hard not to think about all the things that could happen in the city in the middle of the night.

After walking for what seemed like forever, I came to a main thoroughfare which was familiar to me. From there, I knew I could find my way home. What a relief! Being on a busier street, though, brought its own set of worries. So whenever I heard a car approaching, I played it safe and slipped quickly into the shadows of the nearest building.

Once, as a whole succession of cars passed, I impatiently waited against the dilapidated side wall of a run-down store. Shivering in the cold, I wondered how I would ever make it home at such a snail's pace. I sighed. As I leaned my head back against the hard brick, unexpectedly the thought of *angels* came to me.

I remembered the time Jen had come home from a youth meeting and said to me, "You know what they were talking about tonight?"

"What?" I asked.

"They said we each have an angel to watch over us."

"Oh, really."

"Yeah, really! They're called *guardian angels.* And we can ask them to protect us."

"So all of us have these so-called guardian angels?"

She nodded.

"If that's so," I challenged her, "where was Dad's guardian angel when that car slammed into him?"

She blinked. "Well, I don't know, exactly. I guess they don't protect us from *every* bad thing. I just heard that we can ask them to help us when we're in trouble. There's even a prayer that goes, 'Angel of God, my guardian dear—' Jeez, I can't remember the rest. There was something about 'to guard and to guide.' I'll have to write it down next time."

At the time, I blew off her words. If my sister wanted to believe in some sort of heavenly protectors, that was up to her.

But that night, waiting in the darkness, I couldn't stop the words, *"Angel of God, my guardian dear,"* from repeating themselves over and over in my head. As I eventually left the relative safety of the building and continued my lonely walk home, it was oddly comforting to think about an angel watching over me.

When I arrived back in my own neighborhood, there were more and more people out and about. The "night people"—the homeless wanderers and streetwalkers—didn't worry me much. It was the ones who had other business to transact I wanted to avoid. Just as I spied our apartment building ahead, I spotted a group of them hanging around a streetlamp, making deals with drivers at the curb. They were between me and home.

As I halted, unsure what to do next, the gang curiously melted away like a mirage. I was wondering how I got so lucky when I heard the crunch of tires behind me.

My heart racing, I whirled around.

12

I guess angels, like miracles, can come in many disguises. That night, mine arrived in a white police cruiser. A policewoman leaned out the curbside window and scrutinized me.

"What are you doing out here this time of night?"

I sagged against a nearby street sign in relief and mumbled something unintelligible. The policewoman spoke to her partner, then got out of the cruiser to ask my name and age. I heard the other officer call it in, perhaps checking to see if I was a runaway.

"Where are you going?" she asked, not unkindly. "And where did you come from?"

I pointed to the apartment building down the block.

"I live there," I said, "and I was trying to figure out how to get home without having someone jump me."

As for where I came from, I decided that a partial truth was the best course.

"I was out with my boyfriend and he was drinking. And he got too drunk to drive so I decided it'd be safer to walk home."

"Why didn't you call someone?"

"I live with my sister and she doesn't own a car."

"Where was this drinking going on?"

"At his friend's house. I don't remember the address. I just started walking till I came to a street I recognized. And now I'm, uh…almost home," I finished lamely.

She leaned closer to me and sniffed. I hoped the long walk home in the fresh night air had blown away any suspicious odor lingering on my clothes. She looked searchingly into my eyes, then took up her pad and made sure she had my name and address right.

"Get in," she said. "We'll take you home."

After dropping me off in front of my building, they waited to see if I was really going in. I used my key to let myself in the front door and breathed a heartfelt "thank you!" to no one in particular. I had never been so glad to come home to that place.

The next morning, I was relieved to find out Jen assumed I had been at Leona's for the night. Actually, that *was* where I went after seeing Killer's truck parked across the street. I felt terrible waking Lee up in the middle of the night, but she took me in without question. I led her to believe I was there because Jen's boyfriend had come over.

I hoped my life wasn't becoming impossibly entangled in a knot of lies. Up until then, I had always considered myself basically honest. Now that Kenny was out of my life—and I had decided on the long trek home that he *was* out of my life—maybe I could start to become a better person.

Jen was hung over again on Sunday morning. When she perked up in the afternoon, I asked if she'd like to come with me to the library. I mentioned that was where she would find lots of books with craft ideas using fabric.

Her bloodshot eyes brightened. "I never thought of that! Let's go!"

At the library bus stop, as I fought my way off the crowded bus, I spotted Jen way ahead of me on the sidewalk. She turned and beckoned impatiently as I struggled to catch up.

"Hurry on, Antonia!" she called. "Hurry on, would you?"

I glared at her. She knew I hated being called by my full name. I also hated the way she always said "hurry on." I mean, didn't most people say "hurry up?" She claimed our mother had said it that way, too, but I didn't remember. I was sure Jen just did it to annoy me.

We came home with stacks of craft books. She eagerly poured over them while I shoved two pre-packaged dinners in the oven. I scraped pudding from a can, opened a bag of bright-orange cheese puffs—and dinner was ready. She ate with one hand while flipping through the pages of a book with the other.

"Here's a fantastic idea!" she exclaimed. "I wonder if there's enough material in that old jumper to make a vest like this."

And, "Look at this, Tony! It's just a sweatshirt, but it's cut open up the front and the edges are bound with yarn. Then you sew on buttons and embroider around them for flowers. Isn't it cute?"

And again, "There's a couple of dress shirts in those bags. I could cut the collars off—like this, see?—shorten the sleeves and bind the raw edges with fabric from another shirt. Then add button flowers, just like the sweatshirts!" Her voice trailed off as she skimmed other ideas. It looked like I would get stuck with the dishes for another night.

Jen came home Monday afternoon carrying a black coat. It was nearly as ugly as the one she had originally transformed, but it did have a beautiful gray pile lining.

"Sasha didn't have an old coat," she said. "She found this one for five bucks at the Salvation Army. I never thought of that. I bet I could pick up a lot of bargains there."

She tackled the coat right away, setting it aside only long enough to attend her class that evening with Jules. I was amazed how Jen never paid any special attention to either Carlos or Jules. She was grateful for the free rides but, unless she was telling me about her class, she never mentioned them. For my part, I hoped neither of them ever showed up on the same night as Killer. I liked their faces too much to see them rearranged.

Meanwhile, I was having my own guy problems. After the night of the party, Kenny was absent from class for quite a while. I figured when I saw him again he would be chastened, eager to apologize. But when he finally returned to school, he was mad at *me!*

"Where were you?" he demanded. "Why didn't you get me out of there before the cops came? I'm in a ton of trouble! And my car was impounded!"

"Why, you...you—" I was furious, hardly able to speak. "You *chose* to take *whatever*, and I had to walk home and I could have been raped or murdered! You don't care about me! You never did! *Get out of my life!*"

Other kids were pointing at us and laughing. Angry and embarrassed, I swiveled on my heel and started to stalk away.

"Tony!" Kenny grabbed my arm and I jerked it back.

"Stay away from me! Forever!"

After that nasty scene, I put Kenny out of my mind and concentrated on school and my job. Management had changed at the Barn and the new regime was a pain to get along with. On top of everything else, my hours were cut back just when we needed money the most. Jen still wasn't working full-time and we were behind on bills. Just that morning, she had peered into the coffee can where we pooled our money.

"Did you put your last paycheck in?" she asked.

"Sure did," I replied, "all but ten dollars which you said I could keep for myself."

"You might have to throw that in, too. The school sent an order form for your cap and gown."

"But graduation's not till June!"

"They need the money now. Or else you won't get one and you'll have to graduate in blue jeans."

The thought of parading across the stage without a cap and gown was too awful to contemplate. I wailed loudly and Jen frowned.

"Well, don't have a hairy. Sasha's going to pay me for the coat. I'll hurry to get it done."

She had the coat finished sooner than I would have thought. She also made more purses and pillows, and transformed shirts and pants into items that would sell at trendy boutiques. A few of the things she sold to her fellow employees and the rest she piled on a chair in the living room.

When Frank and Beatrice stopped by one Sunday in October, Jen exuberantly welcomed them.

"Well!" Beatrice beamed at her. "What makes you so happy to see us?"

"I can't wait to show you what I've been working on!"

Jen seated them on the sofa. I smiled wryly when I saw them glance furtively around the apartment. Bet they didn't recognize the place.

"Look at these." Jen showed them the items she had created. "I made them out of old clothes someone gave me."

"Oh! You must have spent *hours* on these," Beatrice said, examining the workmanship. "They're absolutely lovely! And so unique!"

"What are you going to do with them all?" Frank asked.

"Dunno yet. I made a coat, too." She brought out her coat and showed them. "A girl at work liked it so much, I made one for her."

"Good heavens, you could sell these things at a craft show!" Beatrice held up a decorated sweatshirt. "People would love them!"

Jen's eyes lit up. "A craft show! What a terrific idea! But where would I find one?"

"There's going to be a Christmas bazaar at our church," Frank said. "Would you like me to call the lady who runs it and get more information?"

"Uh...do you know if there's an entry fee?" Jen asked. "I'm kind of short right now."

"I'm not sure. Let me find out, okay? I'll let you know."

While Jen wrote down our phone number and handed it to him, I jumped into the conversation.

"The weather's getting colder, and the two of you are still going around the neighborhood?"

Frank said, "Actually, we're just doing some follow-up calls with the people we visited before. Do you know Dolores down on the second floor?" Jen and I shook our heads.

"She's in 2H, a Mexican lady with several children. She's asking some of the other tenants over to pray the Rosary this afternoon at four. Would you like to go?"

I *had* seen a Hispanic family around occasionally, but never paid much attention to them. Now they were inviting us over to pray *what?*

"Oh, I'd love to!" Jen enthused. "Tony, how about you?"

One more thing Jen was trying to drag me into. I shook my head.

"But I don't own a rosary," Jen told our visitors. Or know anything about it, I might have added. That was classic Jen, jumping into something new without thinking how ignorant she was of the whole thing.

"Here, I have one you can have." Beatrice pulled a circlet of blue plastic beads out of her pocket.

Jen reached for it. "But I don't know how to use it."

"Don't worry, you'll pick it up. It's not hard. We'll bring a little pamphlet with the prayers in it so you can follow along. See you at four."

13

"—and the boys are named Joachin and Miguel, and the little girl's the cutest thing you ever saw, maybe four years old, with these big, dark eyes! They call her Nina. And the mom's expecting another baby next year."

Working on my math homework, I was only half listening to my sister who seemed determined to tell me everything that had gone on at Dolores's get-together. I kept trying to concentrate on the indecipherable algorithms in front of me.

"The dad's name is Joachin, too," Jen went on, "and he works in one of those factories over on Fort Street. Dolores has some trouble with the language, but the little boys rattle off English just fine. Even though they don't have a lot of things, the kids seem happy enough. They're not allowed to go out and play because the neighborhood is so bad. That's why we haven't seen them around much.

"There were others there, too. Frank and Beatrice, of course, and also a woman named Wanda who lives in the apartment over Leona. And Bobby, the trapeze artist."

That got my full attention. "The what?"

"The trapeze artist. You know—of the Flying Fantini Brothers?"

"You're kidding, right?"

"That's what he said, Bobby Fantini of the Flying Fantini Brothers."

"Why would a trapeze artist be living in this slum?"

Jen brought her sewing box to the table and threaded a needle. "I don't know. I didn't have much time to talk to him. But I guess anyone can be down on their luck. Right?"

She glanced at me before starting to sew. I had to agree. After all, *we* certainly were.

"Was Leona there?"

"No. Beatrice said they'd been invited, but I gather Baptists don't go for the Rosary much."

"What's a Rosary like, anyway?"

"Well, there's different prayers you say. There's the Our Father prayer, the Hail Mary and the Glory Be. You say a prayer for each bead as you go around."

"That's an awful lot of beads. And prayers."

"Yeah. But Frank said once you learn the words of the prayers, you don't think about them so much. You concentrate more on thinking about Jesus, like he was right there with you."

"Seems like it would be hard to say all those prayers."

"It was at first, but once I got the hang of it, it just started to flow. I tell you, Tony, I had such a feeling of peace by the time we got done."

I looked at the top of my sister's head as she stitched a flower onto a bag. Peace, I knew, was something Jen definitely needed in her life. I turned back to my homework but she wasn't done talking yet.

"After the Rosary, Dolores served cake and I had a chance to ask Frank some questions."

"Like what?"

"I asked him if it was better to pray the Rosary or to pray in our own words."

"What a dumb question! What'd he say?"

"Well, *he* didn't act like I was dumb! You know, I really like that old man. Anyway, he said both kinds of prayers are good. That it's important to spend time every day just talking to God in our own words—informally, as he put it. But he said formal prayers are good, too, like the Rosary or other ones, and that there's beautiful prayers in the Bible and ones written by saints. He said that praying those prayers along with our own can lead to a very deep prayer life."

She stopped sewing and looked up.

"Then he asked why I was so interested in prayer."

"So, why are you?"

"I told him that I want so much more for my life, something better than what I've got now. Then he asked what I wanted the most and I told him a house. My own home."

I was surprised. I thought my sister might say she wanted nicer clothes or a car—or money. I would have mentioned those things myself.

"You want a house? So you can get out of this place?"

She stared past me, her thoughts far away.

"Not just because of that," she answered in a soft voice. "I dream about a home that's permanent, where you can feel secure. I feel that when you have a home of your own, all sorts of good things can happen there. Do you remember the house we lived in before Dad died?"

She was speaking of *my* father—her stepfather. I shook my head.

"I guess you were too young," Jen said. "Mom had to sell it after he died, because her cancer came back and there were bills to pay. I never felt any of the places we lived after that were really our home. *Home* has a front porch and a big living room for friends to gather and a yard with trees in it."

I was spellbound. My sister hadn't talked to me like that in a long time. The math problems could wait.

"And what did Frank say?"

"That it's good to bring all our desires to God in prayer, because he's a loving Father who delights in giving good things to his children. And sometimes he *does* give us what we ask for. I asked Frank, 'Do you think God will give me a real home?' He said he didn't know, but God doesn't mind if we keep asking. He said if we pray enough our prayers will start to .change, from wanting the less important to wanting the more important. And the most important thing, he said, is wanting God more than the things he can give us."

Wanting God? What did that mean?

Jen pulled a small card from her pocket. "Frank wrote something down for me." She read from the card, "*Our only need is for God. When that need takes over our life, all other things fall into place.*"

I was trying to figure out what she was talking about. I needed a lot of things I could taste, feel, hear and, especially, spend. How could a person need only God?

Jen set the card aside and picked up her sewing, but I wasn't ready to let the conversation end yet.

"You didn't say anything about this Wanda. I don't know if I've ever seen her. What does she look like?"

Jen looked crossly at me. "Crying out loud, Antonia! Are you ever going to stop talking? I'm trying to get some work done here!"

Frank called the next afternoon. Jen was at work so I offered to take a message.

"That would be great, Tony. Would you please tell her there's a table available at our church's Christmas bazaar? She needs to call as soon as possible and they'll give her all the information. Here's the phone number."

I jotted it down. "When is it?"

"Saturday, December second. Nine to four."

I hated to ask the question, but I had to. "Is there any cost?"

Frank said heartily, "Oh, no, none at all. There was only one table left and it was in a back corner. So they said she wouldn't have to pay for it. But there's just one thing. Every craftsperson has to donate an item for the raffle table. Do you think she can do that?"

"Oh, I'm sure she can! Thanks! I'll give her the message."

Jen was ecstatic when I told her. She immediately began combing through the remainder of the old clothes. "Hmmm. Not much left." She went over to the refrigerator box in the corner and opened it.

"Hey! What do you think you're doing?" I demanded.

"You don't need all these clothes."

"What? Get your paws off my things!"

She looked wounded as she closed the cardboard door. "I was going to ask before taking anything. Well, maybe I can pick up a few things at the Salvation Army."

I remembered our nearly-empty coffee can. "Don't count on it. The first of the month's coming up and the rent's due."

Jen pushed her hair back from her face. I noticed her roots were showing badly and she needed a hair cut. "Can't you ask your boss for more hours?" she asked.

"Last time I tried talking to him about it, he made it a point to mention I wasn't wearing regulation shoes. So I've been trying to keep out of his sight as much as possible. And hide my feet. How about you? Can't you get your hours back?"

"I've asked. It may happen soon with the holidays coming up and all. But I still want Monday nights off so I can go to RCIA."

Jen hadn't missed a class since she started. If no one could pick her up, she took the bus.

"What are you studying in this RC-whatever that's so important?"

"All kinds of things. The priest talks about God and how we can know he exists and why we should pray. And he talks a lot about reading the Bible. I finished the Psalms and the Gospel of Mark, and now I'm on the Gospel of John."

My jaw dropped in astonishment. My sister was reading the Bible and praying—and getting drunk and sleeping with Killer. Somehow, it all didn't seem to fit together. There must be something in the Bible about that. I would have to ask Leona next time I saw her.

Jen was saying, "And next week we're going to start learning about the sacraments."

"The what?"

"Remember when I told you about that youth group with the weird scientist talking about the 'power' of God? P-W-R? Where *P* stands for prayer and *W* is for the Word of God? I finally found out what the *R* stands for—*receiving the sacraments.*"

"So what are sacraments?"

"Dunno. Haven't learned that yet."

I returned to the topic of the craft show. "Why don't you ask the girls at work to go through their closets and bring you their old clothes? In return, maybe you could make them each a small gift, like a purse or scarf or something."

"Tony," Jen cried, "you're brilliant!" But I already knew that.

The next week she began bringing home bags of clothes. The other women had been most happy to clean out their closets. Irene had even thrown in an entire bolt of material.

"Look at this!" Jen exclaimed, pulling out the fabric to show me. "Isn't it pretty? Irene bought it for curtains for her bedroom and never got around to making them."

There were yards and yards of the cream-colored cotton sprinkled with small pink rosebuds and green leaves. She unrolled the material partway and held it up next to the window.

73

"I could make curtains for *our* window! See how nice it looks? It would hide the broken blinds. And there's so much of it! I could do the window and still have a lot left over. Hey, I know! I'll slipcover the sofa, too!"

I smiled at her enthusiasm. "Sounds great, Jen. But that's an awful lot of sewing."

She re-rolled the fabric and set it aside. "I know. I wouldn't even think of starting it before the craft show. Let's see what else we have here."

Sasha had thrown in some of her husband's things. It didn't matter to Jen, as she was just going to cut them up anyway, and the men's clothes were especially generous in the amount of fabric they contained. I noticed a paper sack and peeked inside.

"Ties? She gave you a whole bunch of men's ties! What are you going to do with these?"

"I'll come up with something," she said.

It was hard for me to imagine what in the world could be made from old neckties. But I needn't have worried.

14

Ever since my sister discovered the value in freebies, I never knew what she was going to bring home next. One evening, I arrived home to find everything in our living room pushed into the middle. Jen stood on a kitchen chair, working away at the wall.

"Now what?" I sighed. It had been a hard day at the Burger Barn and I just wanted to collapse on the sofa and watch a little TV.

"You won't believe what I found today," she said. "Look in the bathroom."

On the edge of the tub were three gallon-size paint cans with dried paint striping their sides.

"Where'd you get these from?"

"I picked them up at the curb over on Chestnut Street. Someone had cleaned out their garage. I left the empty cans and brought home the ones which still had paint left in them."

"What are you going to do with them?"

"Paint the living room! I can't stand how awful it looks. There's those water stains on the back wall, mildew under the window, and it's so dirty! Then there's this hole here that sticks out like a...well, like a hole in the wall."

I watched her attempts to patch the hole.

"Where'd you get the patching stuff?"

"From Mona."

"You talked to Her Majesty when you didn't have to?"

Jen gobbed spackling into the hole but it kept disappearing inside the walls. She muttered a few choice words.

"There has to be a better way to do it," I said. "Why don't you stuff something into the hole first? Then the plaster won't fall in."

Although irritated at me for the suggestion, she nevertheless jammed a balled-up piece of fabric into the hole and topped it with plaster. It held. I refrained from saying, "I told you so."

She followed me into the kitchen, putty knife in hand, and smeared spackle over the deep dent left by the flying soup can.

"Hey, I'm getting pretty good at this!" She stepped back to admire her work.

"What's this doing here?" I pointed to the sink where a white-encrusted paint roller was soaking.

She lifted it out and poked it with a finger.

"No good. It's still hard as a rock. What am I going to paint with?"

I opened a can of ravioli and dumped it into a saucepan for supper. "You'll think of something," I said. And she did.

The next day, I arrived home to find she had rescued an old seat cushion from the dumpster, ripped off the cover and cut the proper-sized rectangle to wrap around the hardened roller. She had already attached the foam rubber with white glue and was holding it together with masking tape until it dried.

After scraping the wall patches smooth with the putty knife, she opened the cans of paint.

"This isn't going to work," I said, peering into the cans. "These are all different colors. And there's not very much in any of them."

"I know." She brushed me aside. "But if I mix them together there will be almost a full can. Do you think that'll be enough to paint the living room and kitchen?"

I had no idea. I watched her pour all the paint into one can and stir with our soup ladle. One can had contained a cream color, another pink and the third light blue. As I watched the hues swirl together in a multicolored cyclone, I wondered if our apartment would turn out some sickly shade of purple. But when she was done mixing, the paint was a soft rose color. I had to wait until after work the next day to see how it would look on the walls.

I came home to find Jen in an old shirt of Sasha's husband. She was dipping the roller into paint which had been poured in a cookie sheet, then applying it to the wall. She had

76

covered almost the entire back wall and it looked good. However, trouble was brewing with the makeshift roller.

"The foam keeps coming unglued," she complained, trying to slip rubber bands around the messy cylinder. With a paint-covered hand, she gestured to me. "See those other pieces of foam I cut up? You can use them like a paint brush. Here, take the can of paint and you can help by trimming around the window and doors."

We were thus engaged when a pounding came at the door. It was Mona.

"I came to get my stuff back," she said, a sour expression on her face as usual.

I quickly handed her the spackle and putty knife, hoping she'd go away, but she elbowed her way in and swept her squinty-eyed gaze around the room. I hoped painting the walls wasn't against the rules. Jen ignored her, struggling to keep the foam and the roller working together as one unit.

Mona watched in silence for a minute before spouting, *"Why* are you trying to use such a useless piece of junk? You need a real roller!"

"Don't have one," Jen said. "I glued foam around this old one and it worked pretty well for a while."

"What kind of glue did you use?"

When Jen told her, Mona gave a derisive laugh.

"Of course it didn't hold! The water-based paint soaked right through the water-based glue!" She didn't add, *how stupid can you get?* But it was hard to miss the implication.

"I got new roller covers in the maintenance room," she said. "I'll bring you one."

Jen and I looked at her in amazement. She had painting equipment when it was clear the place hadn't seen new paint since the Middle Ages? And she was offering it to us? For free?

Of course, Mona couldn't leave on such a pleasant note. Before striding out the door, she pointed and snarled, "Ya can't paint over the blasted mildew! Wash it off with some bleach!"

The next interruption wasn't any more pleasant. Killer arrived with Weasel. Jen had gotten so caught up in the painting, she forgot she had promised to go to a movie with them. Killer took one look at the paint smears on her face and spatters in her hair and demanded to know what she was doing.

"I completely forgot, Maxie. Sorry." Jen was genuinely contrite. "If you can wait while I finish this wall and take a shower—"

Bang! He dropped the six-pack he was carrying on the table. "The movie starts in twenty minutes. How you gonna get done that quick?"

"You could help," I said. Weasel sniggered and I felt my face flush. "I mean…you could finish painting while Jen takes a shower."

"I don't think so!" Killer folded his arms and leaned against the wall. Too bad it was already dry. A nice rose-colored swatch on the back of his black leather jacket would have been entertaining.

"I said I was sorry!" Jen sounded testy. "Besides, you cancelled on me that time you *said* you had to take your aunt to the doctor's. On a Saturday night."

Killer's eyes narrowed. Weasel sneered with cruel amusement and I just kept painting.

"I think you're jealous," said Killer.

"I am not! I was just pointing out that you stood *me* up."

"I had a good reason!"

"Well, I have a good reason, too!"

"Maybe you're just trying to get rid of me!"

"Maybe I am!"

"And maybe you're seeing someone else!" Killer strode over to where Jen was holding the dripping paint roller. I wondered what he'd look like if she rolled it down his face. It probably wasn't a good idea to find out.

From his full height he glowered down at her, but she managed to declare calmly, "Now, Max, don't be upset. You can think whatever you want, but I swear there's nobody else. The only reason I'm not going out with you is because I'm in the middle of something I want to finish. Take it or leave it."

I could hardly believe Jen was talking back to Killer. Hadn't I seen the bruises on her arms? And once even a red mark on her face? She never admitted Killer was the cause. I often wondered what would happen if she ever grew some backbone.

Surprisingly, after a tense moment or two, Killer wheeled and strode out with his cousin following. I let out my breath, which I hadn't realized I'd been holding. With a shrug,

Jen opened one of the cans Killer had brought and tossed down a swallow.

"I didn't mean leave the beer, but I'm glad he did!"

It was my firm hope Killer would stay gone for good. No such luck. When he showed up the following night, there was a lot of shouting and cussing and name-calling, but eventually the two of them made up. And since it looked like Killer was staying the night, I headed to Leona's once more.

"How's the paintin' job comin'?" she asked as we finished what was left of her sweet potato pie.

"It's done," I said. "We ran out of paint by the time we got to the kitchen. But at least the living room's finished. We even painted the cardboard closet and it almost looks like part of the room. You'll have to come up and see it sometime. The color is the coolest shade of light rose, and Jen's going to make curtains and slipcovers with some material she got. The apartment's already looking a lot different!"

Leona smiled. "Your sister's a lot different, too."

"I don't know about that, Lee. I mean, she's reading the Bible and praying, and she goes to stuff at the church, but I think she's the same old Jen underneath. She still drinks...and then there's her boyfriend."

Thoughtfully, Leona rested her chin on her hand. "Well," she said, "sometimes the first fruit of prayer is a longin' to have some order in your life. Didn't she say she thought God told her to 'clean up'?"

I nodded, not quite following.

"Maybe God wasn't talkin' about the apartment. Maybe he meant she should clean up the other parts of her life. But your sister isn't quite ready to hear that."

"Why don't you tell her? Maybe she'd listen to you."

Leona shook her head. "No, Antonia. I believe God is workin' in that girl's heart and he don't need me to interfere. But I will pray for her—and for you too!"

I stared down at the crumbs on my plate. Should I tell her I didn't believe much in prayer? Sure, some things had happened recently that almost seemed like answers to prayer. But I had *not believed* for so long that I really found it impossible to think any differently.

Leona laid a hand on my arm.

"Don't you worry, Antonia," she said softly. "God has a way of takin' what's ugly and makin' it into something beautiful. Jes' like Jennifer is doin' with the apartment, you'll see God do with Jennifer. Mark my word."

15

In November, I almost let Jen's birthday pass by without a second thought. But at the last minute, I decided to stop at the drugstore to see if I could find a little something for her. I spent quite a bit of time searching the entire store before finding the perfect gift. Then, on my way to the checkout, I spied cake mixes on sale for only a buck. Now that would make it a real birthday!

Back home, I realized I should have read the package directions before buying the mix. It said to add an egg, but we didn't have even one egg in the apartment. If Leona had been home, I could have borrowed one from her. As it was, I would just have to do without. I dumped the package's powdery contents into a bowl, added the right amount of water and then noticed I was also supposed to add oil. I searched every cupboard for cooking oil with no results. Now *that* was a problem. If I was eliminating the egg, I couldn't leave out the oil, too!

Opening our fridge again, I spied some whipped margarine. It looked kind of watery after I melted it, but I dumped it into the cake mix anyway. Next, the directions said if you didn't have a mixer—which we didn't—you had to beat the batter three hundred strokes by hand. Three hundred! That seemed like an awful lot and I didn't have that kind of time. So I just mixed the whole chocolaty mess together as best I could. Since we didn't own a cake pan, I greased and floured a large saucepan and spooned in the lumpy batter.

When the cake was done baking, I removed the pan from the oven and turned it upside down over a plate. The cake fell out with a *clunk*. I poked it with my finger. It seemed a little dense and was only an inch high. Maybe I had used too large a pan.

We didn't have any powdered sugar for frosting, so I warmed a blob of strawberry jam and spread it for a glaze. On top I placed the only candle I could find. It was a half-used pillar candle, but it didn't look half-bad after I cleaned it up a bit.

There! The cake was ready. I left it on the counter, covered with a large bowl to hide it from both my sister and the cockroaches.

When she blew in after work, Jen was surprised to discover I had put together our entire dinner. She was *really* surprised when I trotted out the cake with the candle lit. I set it in the middle of the table along with the present I had bought for her.

She chuckled at the wrapping, a sheet of lined paper from my school notebook, and smiled quizzically when she opened the gift and saw an eight-pack of colored thread.

"I know you have a lot of thread already," I said. "But at the rate you're sewing, you'll run out sooner or later."

"You're right! It's a great present. Now I feel kinda bad I didn't get you anything for *your* birthday!"

"Forget it. Let's have some cake!"

The doorbell rang, and Leona and Lucy came in with a carton of ice cream.

"Happy birthday to you," sang Leona, with Mama adding, "May the dear Lord bless Jenny, may the dear Lord bless you!"

"We had a note under our door when we arrived home—" Leona winked at me, "—invitin' us for cake. And what's cake without ice cream? Dish 'er up, girl!"

They all got a good laugh when they bit into the cake and found it strongly resembled chocolate-flavored rubber. I was chagrined but Jen assured me it was the thought that counted.

Leona glanced around the apartment and her eyes grew wide. "What a difference in here! It looks so nice!"

"Yes," agreed Mama, nodding vigorously. "What a diligence! A little paint is all it takes to translate a room."

"And what do you think of this?" Jen unrolled the bolt of flowered fabric and held it up. "I'm going to make curtains!"

"How pretty!" cried Leona.

"How bountiful!" cried Mama.

Jen grinned. "I've never had so much fun. Well, not since Mom died, anyway."

Her smile faded. "Cripes, Lee, it's been such an awful struggle. I still miss her so much."

I don't know if Mama understood, but she nodded sympathetically.

"Sometimes," Jen said, "I wonder how she managed to hold up with all she went through. First she lost her husband—my father. Then she got married again, and after Tony was born she got breast cancer. She had surgery and did pretty well for awhile, but Dad was a traveling salesman and we had to move around a lot. When he died, she had to go to work. Eventually the cancer came back and it killed her. I don't know, Lee. I feel like I've had a hard time. But Mom had it worse and yet she never gave up."

"Was your mama a Christian?"

"I dunno. She didn't talk much about that kind of stuff."

"But jes' to manage like she did, it's likely she knew the power of prayer."

"A tower of prayer," murmured Mama Lucy. I patted the old lady on the arm.

"Do you really think that prayer has power?" Jen asked Leona. "Do you really think prayer can change things?"

"I sure do, honey!" said Leona. "Prayer can change things—instantly, if God wills it! But usually prayer changes us, and then *we* have the strength we need to change things. But then again, sometimes prayer simply helps us see things differently, accordin' to God's plan instead of our own. Even if we don't quite understand it, we have that hope deep inside us which don't quit."

Jen, still holding the bolt of material, was chewing her lip. She did that a lot when she was thinking.

"I don't know," she finally said. "I don't think I really know *how* to pray. I never feel like I'm doing it right."

Leona chuckled. "Oh, I can't imagine there's a wrong way to pray! God's lookin' at your heart and he's jes' happy you're talkin' to 'im! When you spend enough time praying, God himself will teach you how to pray."

"Well, I hope he hurries up!" Jen twirled around and the fabric wrapped her in rosebuds. "I intend to pray for a miracle!"

Neither of us realized it at the time, but a miracle—albeit a well-hidden one—was waiting on the threshold.

I was coming to believe that a tremendous struggle was going on in my sister's soul. Maybe it was a struggle *for* her soul. I just stayed out of the way as best I could.

One morning shortly after her birthday, Jen happened to glance at the back wall of the living room. She went over to inspect it more closely and there was an explosion of swear words. What had been, a short time before, a clean-looking expanse of delicate rose, was now riddled with ugly brown blotches. The old water stains had seeped through the new paint. It looked terrible.

Jen launched a bunch of shoes and a lot more unprintable words at the disaster. At the top of her lungs, she screeched, "All that work—for nothing!"

I knew there was no paint left to re-do the job, so I didn't say a word but simply stayed out of her way while getting ready for work. I left her moping on the couch, guzzling a beer and glaring malevolently at the wall.

When I came home later that afternoon, I noticed right away the blinds were closed even though it was still daytime. Then I clapped a hand over my mouth and nose. Ugh! What was that awful smell?

I found Jen prone on the sofa with a wet washcloth over her eyes.

"Jen," I said through my closed fingers, "what stinks?"

She moaned, peeled back a corner of the cloth and squinted at me with red-lidded eyes.

"I'm sick."

"Sick! Did you barf? Where?"

She pointed to the carpet near where I was standing. I grimaced and moved away.

"Couldn't you make it to the bathroom? Why didn't you clean it up?"

"I did—as best I could. I had to crawl on my hands and knees 'cuz my head feels like it's in a vice." Jen dropped the cloth back over her eyes. It was hours before she was able to even sit up.

"What's wrong with you?" I demanded, thoughtlessly eating a bowl of cereal in front of her. "Do you have the flu?"

She avoided looking at my food. "I don't think so. I felt fine till I finished the beer."

"And how many did you have today?"

"Just one."

"Oh, sure!"

"Honest, that's all I had. Just one. It hit me so fast I couldn't move."

"Have you ever gotten sick from drinking before?"

"Never. And it was horrid. My throat burned like fire and I thought my stomach was turning inside out."

"Do you want something to eat now?"

She looked green at the thought. "I think I'll just go to bed."

The next day Jen felt fine, much better than me, who had had to sleep near the bad spot.

"Jen, you gotta try cleaning the carpet better," I insisted.

So she scrubbed it again, using soap, water and a lot of elbow grease. But the odor, like a bad memory, lingered on.

"It's probably soaked through to the padding," I said. "What are we going to do?"

"I think the only thing we *can* do is tear out the carpet. It's in bad shape anyway—and the color is ugly."

When Carlos called to see if Jen wanted a ride to RCIA the next evening, she told him about the problems we were having trying to pry up the carpet with a kitchen knife. He offered to bring over some tools. With the proper equipment and the friend he brought, it didn't take long for the four of us to pull up the carpet.

"Now, how are we going to get rid of it?" I asked.

"We'll have to cut it into strips, roll 'em up and put 'em in the dumpster." Jen smiled engagingly at Carlos. "And Carlos will help—won't you?" Somehow I figured he would.

It took all afternoon, but we finally had a pile of tied carpet and padding rolls on the balcony. We swept up the grit on the floor and then swept again.

"At least it's a hardwood floor," said Carlos. He wiped perspiration from his face, leaving dirty streaks behind. With his boyish grin, he looked like an urchin. A really cute urchin. Jen didn't seem to notice.

"It's not in the best of shape," he continued, "but with a good scrubbing the floor should be passable. We'll go down to the alley and you girls can drop the rolls over the railing."

"Wait till Mona finds out!" I warned.

It seemed strange when Mona didn't notice the carpet rolls raining down outside her back window. At the time, it never occurred to me she might have had bigger fish to fry.

Carlos and his friend, Jim, came back upstairs to wash before leaving. "I was just wondering," Carlos said. "Thanksgiving's only a few days away. What are the two of you doing that day?"

Jen and I looked at each other. *The same thing we've done every Thanksgiving for the past few years,* I figured. *Sleep as late as possible and watch TV.*

"Why don't you come with me to Frank's house?" Carlos asked.

"What?"

"Frank's invited some of us who don't have family in the area to come over for dinner."

"Doesn't he have family he wants to spend the day with?"

"His daughter is going to the in-laws. So he said he'd supply the house and turkey and the rest of us can bring everything else."

"We don't want to barge in uninvited."

"Well, Frank told me to bring a friend. Jim's going, but there's room for two more!"

"Are you sure?"

"Positive. I'll call him tonight and check. So—what would you like to bring?"

That could be a problem. What kind of canned or boxed food could be taken to a Thanksgiving feast?

"I could bring cranberry sauce," said Jen, thinking fast. "How 'bout you, Tony?"

"Uh...maybe I could bake a cake." My sister tactfully suggested a bag of after-dinner mints.

That evening after turning on the TV, I got myself a can of pop and asked Jen if she wanted a beer.

"No," she said, assembling a purse while listening to the program on TV. "I've given it up."

I laughed. "That's what you say now while getting sick is still fresh in your mind. Just wait till the next time Killer comes over with booze!"

She ignored me, just like I was ignoring all the little miracles in our life.

16

Jen eventually had her full hours restored at work, but the craft show was so close she spent every free moment sewing. I was amazed when I saw she had taken Sasha's husband's ties, opened them up, ironed them flat, cut rectangles from them and was piecing them together to make a vest. She already had the lining for it cut out of an old silk shirt.

The next time she went to her class, she put her project into a plastic bag to take along. She must have sewed while listening to the talk and, when she came home that evening, she sewed some more while I listened to *her* talk.

"We learned about sacraments tonight," she told me. "The priest said a sacrament is a way that God gives us grace."

"That's nice. And grace is…?"

"Grace is a sharing in God's own life and love. He gives us a share in his very life, his grace, to help us love him and each other the way we should. And we can wear things like this—"

She showed me the Miraculous Medal she still wore around her neck.

"—to remind us constantly to live out that love. I like wearing the medal because sometimes I forget God loves me. Especially when the rent is due."

"Yeah. Are we going to have enough for this month?"

"Barely…even though soon I should be getting my full paycheck again. For now, we'd better hope this stuff sells at the craft show so we can eat."

She tied a knot and cut the thread before saying, "One of the sacraments is *baptism*. Do you remember Mom ever mentioning if we were baptized?"

I shook my head.

"I don't either," she said. "Baptism makes us members of Christ's family, and you have to be baptized before receiving any of the other sacraments."

"Like what other ones?"

"Well, for one thing, there's Holy Communion. You can't receive Communion if you're not baptized. So much to learn," she said with a sigh. "Oh, yeah, I'm going to start going to Mass every week. That's their Sunday service."

She didn't look up but kept sewing away on the multicolored vest.

I was perplexed. "What do you want to do that for?"

"Carlos told me the Mass is at the center of their faith as Catholics—and if I really want to understand the faith I need to go to Mass."

"Aren't you scheduled to work next Sunday?"

She nodded. "But there's a Saturday evening Mass I can go to."

"Well, *that* will be different than partying with Killer on Saturday nights!"

"The Mass is at five. I'll still have time afterwards to go out with Max."

"I wonder what he'll say when he finds out you've sworn off booze."

She shrugged. "Maybe he'll be glad to save some money!"

On Thanksgiving Day, Carlos and Jim picked us up. As we drove along, the scenery changed from run-down apartment buildings and housing developments to gated stores, then to blocks of factories, and finally to wide, tree-lined streets with larger houses. On Frank's street, well-maintained homes with security grates on their windows and doors sat side-by-side with shabby houses. Frank had one of the nicer places, a gracious, square brick house set on a double-wide lot. Several sprawling maple trees dominated the yard in front of a balustered porch.

A warm smile on his face, Frank bid us welcome as the mouth-watering smell of roasting turkey wafted our way. He introduced us to the others who were in the old-fashioned kitchen working on dinner. There was Rosalie, who seemed to be in charge of the cooking operations, Xavier, a dignified gentleman even in the apron he wore peeling potatoes, and several more.

Frank handed out cups of cranberry punch and invited us into the living room to warm ourselves by the fireplace.

"I could get used to this!" declared Jen, happily ensconced in a soft upholstered chair. "It feels so homey!" She put her head back and closed her eyes while her stockinged feet toasted by the blazing fire.

"Don't get too used to it," teased Carlos. "We have a job, too—setting the table!"

I looked around the spacious living room. It had a lot of comfortable seating by way of sofas and a love seat. On both sides of the fireplace were recessed shelves for books, and the paneled walls glowed warmly in the light of the flickering flames. On the wood floor under our feet lay a beautiful oriental rug.

Frank asked if Jen and I were interested in a tour of the house. We followed our host up the wide, runnered staircase to the second floor. He showed us several closed-off bedrooms and then his own extra-large bedroom, with lace curtains at the windows and flowered wallpaper. It looked like it hadn't changed much since his wife passed away. At the end of the hallway, he opened the door of a small but complete apartment.

"This was for my mother," explained Frank. "When my wife and I had the house built, we added this for my mother who was already widowed at the time. Her arthritis was getting worse, so we tried to make it as easy as we could for her. Come on, I'll show you the elevator we had installed."

An elevator? I was intrigued, even though it turned out to be not *quite* an elevator. It was actually a little chair you sat in which ran down the side of the back staircase and dropped you off in the kitchen.

Frank rode it down while we trotted down behind him. There was one more bedroom off the kitchen to poke our noses into before he led the way to the basement. In the middle of the cavernous basement sat a ping-pong table. My eyes lit up in anticipation of a game later.

"My children loved table tennis," Frank said.

Remembering all the bedrooms upstairs, I said, "You must've had a lot of kids."

He shook his head. "My wife was the youngest of fifteen and always wanted a large family. When we got married, we built this big house hoping to fill it with our own children—and ended up with only two!" He sighed. "Ah, well, the Lord's ways are mysterious indeed."

"Do you have grandchildren?" asked Jen.

"My daughter has three boys—and I also have a little granddaughter." He changed the subject, pointing to the unfinished basement ceiling. "Did you notice how high it is? Most basements have low ceilings, but I had the builders dig extra deep because we wanted to use this for a recreation room. And over there is the laundry room and another bedroom that's roughed in. We were going to finish it all off eventually, but never really needed the space."

We heard Carlos call down to us, "Jen and Tony, your services are requested!"

The dining room table was enormous. Eight chairs fit on the sides and two at each end. From a linen closet Frank took out a long lace tablecloth. We spread it over the table and set out the china and silverware.

"Where'd you ever get such a giant table?" Jen asked. Frank's blue eyes twinkled.

"It belonged to my wife's parents," he explained. "With so many children, her dad had it custom built. By the time we got married, her folks were downsizing and my wife wanted the table. We only used it when we had company, though. Usually we ate in the kitchen."

As big as it was, the table seemed to shrink when we loaded it with food. The last thing to be brought in was a huge platter of turkey, expertly carved by Xavier. He placed it in the center of the table and Frank asked us to bow our heads for prayer.

While he prayed, I stole a glance at my sister across the table. Her head was down so I couldn't see her face. I wondered if she was feeling the same way I was. I could barely recall holidays when our mother was still alive, and I doubted they were much like the present one, anyway, since there had been just the three of us and never any money to spare. At that moment, I missed my mother more than I had in a long time. I tried to be grateful on that day of giving thanks, but the ache stuck like a knife in my heart long after prayers were done and the food was passed around.

As I tried to bring my attention back, I realized the others were deep in a discussion about Frank's house.

"But how does Jill feel about it?" Rosalie wanted to know.

"Jill doesn't want this big old place," Frank said. "She married well and has a beautiful home in the suburbs. Besides, this area, years ago, was rezoned for mixed use. Most of the residents have moved away."

"There's still people next door," Xavier said, his gnarled hands passing me the gravy.

"But it's a group home," explained Frank, "for men and women with closed-head injuries. During the day they're bused to a rehabilitation facility. And many of the other houses on the street have been turned into businesses, like a day care center or insurance agency, or they're sitting empty."

"Is that why Jill wants you to go live with her?"

"That's one reason. She's worried about me living here by myself. Also, my eyesight is getting worse. I suppose it won't be long till I can't drive any more."

Rosalie reached over to pat his hand. "Don't you worry none about that. You know one of us is always happy to pick you up for Mass or meetings."

"It must be hard to think about giving up your house," remarked another woman.

Frank nodded. "But I'm happy to know the Legion will be putting it to good use."

"What's a legion?" Jen asked. The others smiled. They all must have been in on the secret, whatever it was.

"The Legion of Mary," Frank explained. "All of us here, except for Xavier, belong to a group at our church called the Legion of Mary. You remember how Beatrice or Carlos and I came to your door? Members of the Legion do the same throughout the whole parish, going door-to-door, inviting people to come to our church. When I'm ready to move out, I'm going to bequeath my house to the Legion of Mary."

"What will they do with a big house like this?"

"Oh, the Legion's much larger than the few people at our church," said Carlos. "There's lots of Legion groups in the city and surrounding areas. By having a house, the members can come together every month for council meetings. And we'd have room for special events, days of recollection and the like."

Xavier was listening closely. "But keeping up a house of this size!" he protested. "Think of the expense! Are you going to pay for it out of your dues?"

"We don't have dues," said Carlos. "But there's all those rooms upstairs. We're planning to rent them out and use the money for upkeep."

"Still, that could get awfully expensive in an old house like this."

"Oh, I've been taking good care of it," said Frank. "I've had the roof replaced, the plumbing and wiring updated and other major repairs done. Now it only needs things like new paint."

"And a new kitchen!" laughed Rosalie. "I could tell, Frank, you don't do much cooking! It's hard to find anything in there!"

"And you know what else?" said Frank with a smile, as he got up and began to stack dishes. "There's no dishwasher, either! So who's going to volunteer?"

17

I was pretty skeptical when Jen first told me she was done with drinking, but I soon found out she was as good as her word. When Killer came over the following Saturday night, he tried to hand her a can of beer and she refused.

"What's the matter, babe?" he asked. "You're not getting religious on me, now, are ya?" I turned away so he couldn't see my grin. If he only knew Jen had returned from Mass just a short time before.

"I just don't want it, that's all," Jen replied. "I was sick the other day and I've lost my taste for it."

"Here, just have a swallow," Killer urged, pressing his own drink into her hand. "It's like falling off a horse. If you don't get right back on, you lose your nerve."

She pushed the can away. "I don't care if I *ever* ride that horse again. I can't even smell it without it turning my stomach. Come on, are we going or not?"

The next day, Jen told me she was getting awfully tired of the bar scene.

"It never bothered me when I was drinking. But last night I realized if you don't drink, you kinda feel like a peg in a hole."

"You mean a square peg in a round hole."

"Whatever. Even the smoke was bothering me."

"You came home pretty early," I said, although *early* for her nights out with Killer still meant sometime in the middle of the night. "Where'd you go, anyway?"

"We left the bar and ended up at one of Max's friends' place. He's got a house somewhere on the northeast side. We played poker and watched movies on the wide-screen TV. After a while I got bored. Killer didn't want to leave so I called a cab."

Jen must really have been bored if she spent money on a cab. She never spent a buck she didn't have to. Speaking of money, that reminded me...

"The craft show is only a week away. Do you have enough stuff?"

"I've been piling all the things in my bedroom. Let's bring them out and see."

I grabbed an armload and dumped it on the sofa. Jen followed with the rest and then we sorted everything. There was a huge pile of purses and bags—large clutch purses and small evening bags, oversized shopping totes and over-the-shoulder bags. Each was different, hand-sewn and decorated with a load of imagination. I was amazed to realize how much work had gone into them.

I pointed to the stack of clothes. "You can't just throw those on a table at the craft show. Besides, you'll hardly have enough room for the purses. Can we hang the clothes somehow?"

"That would be good," she answered. "But how?"

We wracked our brains for quite awhile over that dilemma. We finally decided to check with Leona to see if she had anything we could use.

"There's that," Lee said, pointing to a six-foot wooden coat rack next to the door. "I can get by without it for a day."

"That will be great! Thanks!" exclaimed Jen. "I'll stop by to get it next Friday."

On the way back up the stairs, Jen suddenly took a detour and knocked at a second-floor apartment.

"What are you doing?" I asked, nonplussed. "Who lives here?"

"Wanda. Oh, hi, there," she said as the door creaked open. "Is Wanda home?"

The scrawny woman with a shock of scraggly, red hair silently shook her head. Jen wasn't deterred.

"Do you know when she'll be back?" she asked. "I'm a friend of hers."

My eyebrows shot up at the word *friend.* As far as I knew, Jen had met her only once. The woman shook her head again.

"Well, tell her Jen said 'hi.' Bye for now."

The door closed as slowly as it had opened and we started back to our own floor.

"What were you doing?" I asked my sister.

"Looking for another coat rack. Somehow, though, I don't think Wanda's going to get my message. I wonder who else I can ask?"

"There's always Melvin," I teased, and was startled when she immediately went to knock on his door. When Jen got it into her head to do something, she didn't waste any time. She came home a short time later hauling an ironing board and what looked like an old shower rod.

"Just what are you going to do with those?"

"Melvin was really very helpful," she said. "Maybe we've misjudged him."

She opened his ironing board about ten inches, standing it upright on its square end, and did the same with ours. By spanning the rod between them, she had a place to hang most of the items.

"Great!" she said. "With that and Lee's coat rack, I think we're all set."

Our next task was cutting paper into small squares and writing prices on them.

"How do I know how much this stuff will sell for?" Jen asked.

"Look at it this way. Most of the materials were free."

"Actually, all of it was."

"For now," I said. "If you keep doing this, eventually you'll have to restock thread and buy other raw materials, too. So I'd price it not according to what you spent, but how many hours of labor you put into it."

"That's a good idea. I didn't keep track, but I could estimate."

We spent a good hour engaged in pricing. After we pinned the prices on the merchandise, Jen figured that was it for the day. But I said, "Wait. We have to take inventory."

"What for?"

"It will give you a reference for the future. Having an inventory list is always good, no matter what you're selling."

"You know what, Tony? You have a good head for business. Have you ever thought of doing something along those lines after you graduate?"

"Like what?" I scoffed. "It's not like I can afford to go to college or anything."

"Maybe not now. But if that's what you'd like to do, don't give up your dream. You never know what will come up."

"Sure. I can always hope for a miracle!"

She pondered for a moment. "I keep thinking about what Frank said about needing God. If that's true, I'm not sure anything is impossible." She swept her arm dramatically in a wide arc and exclaimed, "Maybe miracles *can* happen if we put God first!"

Getting ready for bed that evening, I noticed Jen had stuck the small card from Frank in the frame of the bathroom mirror.

Our only need is for God. When that need takes over our life, all other things will fall into place.

That, I thought skeptically, I would have to see.

Jen had arranged for Carlos to pick us up, along with the merchandise, on the morning of the Christmas bazaar. What we didn't expect was for him to show up in a gleaming blue Chrysler New Yorker. He took the clothes from Jen and arranged them carefully on the back seat.

"I borrowed Frank's car," he explained. "I knew I'd never get all your stuff into mine. And besides, it's too dirty! This one may be fifteen years old but it's like new. Frank never drives further than the church or the grocery store. He keeps it locked up tight in his garage. It's as pristine as the day he bought it!"

He maneuvered the ironing boards behind the front seat and the rod went in lengthwise from the front window to the back.

"Everything fits," he said, dropping bags of the smaller items into the roomy trunk, "except the coat rack."

We ended up returning it to Leona before piling into the front seat. We were on our way to our very first craft show.

In the church basement, "Santa's Helpers" assisted in hauling our goods to our designated booth. Frank had lent us a red tablecloth and we draped it neatly over the table. Against the wall behind us we set up our makeshift clothes rack.

"Maybe we should have covered the ironing boards with something," I murmured to Jen. "They look kind of tacky."

"Too late now. Next time we'll know."

Jen chatted neighborly-like with Norma, the crafter at the next booth. Norma was a large woman with a beehive of blond hair, selling beaded angels of every size and description. She got quite a chuckle out of our ironing boards, and suggested we could make them less conspicuous by hanging signs on them. Carlos overheard and rounded up cardboard and markers for us before leaving.

Jen, unsure about the wording for the signs, tapped the marker against her chin. "What should I write?"

I threw out, "How about 'Collectibles from Cast-offs'?"

She thought I was serious. "That's not half-bad."

"Get real, Jen! Why would you want anyone to know these things are made out of other people's old clothes?"

"Are you kidding? In this age of recycling, that could be a hot selling point." She wrote the words on the cardboard and added "Hand-stitched" underneath. I rolled my eyes. Sometimes, I simply couldn't believe my sister.

Norma overheard our exchange and smiled broadly. "One never knows," she said, "what people will buy. By the way, you have free tickets in your registration packet for donuts or bagels. If you're not going to use them, can I have them?"

I thought Norma didn't look like she needed any donuts or bagels. Jen politely replied we hadn't yet had anything to eat. She sent me to the kitchen window, the "North Pole Snack Bar," to get our breakfast. As I returned, I noticed Jen already had her first customer.

Several hours later, Norma dropped over to examine our wares.

"This your first show? How are sales?"

"Not too bad at first," Jen said. "But they've dropped off."

Norma nodded wisely. "Always happens. There's a big rush at the beginning and then things slow to a crawl. It'll pick up at lunchtime. I'll tell you a secret," she said in a conspiratorial whisper. "The best way to sell stuff is to get out there and talk to the shoppers. Explain how you made things and how much time it took. You'd be surprised."

From then on I stayed in the background, keeping items organized and handling sales, while Jen stood in front of our table and talked to anyone who showed the slightest bit of interest. It worked. People listened, admired and bought.

"Told you," said Norma. She looked at the box lunches Jen and I had just purchased from the roving "Santa's Sandwich Cart."

"If you're not going to eat those potato chips," asked Norma, "can I have them?"

After lunch, Beatrice came by and introduced her daughter Isabella, a sweet little thing with lively black eyes and corn-row braids. Isabella fell in love with one of Jen's small shoulder bags and her mom bought it for her. Then Beatrice noticed our sign.

"'Collectibles from Cast-Offs!' I love it! Whoever came up with such a clever name?"

I smiled modestly and nodded in humble recognition of my genius.

"I was kind of hoping to see Frank today," Jen said to Beatrice. "I want to thank him for arranging for me to be here."

"He hasn't been feeling very well," Beatrice replied.

"Oh, no! I hope he's all right!"

"He has his ups and downs, but I'm sure he'll be fine. Sometimes I think he just suffers from a broken heart."

"What do you mean?"

"It's his granddaughter. He hasn't seen her in years. He misses her and prays all the time he'll see her again."

"Where is she?" I asked.

"He doesn't know." Beatrice moved out of a customer's way. "Oh dear, I'm blocking your business. Good luck today. See you around."

In the middle of the afternoon when things slowed down again, I took some time out to visit the other booths. I was amazed at all the creativity on display. There were felt gingerbread boys, knitted scarves and hats, hand-carved wooden toys and Christmas wreaths and decorations of every description. The Girl Scouts were selling "Christmas spiders"—sparkly pipe cleaners stuck into styrofoam balls—and "mini-shrines" made from empty decorated Kleenex boxes housing Christmas card cut-outs. I guess Norma was right. You never know what people might buy.

The tables I lingered over the longest, though, were the ones displaying handmade jewelry. I was irresistibly drawn to the sparkle of purple amethyst pendants, jade bracelets and turquoise earrings in silver settings. At one booth, I tried on a stunning Swarovski crystal necklace, admiring myself in a large oval mirror placed strategically on the table.

"It looks beautiful on you," the artisan said as I turned one way and then another to see the brilliant rainbows shoot from the stones. I loved the necklace and loved the way I felt wearing it, but that piece and the others were way beyond my means. With a sigh of regret I removed the gorgeous piece, placed it back on its stand and moved on.

Not long after I returned to our table, "Santa's Elves" came around selling homemade cookies and brownies, and "Mrs. Santa's Minstrels" strolled by, entertaining guests and crafters with Christmas carols. All the donated items were raffled from "Santa's Workshop," and we had a good laugh over the rather beefy man who won the button-bedecked sweatshirt made by Jen.

At closing time, we packed our remaining items and "Santa's Clean-up Crew" swept in behind us with push brooms. As we followed Carlos to the car, we overheard Norma accosting one of Santa's Elves.

"If those cookies are left over, can I have them?"

Back at our apartment, Jen returned Melvin's ironing board and then she and I sat at our kitchen table to count the proceeds.

"Five hundred and sixty dollars!" whooped Jen. "Not bad for a day's work!"

"It wasn't exactly a day's work," I said, remembering how many hours she had spent sewing.

"Well, you know what I mean." She retrieved our coffee can and peered into it. "Just in time, too. Hardly anything left after paying the rent." She dropped in the roll of bills and put the can back in its hiding place in the kitchen cupboard. Then she said, "You know, Tony, I've been thinking...we haven't done much for Christmas lately."

That was an understatement. For years, Christmas had come and gone pretty much like any other day.

"Why don't we plan to use fifty dollars from today's proceeds for each of us to buy a Christmas present for ourselves?"

"You should get yourself a warmer coat," I said immediately. "You know how cold January can get."

Deep in thought, she nodded. "Maybe I will."

For my part, I was elated. I already knew what I wanted to do with the money.

18

A bell jangled as I pushed open the heavy glass door and stepped inside. I was immediately assailed by the smell of oil and machinery. In sharp contrast to the bright, crisp air of the December afternoon, it was dark and rather stuffy in the shop. In the dim light, I squinted at the price tags on the merchandise closest to the door. My heart sank.

"Can I help you?" came a voice. I looked up to see a wizened fellow whom I guessed might be in his eighties. Easily.

"Yes," I said. "I'm looking for a...um...sewing machine."

He grinned and his breath whistled through the few yellowing teeth left in his gums.

"Well, young lady, you've come to the right place." He stretched a bony hand towards the shelves. "Have you had a chance to look around?"

I nodded, but I had no doubt whatsoever I was in over my head. I couldn't imagine what all the knobs and dials and fancy gadgets were for. The machines I saw looked like they could not only sew up a seam, but fit the garment and press it, too. And the prices ranged up into thousands of dollars.

"I thought your store sold *used* sewing machines," I said in dismay.

"These *are* used." There was obvious pride in his voice. "They're reconditioned machines, guaranteed to perform as good as new."

When I said I didn't need anything so fancy, he led me further back in the store to merchandise more along the lines of what I was looking for. Bypassing the larger machines with tables, I looked at small portables with carrying cases. However, the cheapest one was still over a hundred dollars.

"I'm just looking for a small sewing machine that can do basic stitching," I told the old man. "I don't have much money."

"What kind of sewing do you do?"

"It's not for me, it's for my sister. For Christmas," I added. "I was thinking of something that just sews straight lines, so she doesn't have to make curtains and stuff like that by hand."

He shook his head. "You'd have to get a pretty old one to get something that basic. Everything for the last forty, fifty years has at least a few extra stitches—zigzag and the like. You get anything older than that and it could be unreliable."

He went behind the counter and hauled out a medium-sized machine, setting it up to show me.

"Now this one," he said, "is maybe thirty years old. It has a carrying case that comes with it. You can see that it's well-made. The body is metal, not plastic like so many are today. It has not only straight and zigzag stitches, but also a blind-hem stitch. And this here—" he pointed to a mark on one of the dials, "—is for stretch fabrics. It's a great deal. I just got it in last week. I can let it go for ninety-five dollars." He smiled a toothy smile and waited expectantly for me to agree it was really quite a good price.

I felt like crying. "I don't have that much money. I'm sorry."

I turned to leave, and was almost to the door when he said, "Miss, wait a minute." He disappeared into a back room and returned a few minutes later with a small black sewing machine.

"I picked up this one just two days ago at an auction. I haven't even had time to check it out yet, but I could let it go for sixty dollars."

Sixty dollars! I could manage that!

"There's no carrying case for it, but it's a solid little machine with straight and zigzag stitching. Unfortunately, instructions didn't come with it. But if you can leave it with me a couple of weeks, I'll clean out the dust, give it a tune-up and make sure the tension is set right. I'm sure it would give your sister years of fine service."

I was elated over my good fortune. Then I realized I had forgotten to bring the cash from the coffee can with me.

"I don't have all the money today," I said, checking my wallet and pulling out my last ten dollars. "Will this be enough to hold it?"

"Sure thing. I'll write you up a bill of sale."

I couldn't wait to see my sister's face when she saw what I got her for Christmas! It was unfortunate, though, that I hadn't remembered to bring the fifty dollars with me.

I watched Jen cutting small swatches of fabric from project leftovers.

"What are you doing?" I asked. "The craft show's over."

She didn't miss a beat—or a stitch. "I thought I'd make Christmas ornaments for all our friends."

"Like who?"

"Well, first of all, Leona." She looked over at Mama Lucy sipping a cup of tea at our kitchen table. "Now, Mama, that's a secret. Don't tell Leona."

"Don't worry, dear," Mama replied. "My zips are lipped."

I laughed. "Mama, you're hilarious!"

Her white head nodded. "Leona says I have a real bunny phone. But it's beyond my apprehension."

Still smiling, I turned back to Jen. "What exactly are you making? And for who else besides Leona?"

"They're stars. Maybe you can help me with them and that way they'd be from both of us. They're for Beatrice and Frank, for sure, and Carlos and Dolores, and maybe a few others—depending on how many we get done between now and Christmas."

"Speaking of Carlos," I said with a grin, "I was sure surprised this morning when he picked us up for church."

"Did you say Carlos?" Mama asked. "Isn't he that illegible bachelor?"

Jen's face reddened and I snickered. It looked like Lee had been talking.

"Lucky I came with you," I teased, "to chaperone!"

With feigned nonchalance, Jen tossed her hair back and changed the subject. "You weren't even planning to go. Remember? I practically had to drag you."

I certainly did remember how she wanted me to go to church that morning with her and how I tried to think of every excuse not to. Neither of us was scheduled to work and I couldn't imagine why I would want to spend my day off at church. But when she asked me, "What else could you do today that's as important as spending time with God?" I had to think quickly. I had planned to wash my hair, work on a paper due the next day, polish my fingernails, call Annalisa to see if she knew the answer for a math problem, go to the store to pick up a few things and look through my magazines to solve some fashion dilemma or other. But after Jen put it that way, I wasn't about to run all that by her. I decided to stick with the excuse most likely to pass muster— "I have homework to do."

"You've got the rest of the day," had been her quick comeback. "Besides, they've got wonderful cinnamon rolls in the social hall after Mass. You'd love them."

I wasn't exactly sure why I agreed to go with her. Maybe the cinnamon rolls did have something to do with it.

I poured more tea for Mama and complained, "But I didn't really get anything out of it."

Jen nodded. "That's how I felt at first, too. But Carlos told me we go to Mass not to get something out of it, but to give something to God. That is, our praise and worship. Because he has given us everything we have, we owe that to him.

"And you know something else?" She trotted to the kitchen and came back with crackers for Lucy to go with her tea. "When we go to Mass, we do get something out of it. Or rather, *someone*. God gives us *himself*. In the first part of the Mass, we receive his Word in Scripture. In the second part, if we're Catholic, we receive him sacramentally in the bread and wine."

"Huh?"

Jen patiently explained, "The bread and wine at Mass, when they're consecrated by the priest, become the Body and Blood of Jesus Christ."

"You must mean symbols of him," I said, but Jen shook her head.

"No, they become the Body and Blood of Jesus, because he said so in the Bible. On the night before he died, he took bread and said, 'This is my body.' And he took wine and said, 'This is my blood.' It must be true because Jesus is divine and could never lie."

Evidently Mama agreed, as she began to sway a little, singing, "Jesus never lies, no, Jesus never lies. He's the Way, the Truth, the Life. No, Jesus never lies."

We both waited, expecting her to burst into a hymn, but she fell silent again.

"That's all beyond me," I said. "I did like the choir, though. And the cinnamon rolls."

We heard a knock on the door and Jen quickly hid what she was working on. Leona came in brushing snowflakes from her hair.

"Sure feels cozy in here," she said. "The weather couldn't be more miserable. It's freezin' and the snow's really blowin'."

"Come in, dear," Mama graciously invited. "Come in out of the buzzard."

Whenever we had a little time during the next week, my sister and I worked on the stars. She stitched the edges together and I turned them inside out and stuffed them with odd fabric bits. Then she sewed them closed and I attached the yarn loops. When they were done, we lined them up on the table to admire them.

"Perfect!" Jen exclaimed. "This blue one with white yarn is for Frank. It reminds me of his blue eyes and white hair."

"And this bright yellow one has to be for Beatrice," I decided. "It's just like her colorful dresses."

I thought Jen's idea of making ornaments was an ideal way to get into the Christmas spirit. For too many years we had let the holiday season slip by without doing anything special. I had a sudden flashback to our childhood Christmases when our mother would roll out gingerbread dough for Jen and me to cut out reindeer and bells, wreaths and angels.

"Jen, don't they sell refrigerated dough at the grocery store? What about if you bring some home tomorrow? We could cut out Christmas cookies."

She looked at me in surprise. "Well, okay. I didn't know you liked to do that kind of stuff."

"Well, sure. I mean, it *is* Christmas, isn't it?" I didn't tell her how excited I was at the simple thought of making cookies.

"I'd better take some extra money with me. I'll need to get cookie cutters, too."

She brought our coffee can to the table, flipped off the plastic lid and peered in. Her face froze in shock.

"Tony! What happened to the money?!"

19

"What are you talking about?" I grabbed the can out of her hand to look for myself.

"It's gone!" she whispered hoarsely, her eyes wide. "How could it be gone?"

My heart sinking, I dropped the empty can and ran to search wildly through the kitchen cabinets. It was crazy, I knew, to think the money had somehow leaped out of the coffee can and was hiding behind a box of cereal or a two-liter of pop. But desperation makes a person do strange things. Jen was pawing through her grandmother's sewing box and checking under piles of fabric.

For several long minutes we hunted in silence. Then, in tears, I returned to the table and dropped heavily into a chair.

Jen began to rant, yelling at me, "Are you sure you didn't borrow the money for something?"

I stared at her in disbelief and yelled back, "Are you crazy? What would I do with hundreds of dollars? Maybe *you're* the one who 'borrowed' the money and forgot about it!"

"Don't be stupid! That money was for paying bills—and for Christmas! I haven't even bought groceries this week!"

"So you think I stole it?"

"I didn't say that! No, I don't think you stole it! But where did it go?"

Casting about to come up with an answer, Jen jumped up to check our doors.

"They're locked now. Do you remember coming home any day this week and the door wasn't locked?"

I shook my head. "No, I'm sure I used my key every day."

"What about the back door? Was it left open recently?"

I rubbed my eyes with my knuckles. My brain felt fried with Jen firing questions so rapidly at me.

"I don't know," I said bleakly. "I don't remember."

"Did you put the garbage out this week?"

"Yeah." Like usual, I had launched the bags over the balcony railing into the dumpster.

"Did you have to unlock the door? Or was it already unlocked?" Her strident voice was like an interrogator's.

"I don't know!" I shouted. "I don't remember! I think I had to unlock it, but I can't say for sure!"

I was desperately trying to focus. *Had* I forgotten to lock the door behind me? I recalled how easily I had climbed up the balconies to our apartment. Could someone else have done the same? Oh, why couldn't I remember?

Jen called the police and filed a report, but neither of us was so naïve to think the thief would be caught and our money returned. The rest of the evening was spent in grim silence. After my sister turned in early, I sprawled on the sofa in the darkness, staring at the play of shadows across the ceiling. My stomach churned in turmoil. Not only the money from the craft show was missing, but also what was left from our last paychecks. It was fortunate we still had a little food left in our cupboards.

But...Christmas! The first Christmas in years when we were actually going to celebrate a little! We were going to have Christmas cookies...and presents—

Oh, no! I sat bolt upright. The sewing machine! The fifty dollars was due the next week!

In anger and frustration, I punched my pillow and lay down again. How the heck was I going to come up with fifty dollars? My next paycheck would be needed to help with the rent. No matter which way my thoughts went, I kept coming up against a blank wall. For the longest time, I lay awake pondering the hopeless situation. A miracle was needed, but I had no idea how to go about getting one.

Many restless hours later, I slid my hand under the sofa cushion, pulled out the hidden Miraculous Medal and slipped it around my neck.

Christmas was rapidly approaching when Jen called an emergency meeting at our kitchen table.

"As you know," she said, one hand propping her chin and the fingers of the other drumming absentmindedly, "we've got some real problems. I've been adding up the bills and I don't see how we're going to cover everything. Today I took the leftover stuff from the craft show into work, but no one's interested. I guess everyone's done with their Christmas shopping by now."

Except us, I thought glumly while saying, "Since I'll be off school next week, I can work extra hours. Then again, it won't show up in my paycheck till January. Do you think Mona would give us some extra time to pay the rent? Being it's Christmas?"

She raised an eyebrow. "Would you like to ask her?"

"Uh, no…not really. Didn't we try that once before?"

"Yeah, and if she could have, I really think she'd have pitched me in the dumpster!" Under other circumstances, the memory might have brought a chuckle. But Jen just made a wry face and continued with the sad litany.

"It's been so cold this year, our heating bill is higher than ever. And, of course, there's the dentist's bill from back in the fall when I had my teeth worked on—"

"Okay, okay, so what's the bottom line?"

"We can pay the rent—or eat. Not both." She pushed the paper with scribbled figures over to me. Before even looking at it, I tossed out a random thought.

"I bet if you'd say something to your friends at church, they'd help us."

Her eyes narrowed. "Antonia, I am *not* going to ask for charity!"

It was then I almost told her what I suspected about the craft show at St. Therese's. That Frank had either talked the coordinators into a free table or he had paid for it out of his own pocket. But in the end, I decided to keep my mouth shut. There was no way to be certain, anyway.

I perused the numbers she'd written. "Looks like we have a little money for food."

"Sure, as long as nothing else comes up! Anyway, we usually spend four times that amount." She sighed. "And I *was* thinking it would have been nice to get a ham for Christmas this year."

Well, what a surprise! It seemed like Jen, too, was getting into the spirit of the season!

"You know," I said, "I don't think it's as bad as what you make it out to be. I think we can eat a lot cheaper than we do. After all, look how much we're saving since you stopped buying beer!" I grinned at my sister, thinking not just about the money. Since she got sober we were saving our friendship, too.

"You know," I pointed out, "we spend an awful lot on take-out food. Why don't we try making our own pizza instead of always picking one up?"

"That's not a bad idea." Jen looked thoughtful. "That would probably cut the cost in half right there. Actually, I bet if we eliminated all the junk food, we'd save a bundle."

"Junk food! Like what?"

"Like those Twinkies, cheese puffs and potato chips you're so fond of."

"What? Wait a minute! Those are necessities!"

She did some more figuring on the paper. "What say we give it a try? No more junk food and we'll cook from scratch. If it turns out we don't save anything, we'll throw out the experiment."

We'd likely be throwing out more than that, especially if our meals turned out anything like my cake. But for the first time in days, there was a look of hope on my sister's face, so I reluctantly agreed. I came home the next day to find her hovering over a hot skillet, frying sliced potatoes.

"I asked Leona what would be the least expensive foods and she said potatoes, pasta and beans," Jen said. "I thought we'd start with potatoes, since they were on sale this week for a dollar a bag."

"That's all we're eating? Potatoes?"

"Nope. Cheese was on sale, too, so I'll sprinkle a little over the potatoes. I bought some day-old rolls and made a salad. How's that sound?"

Personally, I didn't think it sounded too good, but Jen seemed so proud of her new-found culinary skills that I didn't want to toss cold water on her good intentions. At least, I consoled myself, it wasn't beans.

After dinner, my sister had a date with Killer. For once I was happy Jen was going out for the evening, as I had been looking for a chance to act on an idea which had been percolating in my head. After they left I sat cross-legged on the floor, thrust my arm under the sofa and extricated a slightly crushed shoebox. I blew off the dust and removed the top.

Before my eyes were so many of my prized keepsakes, and I took them out one by one. A worn yo-yo with frayed string—a gift for my tenth birthday. A well-loved Barbie doll in a party dress. A dapple-gray pony with silky tail and removable saddle. A rather squashed-looking stuffed dog with matted yellow and brown fur. There was also a faux pearl necklace, worn for my fifth-grade graduation, and a small painted plaque that Jen had made me years ago. I had so little from my childhood that I thoroughly enjoyed looking at each thing before laying it on the floor. Finally, only one treasure remained in the box.

I lifted out a roll of soft brown velvet material, laid it in my lap and unrolled it. Almost reverently, I picked up by the clasp a stunning pendant necklace. It had a fine silver chain and a single teardrop-shaped diamond. A slender ray of setting sun which stole through the back window lightly touched the gem, and sparks of fire and ice sprang out of its depths and danced over the walls and ceiling.

Although it wasn't in need of any cleaning, I gently polished the diamond on the velvet. As I did so, a tidal wave of memories flooded over me, especially of that unhappy day shortly before my mother's death. That was when she had called me to her bedside, placed the necklace in my hand and pressed my fingers tightly around it.

"Tony, love, this is the only thing I have to pass on to you from your father's family," she said. "His mother wore it on her wedding day and I wore it when I married your dad. I want you to wear it for your own wedding some day."

"And what if I don't get married?" I shot back, not really thinking about what I was saying.

I couldn't help but see the sallow skin and the pain hiding behind hazel eyes. Her long, honey-colored hair lay tangled against her shoulders. Up until then I hadn't noticed how much grey was in it. It suddenly hit me how terribly *old* my mother looked. Tears threatened as I bit my lip and tapped my foot in an uneven staccato against the floor.

She made no response to my flippant remark, but went on speaking so softly I almost missed the rest of what she was saying.

"All I had to give Jenny was the sewing box that belonged to *her* father's mother. When Grandma Alice died, her grandpa gave it to me to pass along to Jenny. I wish I had more to leave you girls, but everything else I had to sell—" A ragged breath, like a sigh of regret, escaped through parched lips.

With a muffled sob, I insisted she was going to be around for a long time, so why did she need to tell me all that? Yet deep down I knew that was a lie, and saying it out loud wouldn't make it true no matter how much I wanted it to be so. Her watery gaze held mine as she lifted a weary hand to brush away a teardrop clinging to the end of my nose.

"Just remember," she said in a resolute whisper, "it's not *things* which are important. You and your sister stay close and take care of each other. That's what really matters."

Sitting on the floor of our apartment, the diamond pendant still cradled in my hand, I reminded myself all over again, *That was really what mattered, wasn't it?* Trying not to think about anything else, I leaned forward until my forehead rested on the rough edge of the sofa cushion. For so many long years I had kept all those painful memories boxed up like my treasures, but at that moment they spilled out with the rivers of tears coursing down my cheeks.

The dark of night had crept into our apartment long before I finally sat up, wiped a hand across my wet face and carefully, resolutely, wrapped the necklace back in its velvet shroud.

20

"There was no name on it or any writing on the envelope. I wonder who might have given it to us? Somebody from church? Couldn't be Leona—she doesn't have money to throw around!"

It was Christmas Eve, and Jen was relating to me the tale of finding a gift certificate in our mailbox when she got home from work. Too tired from a long day on my feet at the Barn to play guessing games, I said, "Maybe it was Killer." She snorted, which told me what she thought of *that* idea.

"Let me see it," I said.

"Can't. Went right back to the store and used it to buy groceries."

My weariness vanished. I ran to the fridge and threw it open.

"Yeah, a ham! Ham for Christmas! No potatoes!"

"Well, actually," Jen said from behind me in a serious voice, "I thought maybe I'd stretch the ham by cooking up some potatoes and pasta—"

Incredulous, I spun around, only to see her grinning at me.

"Okay, okay, if you insist! No potatoes or pasta on Christmas! We'll serve the ham with something else." She opened the cupboard to show cans of yams, cranberry sauce, peaches and mandarin oranges, and a tray of brown-and-serve rolls. Then, from the fridge, she took out a roll of cookie dough I had overlooked in my excitement.

"Come on, sis! What are you waiting for? Let's do cookies!"

Naturally, after we finished the cookies, we had to trim the tree. It took a real stretch of creativity to come up with ornaments. First, Jen popped a large bowl of popcorn which we tried stringing

111

with needle and thread. It turned out to be more difficult than we anticipated, so we ended up simply dangling truncated strands of popped kernels from the branches. Then we fashioned icicles and stars from aluminum foil and hung small balls of colorful yarn with paper clips.

I stepped back, looked at our efforts and laughed. "This will never qualify for 'best-dressed tree!'"

Not only was it not well-dressed, it wasn't even a tree. Earlier in the week, Jen had rescued several sawed-off evergreen branches which had been dumped curbside. We arranged them in our large pasta pot and added water. In her bag of sewing leftovers, she found an old green and red plaid skirt. When arranged carefully around the pot, the large stain in the middle of the fabric was hardly noticeable.

Later that evening, long after Jen had gone off to bed to dream of sugarplums, I was still up. There was one more thing I needed to do.

It was way too early on Christmas morning when I heard my sister humming "Jingle Bells" and slamming kitchen cupboard doors. I groaned, rolled over and pulled my pillow over my head. Only the buttery aroma of frying eggs finally roused me off the sofa. I jump-started my heart with a cup of strong coffee while Jen fiddled with the dial on her radio. As Christmas carols blared, we lingered for some time over our breakfast. Finally, I couldn't wait any longer. I hopped up and told Jen to close her eyes, that I had a surprise for her.

From the bottom of the refrigerator box closet, I hauled out a heavy package. Of course, I had forgotten about wrapping paper until too late the night before, but a pillowcase, tied with a loopy bow made of yarn, served the purpose. Pushing the dirty dishes aside, I set the present on the table.

"Merry Christmas, Jen!"

She opened her eyes. "For me? Oh, my gosh!"

"Open it up!" I was so excited you'd think it was me getting a gift.

She untied the yarn and pulled off the pillowcase.

"A sewing machine! Tony! How did you ever manage to get me a sewing machine?"

"Well, it's not new, but—"

"Who cares? A sewing machine! I can't believe it!"

She quickly plugged in the cord and placed the foot pedal on the floor under the table. With her sleeve she polished a few fingerprints off the shiny machine, then picked up a little box lying in the middle and shook it.

"What's this?"

"Extra bobbins the sewing machine guy gave me. He also threaded it, as you can see. It didn't come with instructions, so he wanted you to know how the thread went through all the little loops and things."

Jen bit her lip and looked at me with that sappy look big sisters get when their little sisters do something especially touching. She started to say something but I cut her off.

"Go ahead!" I urged her. "Try it out! I hated to see you sewing all that curtain fabric by hand. Now you'll be able to zip through it like anything! Before you know it, our place will be transformed!"

If I had been paying closer attention, I would have seen her smile freeze in place. But I was too pumped to notice. I scurried for the bolt of flowered material and brought it to her.

"Here. Try hemming up the end on the sewing machine so we can see how it works!"

When she didn't make a move to take the fabric from me, I looked at her more closely and was puzzled by the odd look on her face.

"What's the matter, Jen?"

"Sorry," she said with a hesitant smile, "I can't make the curtains—"

"Why not?" I broke in. "It should be easy now."

She cleared her throat. "Well, you see, I asked Irene if she'd like me to make the curtains she wanted for her bedroom. I mean, it *was* her material, you know."

"Oh." I had to think about that for a moment. "But she gave it to you," I said. "Why are you giving it back to her?"

"Uh…well, actually, she gave me cash in advance to sew the curtains for her." Jen seemed reluctant to continue and I figured I'd better let it drop. She must have needed the money for something.

"But it doesn't matter," she assured me brightly. "I can use the machine for all my other sewing. And I still have to make the curtains, even if they're for someone else. So you can see how much time this will save me!" She hopped up and gave me a hug.

"And now, sis, you just sit yourself in that chair, 'cuz I have a present for you!"

I grinned. I hadn't expected anything, but neither was I going to refuse it! From her room she brought out a wrapped package, about a foot square and six inches high, and set it in front of me.

"Okay, it's your turn! Open it!"

Ripping the wrappings off, I saw a polished wooden box. Stained a rich ocher, its top was inlaid with an exquisite mosaic of tiny turquoise and gold tiles.

"Oh, it's gorgeous!" I ran an appreciative finger over the gleaming tiles. "How did you ever find such a thing?"

"As soon as I saw it, I just knew I had to get it for you! Look, when you open the top, there's a tray." The sectioned tray was lined with navy blue felt like the rest of the inside. "I know how much you love jewelry, and someday you'll be able to keep all your pretty things in this jewelry box. For now, you can put your grandmother's necklace in this section here," she pointed with enthusiasm, "and it won't get all tangled. Better than that old shoebox, huh?"

I tried to smile, but my mouth felt like it was encased in hard plastic. I made an effort, anyway.

"Thanks," I murmured. "The box is beautiful. I love it."

I dreaded what she was likely to say next and, sure enough, that's exactly what she said.

"Go on, get your necklace! Let's see how it looks in a place that's fit for it." She laughed happily, but I didn't move.

"Tony?" she asked, her smile fading. "What's the matter?"

"Well, it's just—" I started slowly, "—um...someone else has it right now."

Her face froze and her voice rose a few decibels. "Someone else! Who else would have your necklace?"

I squirmed. "Well, you see, uh, what happened was...I found the sewing machine and put a down payment on it, but after the money was stolen, I didn't know where to get the rest of the money—"

"Antonia!" shouted my sister. "You went and sold your grandmother's necklace? A sewing machine isn't worth that!"

"I didn't *exactly* sell it!" I said in my defense. "I...I took it to a...um...pawn shop—" I stopped. The memory wasn't exactly a pleasant one, especially when I found out how little they would give me for my precious heirloom.

"A pawn shop! And how much time do you have to redeem it?"

"Three months," I said in a small voice. I started to sniffle.

Jen quieted down then and a wall of silence sprang up between us.

At last she said, "We're going to get it back for you, no matter what. You...you silly old—"

Tears began to trickle down my sister's face. Mine, too.

"Tony," she continued more softly, with a hint of a smile breaking through her tears, "I was just remembering how Mom always told us we had to take care of each other."

She took a deep breath before continuing.

"We're a hoot, aren't we? But somehow, in spite of everything, we're doing just what she asked!"

21

Crammed in next to a laundry basket full of clothes in the back seat of Carlos's old Honda, I was eyeing the junk on the floor. It seemed like the guy kept everything he owned in his car, including what he needed for his classes. I picked up a heavy textbook with the word *Theology* on the front. What in heaven's name was theology? I didn't want to ask or it would look like I was nosily poking through his things—even though I was.

There we were again, on our way to Frank's house. Earlier that day, after attending Christmas Mass at St. Therese's, we had given Beatrice and Carlos their ornaments. Jen told them, "I was hoping to see Frank at Mass today. We have a star for him, too."

"He probably went to an earlier Mass. Even during the week, you'll find him at the earliest one possible," said Beatrice.

"There's Mass during the week, too?" I was surprised. "Seems like an awfully big production to do every day!"

Carlos laughed. "That's only because today is Christmas. There's more music, more readings from the Bible, more everything. Daily Mass is a little simpler, but all the essentials are there—prayers, Scripture, consecration of the bread and wine and, of course, Holy Communion."

"I always wonder why you call it the 'Mass,'" I said. "That's a weird name for a church service."

"It comes from the Latin word *missio,* which means 'to send,'" he explained. "At the end of every Mass, we are literally sent out into the world to bring Christ's love to others by serving them."

Carlos must have taken that mandate seriously himself because, before we knew it, he was driving us to Frank's so we could drop off the ornament. As the Honda chugged and backfired through the holiday-quiet streets, Jen and Carlos talked up front.

At a pause in the conversation, I piped up from the back seat, "Hey, Carlos? I've been wondering about something. Did the Legion of Mary give us a gift certificate on Christmas Eve?"

His glance at me in the rear view mirror showed surprise.

"You got a gift certificate? Well, it can't be from the Legion because we're not allowed to give material help. We only do spiritual things, like calling at homes in the neighborhood to invite them to church. Or visiting the homebound or bringing Communion to the sick. We also encourage praying the Rosary as a way to bring people closer to Jesus with Mary's help. But, like I said, the Legion can't give anything like money—or gift certificates. Of course, one of the members could have done it on their own. There's nothing to prohibit that."

I wondered if *he* had been the one who had been so generous. However, the more I shivered in the back seat of that old junker which didn't seem to have a working heater, the possibility seemed less and less likely.

Carlos said, "Probably best to stop wondering and just thank God for it. Whoever it was apparently didn't want you to know—and you may never find out, anyway."

Carlos was right about that. We never did discover who our benefactor was.

"Oh, dear," Jen said as we pulled up in front of Frank's and noticed several late-model cars in the driveway. "He's got company. Carlos, just take us home."

Carlos shook his head. "You're here now. Might as well give it to him. Go ahead." He turned to me. "You too, Tony."

Frank's face lit up when he opened the door. "What a wonderful surprise! Merry Christmas, girls! Won't you come in?"

Jen handed him the blue stuffed star. "Merry Christmas to you, too, but we're just dropping off this ornament, and Carlos is waiting for us so we won't keep you," she said a rush of words.

"Don't be silly," Frank said. "You can't go running off on Christmas. Come in and have a cup of hot cider."

That sounded great! I was frozen. I wondered if I could find a way to stay even if my sister left.

"Tony," Frank said firmly to me, "run and tell Carlos to come in. I'm sure you can all find a few minutes to visit."

I quickly returned with Carlos and the three of us stepped into the front hall. Frank placed our humble star on a beautifully-decorated live fir next to the staircase. While he hung up our coats, he asked Carlos to take us into the living room to meet his family.

Frank's daughter must have known Carlos, as she jumped up to greet him with a warm hug.

"Jill," Carlos said, "I'd like you to meet a couple of friends of mine, Jen and her sister Tony."

Jill, who resembled her father in her slender height and gentle smile, then introduced us to her husband, Harold. A heavy-set, balding man, he greeted us in a friendly manner. The three young men present, ranging in age from about twenty to thirty, shook our hands politely, and the eldest son introduced us to his fiancée, a willowy blond woman.

While Carlos visited with them, Frank brought in mugs of cider and sat with Jen and me, inquiring how things were going in our lives. Jen told him all about the craft show, omitting the story of the stolen money. She didn't say anything, either, about her decision to stop drinking. Maybe it was obvious, anyway, to anyone who knew her.

Before long, she managed to lead the conversation to the topic of her RCIA classes.

"—and they're not having any more until the second week of the new year. I kind of miss them."

"Why is that?" asked Frank.

"Because that's where I ask questions." And I'll bet she has a ton of them, I thought. She continued, "I've been reading the Bible, but there's so much of it I just don't get."

"It's not always easy. Have you considered joining a Bible study at church?"

Jen shook her head. "I don't have time right now. I'm working full time again. Also, I'm spending a lot of time going through cookbooks." Frank looked puzzled at the last statement, but Jen didn't take time to explain. "There was something about, if you're going to pray, you should first forgive those who've done you wrong." It was hard to follow Jen's line of thinking sometimes, but I assumed she was talking about the Bible, not the cookbooks. Frowning, she said, "But I'm struggling with the forgiveness thing. Does that mean it's useless for me to pray?"

"Ah, no," Frank said. "It's never useless. We always have to keep praying, *especially* for the grace to forgive. How can any of us ever hope to do it on our own? If we don't pray, we won't have God's help to love others. And isn't that what forgiveness is really about? Loving others as God loves them—his broken, hurting and hurtful children."

Now *that* was a totally new thought for me. Maybe I, too, had some forgiving to do. I was still angry at Kenny, even though he had again disappeared from school—and, hopefully, from my life. It had never occurred to me to think of Kenny as someone God must love, too.

Well, I figured, there was no accounting for taste.

I brought my attention back to what Jen was saying. "This business of praying is harder than I thought it would be. In class last time, we were told we should sometimes just wait in the presence of God without feeling the need to say anything. But I get antsy and can't seem to do that."

Frank chuckled. "And therein lies the battle, doesn't it? Here's something that has helped me. Did you notice all the trees on my property?"

He did have a lot of trees, but I wondered what that had to do with prayer.

"Every fall I used to go out in my yard and stand ankle-deep in leaves, wondering how I was ever going to get the raking done before the snow came. Believe me, it seemed overwhelming! But one year I realized if I made myself rake for five minutes each and every day, the job would be done before I knew it. Just five minutes. Of course, sometimes the weather was beautiful and I wanted to keep going, so I did. But knowing I only *had* to do five minutes made it easier to get started."

"You're saying to pray for only five minutes? That doesn't seem like very much."

"You'd be surprised. Why not commit to just five minutes a day to being quiet in God's presence? Set a timer or your watch so you're not distracted by checking the time. Maybe the timer will go off and you won't want to quit. That's like when the weather was so nice I wanted to keep raking. There were also days so cold I didn't want to do *any* raking, but I still did my five minutes. Likewise, sometimes your quiet time with God may seem so cold and fruitless you'll want to stop before the time is up. But stick to your commitment to sit in his presence for five minutes and, over time, you'll see results. Like I did with my leaves."

"What's the point?" I asked. "Sitting quietly and not saying anything! I mean, don't you pray in order to talk *to* God?"

"The problem is," said Frank, "prayer can become a one-way conversation. We talk to God and don't take time to listen to him. That's as foolish as telling a doctor all your symptoms and problems, then getting up and leaving before he can diagnose you and give you the remedy!"

Jen wasn't as skeptical as I was. "I guess it's worth a try."

Frank smiled. "Don't worry too much about it," he said. "Just pray as you can, and don't pray as you can't. By the way, is Dolores still hosting the Rosary in her apartment?"

Jen nodded. "Every Sunday. I go when I'm not working."

"I'm thinking that maybe a couple of us could come to the Rosary some Sunday. Afterwards, if you want, we could stop at your place and help you with those questions. Why don't you write them down when you think of them?"

Jen would likely have launched into more questions right then, except Carlos glanced at his watch and said the family he roomed with were probably waiting dinner on him. It was hard to tear ourselves away from the warm fire that afternoon. Of course, the thought of our own ham waiting for us at home helped a little.

Back at the apartment, I couldn't resist teasing Jen.

"You know, those grandsons of Frank's weren't too bad. They could give Carlos competition any day."

She stuck her tongue out at me and said she noticed the youngest son kept looking at me with interest. I laughed. Who were we kidding? Those guys lived in a far different world than either of us could ever aspire to.

Jen opened a can of yams and dumped them into a pan.

"You know," she said, "I can't help wondering about Frank's other child. Didn't he say he had two? We've met Jill but the other son or daughter is never mentioned."

"The only thing we know," I answered, "is that he has a granddaughter he never sees. Wonder why?"

Jen shrugged and began to slice the ham. While we enjoyed our modest Christmas feast, she suggested we deliver the rest of our handmade ornaments that evening. So after dinner, we dropped off a star for Melvin and then knocked on Leona's door. When there was no answer, we decided to return later. Next, Jen led the way to 1B where the trapeze artist lived.

I sure hoped *he* was home. I couldn't wait to meet him.

22

Jen and I were perched uncomfortably on a love seat which felt like the springs in it had sprung a long time ago. But then again, neither of us really noticed it much, as we were busy sampling the most delicious Italian pastries one could ever imagine. There were cannolis with light, tender crusts wrapped around luscious ricotta filling, miniature cream puffs and the tastiest tiny tarts. My hands-down favorites, though, were what our host called *Napoleons*—layers of delicate pastry with dollops of vanilla and chocolate cream.

Bobby had opened his door when we knocked and Jen introduced me. He pumped my hand.

"Nice to meet you," he said. "I'm Bobby Fantini."

After a dramatic pause, when he seemed to be waiting for a response, he went on, "You know—of the Flying Fantini Brothers?" He peered at me with bright, hopeful eyes.

I smiled and shook my head politely. He looked disappointed but graciously invited us in to have a seat in his living room, where Jen handed him a stuffed star. He thanked her and insisted we sample a dessert or two.

While we were thus engaged in that delightful endeavor, I had the opportunity to look around. His apartment décor was a curious mix of old-world elegance and modern-day flea shop. The love seat, you could easily tell, had once been first class. Its solid wood arms and feet were ornately carved with curlicues and fleurs-de-lis, and the brocade fabric still gleamed with faded dignity where it wasn't frayed. There was also a threadbare matching chair where Bobby was sitting. Underneath our feet the area rug, patterned in soft florals, may have been Persian. I wasn't certain, having little knowledge of such things. But even I could see the disparity between the solid furniture and the fabricated-wood bookshelves and end tables.

Bobby himself was quite a study in contrasts. His weathered face put him at about seventy years of age, yet his hair was jet black and hung poker-straight past his shoulders. Although he walked with the stiffness of arthritis, his T-shirt was stretched tautly over muscular arms and shoulders. While I stuffed another pastry into my mouth and tried to figure him out, Bobby suddenly hopped up and switched on a brighter light.

Before that, I hadn't noticed what was hanging from the ceiling near the kitchen. I was incredulous. Could Bobby really have his own trapeze? I poked Jen's arm and pointed to it.

Tossing a grin at us, he trotted to the contraption, leaped high and grabbed hold. A small grimace of pain crossed his face, but he hoisted himself up until he was above the bar. Straight-armed, he supported his body in the air before swinging down again. He kicked his legs forward and then back to get the trapeze moving. The cables creaked a little against the eyebolts in the ceiling—or maybe it was poor Bobby's joints I was hearing.

For the next ten minutes or so, he entertained us with amazing stunts on the trapeze. Over the bar he went and under it, then flipped in a complete lateral turn and managed to grab on again as we watched in astonishment. At the end he somersaulted off, wobbled a bit before getting his balance and then executed a sweeping bow. We applauded appreciatively.

Bobby dropped into his chair with a wince and then his lined face lit up like a spotlight under the Big Top.

"And what did you think of that, m'ladies?"

Both of us exclaimed over his performance and peppered him with questions.

"Hold on!" he said, laughing. "One at a time. Yes, I was with Barnum & Bailey for many, many years, along with the rest of my family. There was me and my brothers, Joey and Freddy and Mickey, and my brothers' wives and eventually their children. I was the only one who never got married—"

He paused and his attention seemed to wander, which made me wonder if there was a girl he once loved. Maybe—and here my imagination ran way ahead of the story—she was tragically killed in one of those high-wire accidents you always hear about. I waited breathlessly for the rest of the tale which never came.

122

He pulled his thoughts back to us and winked. "Eventually I got to an age when I couldn't continue in the air. The old joints got rusty and nobody trusted me as catcher any more. By the way, did you hear the joke about what advice the seasoned trapeze artist gave to the beginner? He told him, 'Never fool around with the catcher's wife!'"

Jen and I stared at him blankly.

"Uh…guess that's an inside joke." After a moment, he chuckled. "Anyway, can I get you something to drink?"

We declined because we wanted to get going, thanked Bobby and bid him goodbye. Jen next knocked on Wanda's door. When Wanda opened it, Jen handed her a stuffed star. The woman took it and closed the door without a word.

"Well, that's a fine way to treat your neighbors on Christmas," I huffed. "She sure isn't very friendly!"

Jen didn't seem as bothered by Wanda's behavior as I was. "Well, living in a place like this can make people unfriendly," she said.

"Huh! *We* don't act like that."

She looked sidelong at me. "We were lucky, Tony, to have parents who loved us. Sure, we went through bad times, but at least we had a good home. Some of these people might have been abused or neglected. I don't like to judge them."

I should have felt chastened, but was simply annoyed with my sister. What made her, all of a sudden, so holier-than-thou? I probably would have said something uncharitable, but we had arrived at Dolores's apartment.

"Feliz navidad," Jen said to the dark-haired boy who cracked the door open at our knock. He grinned and flung the door wide. When his mother saw us, she smiled shyly, beckoning us in.

"Mer-ry Christ-mas," she said, pronouncing each word carefully.

"This is my sister Tony," Jen said to the young mother. "How are you, Dolores?"

"Muy bien, gracias."

The little boy tugged at her arm. "Mama, speak English."

She smiled at him and said to us, "I am *weel*, tank you. Baby *weel,* too." She patted her large stomach.

A dark-haired man came over with another boy and a little girl. He shook hands unsmilingly and went back to his supper.

"'Scuse my husband, *por favor,*" Dolores said softly. "He tired. Works nights." She leaned down and pulled the smallest child to her. "Nina," she said to me, then pointed to her sons. "That one Miguel and this one, like his papa, is Joachin."

Jen handed her the star ornament. "We made this for you."

"Oh! *Muchas gracias!*"

As she hung it on the wall over a painted wooden crèche, I looked around. The nativity scene was about the only bright spot in the bleak room. Over in one corner was a mattress topped with moth-eaten blankets. A battered sofa faced a small TV, and the table where her husband ate was propped on one corner with a length of lumber. There were few toys that I could see. I wondered what the children did with themselves all day.

"Come." Dolores beckoned us to the tiny kitchen. On the counter were set out dozens of Mexican pastries, beautiful even on a chipped platter. She handed us each a plate.

"Please—eat. Here are *mollettes* and *empanadas.*" She pointed to each delicacy while Jen and I stole a quick glance at each other. How could we possibly eat any more sweets? But it would be rude to refuse. We certainly couldn't be rude.

"*Churros,*" she called the cinnamon-sprinkled pastry I bit into. "And would you like a *borrachio* cookie?" I tried one of the anise-flavored treats and told her truthfully how delicious it was. Her dark eyes sparkled with pleasure.

The children were starting to warm up to me. Before I knew it, little Nina had edged so close she was leaning against my knees. I smiled down at her and she held up a well-loved dolly.

"St. Nicholith brought me a banket for my baby."

Jen admired the miniature quilt wrapped around the doll.

"Handmade, right? It's beautiful," she said to Dolores. The woman beamed.

"Did St. Nick bring you anything?" I asked the boys.

Miguel showed me a small metal truck with paint chipped off in spots, and Joachin had an almost-new pair of sneakers. Even though Jen and I exclaimed over the gifts, it saddened me to know that those were all they got for Christmas. And yet—I felt an unexpected prick of envy as I looked into their shining eyes.

Those poor children were far richer than I. They had their mother there to love them.

Jen and I practically rolled down the stairs to Leona's.

"Hope they're back by now," said Jen.

"Hope they don't offer us dessert," said I.

Leona and Lucy were going into their apartment when they saw us coming. Lee waved.

"Hey, ladies! Ya'all come for a Christmas visit?"

"Happy Christmas!" piped up Mama Lucy. She had on her Sunday-going-to-church coat topped with a red scarf. Her bright eyes twinkled at us. "And Merry New Year!"

We all tumbled into their place together. Jen and I collapsed on the couch while Leona got her mother settled into her favorite chair and made coffee while talking about their holiday visits with friends. When we, in turn, told her about our visit with Bobby, she exploded with laughter.

"You're pullin' my leg," she sputtered, shaking her head. "There's no way we got a real trapeze artist livin' here!"

"Honest," Jen said, and described Bobby.

With a final chortle, Leona nodded. "Come to think of it, I *have* seen someone fittin' that description. But a trapeze artist?" She leaned towards us expectantly. "What's his story? I'm waitin' to hear it!"

Lucy also leaned forward. "Me, too! I'm waiting on nins and peedles."

Jen told them everything we knew about Bobby. Then her smile faded as she went on to tell of our visit to Dolores's family.

"I could just kick myself. I could have made a dress or something for that little girl's doll. And something for the boys, too. Why didn't I think of it sooner?"

"You'll have another chance to help them," Leona said. "Sounds like Dolores has her hands full. If you pray about it, maybe the Lord will lead you to do something nice for 'em."

"Something sugar and spice for 'em," agreed Mama.

"I don't know, Lee." Jen's face was glum. "It's hard to figure out just where the Lord is leading me. I try to pray every day, but he doesn't seem to answer."

"Really? Are you tellin' me, girl, there's been *no* changes in your life since you started prayin'?"

I spoke up. "Seems to me there's been a few. Maybe even a few miracles." I hated to admit it out loud, but you couldn't deny the evidence.

Jen ignored my interruption. "But I don't seem to be hearing God very well."

"When that happens to me," said Lee, "it's usually because there's something blockin' it."

"Blocking what?"

Leona chuckled. "Why, blockin' God's sunshine! His love is like the sun pourin' its warm, golden rays down over us. It never stops, no matter what. And if the Lord's always pourin' his sunshine on us, why, the only way we can't notice it is if we done pulled the shade!"

Mama Lucy nodded. "Don't pull the shade."

"Okay," said Jen, "so I'm still angry about our money being stolen. Is that what you mean?"

That probably wasn't the only thing Lee had in mind, but she was too kind to mention anything else in my sister's life which was downright shady.

"Well, there's nothin' wrong," she said, "with gettin' mad 'cuz someone done you wrong. But *stayin'* mad is jes' goin' to be bad for yourself in the long run. And you know, you'll not be able to let it go on your own. You have to let God help you."

Frank, I remembered, had said something along those lines earlier that very day.

Jen sighed. "I guess there's lots of things God has to help me with."

It was late and I was getting tired, so what blurted out of my mouth might not have been the best thing to say. "Well, he helped you stop drinking, didn't he?"

My sister looked like she wanted to pop me. Leona asked gently, "Is that true, Jennifer? Did you pray to stop drinkin'?"

"Well, maybe I did. But I didn't pray to get sick as a dog!"

Lee laughed heartily. "You gotta be careful what you pray for! You jes' might get it!"

"Well, I just don't get it," chimed in Mama Lucy, who probably felt left out of the conversation. "What are we talking about, anyway?" She didn't seem to expect an answer, as she proceeded to rise and shuffle off to the bedroom.

I rubbed my eyes and yawned. "I don't get it either, Lee. This whole business about praying. Sometimes it seems like God answers—and sometimes not. How are we ordinary mortals supposed to figure it all out?"

She laughed again. "Jes' keep havin' faith in him, Antonia, and you'll be surprised. Things will start workin' out. God can bring good out of everything—even when everything seems hopeless."

"I don't know if I have that kind of faith," I admitted, and Jen said, "Me neither."

Leona answered, "Faith don't fall on you out of the sky. You have to live like you *do* have faith, and before you know it, you're really believin'! Jes' keep prayin'."

"Maybe there's something wrong with me," Jen said. "I want to be able to pray well, but it's always such a struggle."

"Well, have you asked God to help you pray?" Jen shook her head and Leona continued, "Why don't you ask him to give you a love of prayer? Even if that seems like startin' at the bottom."

I remembered the *ladder of holiness* that Carlos talked about. He, too, had said to start at the bottom by asking God to grant a desire to pray. There seemed to be a lot of repetition in what people were telling us lately. Did God have a sense of humor—or were our skulls so thick he figured everything needed repeating?

"Maybe that *would* make it easier," agreed Jen.

Leona added, "After all these years, I *still* have to ask God to help me pray."

From the bedroom came Lucy's voice. "Help me pray, Leona! I'm ready for bed."

"In a minute, Mama!" Lee chuckled and looked steadily at Jen. "Don't ever forget," she said, "that prayer is connectin' to what is greater than anything on earth. With that connection, life becomes an adventure and miracles happen."

Leona was showing us to the door when she stopped suddenly.

"Oh, dearies, I almost forgot!" she cried. "Ya'll can't go yet! Set yourselves back down and have a piece of my homemade cherry pie!"

23

Jen continued to tackle everything she did with every fiber of her being. Having discovered the virtue of thriftiness, she began to bring home stacks of library books on the subject. There came a day in January when I noticed she no longer dowsed her cereal with sugar.

"I can get by without it," she said. "Sugar costs money."

I pointed out that sugar didn't cost as much as the cereal she poured it on. "In fact, maybe you should eliminate the cereal entirely and just eat sugar. It would be cheaper."

"You're probably right," she muttered, her nose buried in the '*It Pays To Be Frugal' Guidebook to Saving Money Everyday.* "Hey, Tony, did you know that you can use up wrinkled potatoes by first soaking them in cold water?"

Great, I thought, just what we needed—a way to rescue mummified potatoes so we could eat more of them.

"If bread gets hard before it's eaten," she continued, "mist it with water and warm in the oven." She turned the page. "And if you run out of baking powder, you can substitute baking soda mixed with cream of tartar."

Now *that* was a staple on everyone's pantry shelf. I shook my head, amazed at my sister's penchant for the ridiculous, and began to get ready for work.

"Hang it all!" I exclaimed, examining my black pants. "There's a hole in these! At work yesterday I backed into a table with a broken edge."

"Wait!" Jen enthused. "I remember seeing something about that a few pages back! Here it is! 'If you get a hole in your pants, simply use a marker to color your underwear so it won't show.'"

I stared at her. "You have GOT to be kidding!"

"No, it says right here. Look!" She held the book out to me. When I refused to take it, she realized I was in no mood for such absurdity.

"Okay," she sighed. "If that's the way you want to be, hand over the pants. I'll mend the hole." I never did find out if she was serious about the underwear.

When Killer and Weasel came over that evening, Jen agreed to go to a movie with them—but only if Killer was paying. They argued back and forth for awhile. I was glad when they finally left, especially since Weasel had been prowling around our place in a mightily suspicious way. If he was trying to think of more places we had cash stashed, he would find himself fresh out of luck. After the holidays, Jen and I had opened a joint account at a nearby bank. It was a lot more secure than our coffee can and it heralded our new determination to take control of our lives. We each contributed a proportional amount to our living expenses. Whatever was left over, we designated for our own personal plans.

Jen insisted that I save up to go to college, "so you don't have to work in a grocery store all your life—like me."

I suggested she do the same, but she shook her head.

"My dream," she said, "is a house of my own. I don't care if it's a small one, but that's what I want more than anything else. But our very first priority, Tony, is to get your necklace back!"

And so we did just that.

By the end of the month, we were well settled into our newly-frugal lifestyle. We ate what was on sale, cooked from scratch and cleaned everything with baking soda and cheap vinegar. Jen re-used envelopes from junk mail by ungluing them and turning them inside-out, rescued old shoelaces by dipping their frayed ends in nail polish and dropped scraps of soap into an old sock to use for a shower scrubber.

One day I found a Q-Tip balanced on the edge of the bathroom sink and went to throw it away.

"Hey," said Jen, "I need that!"

"But it's used!"

"Only one end's used. The other end's still good."

My mouth fell open. "Are you nuts?"

"Why throw it away when it's still half-good? Just think— our supply of Q-Tips will last twice as long!"

That was nothing compared to the exchange we had over dental floss. It began when Jen read that floss could be used to cut apart rolls.

"Why would you want to do that?" I asked logically. "What's wrong with using a knife?"

"Well, I guess if you didn't own one, then it would be cheaper to use floss than have to buy a knife."

While we were on the subject of dental floss, I thought of another way to save money. "What about if you washed your floss after using it and hung it up to dry?"

Jen looked up from her book in surprise. "I never thought of that!"

"Tell you what," I went on, getting into the swing of things, "I'll put a strip of masking tape on the inside of our medicine cabinet door. Then every time we wash a piece of dental floss, we can stick it under the tape to dry."

Jen nodded seriously. "That would work," she said, turning back to her research. I sighed. Was this getting crazy, or what?

One day I mentioned to my sister she was looking pretty shaggy. Before I knew it, she had brought home a library book on how to cut hair. She wanted to try it out first on me. I flatly refused.

"Come on, Tony," she wheedled. "With your curly hair, who'd notice if the cut wasn't perfect?"

"You experiment on your own hair!"

So she did, sectioning off each part like they showed in the book, holding it between her fingers and cutting off the ends with her grandmother's embroidery scissors. She made layers around her face, taking off nearly all the bleached hair, leaving her natural honey-blonde color. She struggled a little with the longer hair in back before talking me into helping her. As she walked me through it step by step, I snipped away carefully until it was short enough to suit her. She peered into the bathroom mirror, pleased with her new style. Lucky for me she couldn't see the back.

Ever since she got her sewing machine, Jen had put it to good use. After finishing the curtains for Irene, she shopped the Goodwill store for likely project materials. One day she came across a warm winter coat for herself—"only five bucks!" she exulted—but mostly she brought home super-cheap clothing to be cut up and put together in new ways. She began a fresh round of making unique purses and other things, asking Dolores to help with the sewing. A pile of marketable items began to grow for the booth Jen reserved at the "Springtime Fling" at Leona's church.

One day after the Rosary at Dolores's, Frank and Beatrice stopped by to help Jen with her questions.

"Why do we always start prayers by making a cross on ourselves?" Jen asked them first. "Why do we do that, anyway?"

She was talking about the odd thing I'd noticed her do with her hand—touching her forehead, her chest and then both shoulders. Although trying hard, she looked like she didn't quite know what she was doing.

Jen continued, "And I wonder why Leona doesn't do it when *she* prays?"

Beatrice answered kindly, "I don't know why most non-Catholic churches dropped the practice over the years. Martin Luther always recommended making the Sign of the Cross first thing in the morning and before going to bed."

Martin *who?* I was listening in on their conversation, but not understanding it very well. I didn't have a chance to ask anything because Frank jumped in.

"The Sign of the Cross actually goes back to the ancient church," he said. "When you make the sign, you are praying '*in the name* of the Father and of the Son and of the Holy Spirit.' In biblical times, to use someone's name meant you were declaring you were actually in the presence of that person. So making the Sign of the Cross is, so to speak, telling all evil to stay away, because God is present and you belong to him."

As our visitors opened their Bibles and started on the rest of Jen's questions, I wondered if my sister really wanted to belong to God. Not long ago, she had been addicted to alcohol. Maybe that had changed, but she still seemed to have an emotional addiction to Killer which might be a far more difficult dependency to overcome. And maybe it would have been, if the crisis hadn't come along.

24

It seems that life seldom travels in anything resembling a straight line. It goes up and down, in and out, over and around again. Just when you think you've got things figured out, life comes screaming at you from an entirely new direction.

That's how it was on that particular snowy-cold day. I was at our kitchen table putting the final touches on a history paper while Jen sat sewing on the living room sofa. Mama Lucy was seated nearby. My sister liked to use Mama for a sounding board. The old lady usually didn't give advice but, even if she did, it was the sort you didn't feel guilty about ignoring.

"You wouldn't believe, Mama," Jen said, "how much money we're saving now. And it's all because of a few books I've read!"

"I've bred a few good rooks myself," declared Mama. "And the best one is the Bible." She began crooning, "Jesus loves me, this I know, for the Bible tells me so—" As her thin voice swelled in song, it made even cynical me smile to witness the old woman's uncomplicated love for the Lord.

Jen waited patiently for her to finish before saying, "I'm learning a lot about the Bible. And about God and prayer. Last week in class I heard something pretty cool—'*Prayer enlarges the heart until it is capable of containing God's gift of himself.*' Isn't that beautiful, Mama? Prayer makes our hearts larger so God can live there. Who would have thought God gives *himself* to us as a gift? But that's what happens when we pray."

Lucy nodded. "The Bible sez to pray all the time. While we're working or playing. I even pray while I'm sleeping."

I looked skeptically at Lucy, but I almost believed that's exactly what she did.

Jen chuckled. "Mama, I think you're what they call a real prayer warrior! Will you pray for me? I could use some prayer."

"You sure could, honey," agreed Lucy.

Jen glanced at her sharply, then bent her head over her work and didn't say anything else for quite a while. At last, she put down her sewing to begin supper and, from the kitchen, resumed the conversation.

"Mama," she called, "I've made a decision. I'm going to join the church that Frank and Beatrice and Carlos go to. What do you think of that?"

I looked at her in surprise, but I really didn't mind if she was to do that. Going to church had greatly improved her moods. Maybe going more would improve what else needed improving.

Lucy nodded. "Church is good. I go to church every Sunday."

Before long, Leona arrived to claim her mother.

"Umm, something sure smells good," she declared, dropping into a kitchen chair.

Jen stirred the pot of vegetable soup on the stove. "It's the garlic. Melvin swears by eating garlic. He claims it gives you a long life."

So *that* was the pungent odor which always clung to our neighbor. "How does he know that?" I asked.

"Well, think about it. How many people do you know who've died while eating garlic?"

"I wonder if garlic would do anything for my bursitis." Lee grimaced as she got up. "The other day I was trying to explain to Mama that my bursitis is the inflammation of my bursa. She wanted to know if her arthritis is the inflammation of her Arthur!"

We all laughed as Leona and Lucy headed to the door.

"Bye, Mama," Jen said. "See you soon."

"Not too soon," replied the old lady. "We got a doctor's appointment tomorrow. Leona's taking me in for my annual autopsy."

It was over dinner that night when I first noticed how pale Jen looked.

"Are you all right?" I asked.

"Yeah. Just a little tired. I think I'll turn in early."

I returned to my homework and didn't think any more about it.

Way past midnight, I was awakened from a deep sleep by a sound I couldn't immediately identify. I lay there in a stupor for a moment. It wasn't unusual to hear strange noises in our part of the city—even in our own building. I was turning over to go back to sleep when I heard a soft moan.

"Jen?" I called out. "Jen, is that you?"

I swung my legs off the couch, sat up and rubbed my eyes. At first there was only silence, then I heard a husky whisper from the bedroom.

"Tony...help me!"

I flew off the sofa, crashed through the bedroom door and stumbled to the bed in the dark. I couldn't see anything so I switched on the bedside lamp, squinting in the sudden brightness. My sister had an agonized look on her face.

"Jen!" I cried in alarm. "What's wrong?"

She didn't answer. Beads of perspiration sparkled on her forehead as she plucked at the blankets. I grabbed hold of the covers, threw them back and gasped.

There was blood everywhere.

Leona, whom I called right away after dialing 9-1-1, beat the ambulance to our place by a good fifteen minutes. While she was in the bedroom with Jen, I paced the living room, my stomach in knots.

Finally emerging, Lee said in a subdued voice, "Antonia, your sister's gonna be all right. But she's havin' a miscarriage."

In shock, I stared at her. "A miscarriage! I didn't even know she was pregnant!"

She shook her head and sighed. "Neither did she. So sad."

After the ambulance arrived and left with Jen, Leona called a cab to take us to the hospital. In the room where we were asked to wait, she patted my arm.

"Don't worry. They're taking real good care of your sister."

"But, Lee! How could Jen be so stupid as to have gotten herself into this mess? Maybe God is punishing her!"

"Antonia," she said firmly, "God doesn't reward or punish in this here earthly life. The miscarriage happened because her body, for reasons unknown to us, couldn't carry the baby. It has nothing to do with any punishment. Lots of good people lose their babies and lots of bad people end up havin' babies. Don't try to figger it all out. Jes' pray for your sister. She's gonna need your support in the days to come."

Hours passed, and Leona went home so her mother wouldn't be alone when she awoke. Through the hospital waiting room window, I watched the snow falling steadily, silently. It was gradually covering all the ugly things—the street, the barren trees, the unwashed cars—transforming the bleakness outside. I only wished there was some kind of interior snow which could cover up and transform the bleakness inside me.

Finally, Jen was released. Her face ashen and her progress painfully slow, she climbed the stairs to our apartment. She told me to call work and tell them she was sick, and she went right to bed. A whole day passed before she was on her feet again, and then she wasn't the same Jen as before. While she would go through the motions of whatever she had to do, it was done in silence. If I asked a question, she would answer in a monotone and then withdraw into herself again.

Leona had warned me my sister would probably go through a time of grieving for her lost child. But after a week of watching her act like a zombie, I got fed up.

"Jen, you gotta snap out of this," I said. She didn't even look at me.

I tried again. "You can't go around like this forever. Life goes on."

When there was still no reply, I grabbed my backpack and left. I felt bad for her, I really did. But how long could a person mourn for a baby she didn't even know she was going to have? I didn't understand at all. Besides, who did she have to blame but herself?

After school that day I caught a city bus, intending to go to the library. At the last minute, though, I changed my mind and got off at St. Therese's. Even as I pulled open the heavy door and stepped inside, I wasn't exactly sure why I had come. I slipped into a back pew and tried to calm my thoughts by focusing on the flickering votive candles and the stained glass windows. Except for the muffled hum of traffic outside, there was a deep silence, unbroken by the presence of a few people intent on their prayers.

It was a place of peace, yet peace kept eluding me. I shifted uncomfortably on the hard seat as my annoyance with Jen bubbled, over and over again, to the surface.

All of a sudden, Leona's words came rushing back to me—*You haven't walked in her shoes.*

I guess I hadn't, I admitted to myself, coming to the eventual conclusion that no one had appointed me my sister's judge. Somehow, I knew, I had to set aside what I was feeling and pray for her.

I couldn't even remember the last time I had prayed. My mother's passing so many years ago had left me floundering in a swamp of emotions. If I had prayed previous to that I couldn't remember, but I know for certain her death ended any pretense of prayer I might have made. But now Jen was all I had left. I knew I had to find something—anything—to help her. If prayer was that thing, I needed to give it a shot.

Yet, how was one supposed to go about the business of praying? Should I say *Dear God,* like one would start a letter? Maybe *O Lord* was better, or *Our Father.* How about *Lord Jesus,* like Leona and her mother always said? I was getting more frustrated by the minute. The praying thing wasn't going so smoothly—and I hadn't even begun!

I eventually decided it probably didn't matter much how I started. Maybe God would be so surprised hearing from me, he wouldn't notice how I addressed him.

I plunged in. "Dear God," I said out loud. A woman in the front pew turned and looked at me. I ducked my head in embarrassment and whispered, "Hello, God. It's me, Tony."

Now, that was a silly beginning, wasn't it? God was supposed to know everything, so why tell him who I was? I blew out my cheeks in exasperation with myself.

"I'm sorry," I plunged on. "I know it's been a long time since you've heard from me. I guess I've gotten pretty used to getting along by myself. But right now I don't know what to do about Jen. She needs your help. She's hurting from losing her baby and is acting pretty strange these days."

Irritation started to creep in again, so I figured I might as well be honest about that, too.

"Okay, God, you probably know I'm plenty ticked off at her. She does some really stupid things sometimes. But I'm also worried. So, Lord Jesus, if you can help her in any way, I would appreciate it. Thank you, Father God."

There. I had used all the names for God I could think of—just to cover my bases—and I ended with "Amen." It wasn't a very long prayer but I had run out of things to say.

I looked up again at the stained glass window closest to me, noticing for the first time how brightly the colors glowed in the late afternoon sun. The window had a Christmas theme, complete with angels, lambs and shepherds. In the center sat a blue-robed Mary, holding her precious Infant on her lap. The arms of baby Jesus were stretched out wide and, for a brief moment, it seemed as if the Mother and Child were embracing all the hurting people in the world—including my sister.

I stared at the window, transfixed, for the longest time. It wasn't until I noticed the daylight fading outside that I finally left. After getting off the bus, I ran the rest of the way home. Just inside the door of our apartment, I stopped short. Jen was seated on the sofa, fully dressed. That alone was quite an improvement. Although her eyes were red and her face streaked with tears, she calmly held her rosary beads.

"Glad you're home," she said quietly. "It's almost dark."

Carefully I closed the door, as if I feared the improvement might disappear with any loud noise.

"You're dressed," I said.

She nodded. "It's strange, but for the first time in a long time I felt like getting up and praying the Rosary. And when I got to the third joyful mystery, about the birth of Jesus, I started crying and couldn't stop." She pulled out a tissue and wiped away the last trace of tears. "But I guess that's what I needed the most."

Later, at bedtime, she returned to the topic.

"All this time people have been telling me Mary is my mother and I can go to her with all my needs. Yet it never really sank in. But today, during the Rosary, I just *knew* Mary was praying for me, and that Jesus was holding my baby in his arms and that everything would be all right." Tears welled again in her eyes. "And you know, Tony, I am *so* glad to be joining a Church which has a mother to give me."

After she turned off the lights and went to her room, I lay wide awake in the darkness. I knew I was greatly in need of a mother, too, and wondered if Mary had any extra room in her heart for me.

25

"Carlos called," I told my sister as she mixed up chocolate chip cookie batter. I had already tried sneaking a taste and she had whacked my hand with the wooden spoon. Maybe, I thought, if I could distract her with talk about the handsome Carlos, I could get my fingers into the bowl before she noticed.

"He wanted to know if you were going to RCIA tonight. I told him you were. Since you missed the last two classes, I figured you wouldn't want to miss again."

Jen nodded. "That's why I'm making cookies. I thought I'd bring them tonight. Other people sometimes bring snacks. Did he say he'd pick me up?"

"Yep," I answered, smiling to myself.

I still was hoping to get something started between those two, especially since Jen had been coming up with excuses not to see Killer. I had started to realize things were different between Jen and her boyfriend when I came home one afternoon to find our apartment looking like a tornado had touched down.

"Hey, Jen?" I called over music blasting from the radio.

My sister exited her bedroom with an armload of clothing, depositing it alongside the piles already on the sofa. Her stuff was everywhere and there was barely room to walk. She waved to me as she returned to her room. I followed her through the disorder and stopped at the doorway.

"Wow!" I said. "What are you doing?"

She removed the last of her clothes from the closet. Everything else was gone. Her bed had been stripped and the bureau drawers were empty.

"Are you spring cleaning early?" We had never done any spring cleaning, but there was always a first time.

"Nope. I'm moving out."

My heart stopped. "What?" I shrieked. "What do you mean you're moving out?"

"Crying out loud, Antonia! Calm down!" I followed her back to the living room where she switched off the music. "I'm not moving *out* out. I'm only moving out of the bedroom."

I blinked in confusion. "Out of the bedroom? Where are you going?"

"Right here," she declared, patting the old sofa. "I'm moving out here and you're going to have the bedroom."

"I am?"

It took a minute to sink in. Then she grinned at me and I let out a shout. A room of my own!

We spent the rest of the evening sorting and storing. When we were done, my things were neatly put away in the closet and bureau, and hers were stashed in cartons and the refrigerator box. It was after midnight when we finished and collapsed on the sofa.

"I can't believe it! Now I'll have room to spread out...and a little privacy—" I stole a quick look at Jen. Did changing the bedroom arrangement mean her arrangement with Killer was changing? Her face was inscrutable.

"—and maybe I can come up with some sort of bookshelf for my books," I finished.

"I'll keep my eyes open," Jen said. "Things are thrown out at work all the time." She looked over at a stack of clothes piled high on a kitchen chair. "As a bonus, look at all the stuff I had which I never wear! I can make new things out of them. And now, sis, get off my bed so I can go to sleep!"

Yes, things were definitely changing, I reflected, as I tried once more to sneak a bit of batter while Jen removed a tray of cookies from the oven.

"Keep your paws out of that bowl!" she commanded without even turning around.

After supper I walked down with her to wait for Carlos. It was too early in the evening for the druggies to be out, so we were able to linger in relative safety on the sidewalk. Then she glanced over my shoulder and her face went white. I turned to look. My heart skipped a beat when I saw Killer's pickup approaching.

"Hey, gal," he drawled, after pulling over and getting out. He noticed the plastic-wrapped plate Jen held in her hands. "Well, isn't this nice? Coming out t'meet me with cookies, eh?"

I had always suspected Killer wasn't the sharpest knife in the drawer. Now I was certain.

"Hello, Max," Jen said quietly, then pressed her lips tightly together. She always did that when annoyed.

"You *were* waiting for me, now, weren't you?" The big man peered at Jen and then glanced over at me. I looked away nervously. "I called several times and your kid sister told me you were sick. Seems like you're all recuperated now. So how come you haven't called me?"

Things didn't look good. If Jen *was* planning to break up with Killer, the middle of the sidewalk didn't seem the best place to go about it. I kept sneaking worried looks down the block. What if Carlos showed up? The young man was strong enough, but he was no match for the towering hulk waiting impatiently for Jen's explanation.

She said, "We need to talk. But right now's not a good time. I have a meeting at church tonight."

He scowled at the word *church*. "You *are* getting religious on me, aren't you!"

"Oh, Max," sighed Jen. "Can't we talk about it some other time?"

"What's the matter with right now?" Belligerently, he moved closer. "Those cookies *aren't* for me, are they? You waiting for someone else? Gal, you holding out on me?"

When Jen said nothing, his hand struck out. I caught my breath, fully expecting my sister to get socked in the nose. But instead, the plate of cookies flew up, cracked against her face and spun off to crash onto the concrete. Tears sprang to her eyes as blood trickled down her chin from a split lip.

"Hey!" I yelled, just as there came the sound of tires squealing to the curb.

I whirled around. Oh, no! It was Carlos! Killer was going to cream him!

I was surprised to see both Carlos *and* Jules jump from the old Honda and sprint over. They came to a stop just out of Killer's reach, one on each side, and eyed him cautiously. He turned his gaze from one to the other with a smirk on his face.

"Well, ain't this nice? *Two* pretty boys, huh, gal? It seems I'm not good enough for you. Now you need two fellas to keep you happy!"

Carlos's cheeks reddened and his jaw tightened as he clenched his fists. Jules crossed his arms, steely-eyed as he stared at Killer without flinching.

"Come on, now, Max," pleaded Jen. "They're just friends."

At that, any common sense Killer might have had left him. His arm swung out as he lunged towards Jen. Jules moved quickly, intending to yank her out of harm's way. Carlos grabbed Killer's arm. I wasn't any help at all. I just screamed.

In that instant, Jen did something so unexpected that everyone froze. Her right hand went up to her forehead, then to her chest and to her shoulders, making a distinctive Sign of the Cross over herself.

We all gaped at her as she said calmly, "Max, I don't belong to you anymore. I belong to God. So if you do anything to me, you'll have to answer to him."

Then she turned her back on him and headed down the sidewalk as if she was totally unconcerned about his reaction.

Carlos quietly released Killer's arm and both younger men took a step backwards. Killer paid them no more attention than if they had been ants crawling on his shoe. He stared after Jen for a full minute with an almost comical look of confusion on his face. Then he turned on his heel and marched to his truck, all the while hurling invectives at Jen's receding back—the gist being that, if God wanted a loser like her, well, he could have her because there were better fish in the ocean. Or something to that effect. I was scared he would go after Jen, but he rocketed off in the opposite direction.

I was almost afraid to hope he was gone for good. But as it turned out, we never saw him again. If only it had been that easy to get rid of another loser.

Jules looked at me and I looked at Carlos, who said tersely, "Get in!" We all piled into his car and took off after Jen, catching up with her at the bus stop. I opened the back door and called to her, and she squeezed in next to me and the laundry basket.

We drove in silence for awhile. Neither guy mentioned Killer or asked what the altercation had been about. Jen pressed her swollen lip with the back of her hand. I wondered if I should give her one of Carlos's T-shirts from the laundry basket to wipe off the blood, but thought better of it. Maybe he read my mind, because a box of Kleenex flew over the seat and landed in my lap.

Eventually, Jules turned and asked, "You okay, Jen? You still want to go to RCIA tonight?"

She took a deep breath. "Yes, I do."

I asked him, "How come you happened to be with Carlos tonight? You don't usually go to the class, do you?"

"Not usually. But tonight's talk is about the Blessed Mother. I've always had a devotion to her and wanted to hear it. I guess I was there when your sister needed help because I was supposed to be."

Next thing I knew, we were pulling up at St. Therese's. I hadn't intended to go to Jen's class with her, but maybe I, too, was there because I was supposed to be.

26

At the library, we sat across the table from each other with my math book traveling back and forth between us. I was scrawling numbers on a piece of paper in a determined effort to plumb the unfathomable mystery of mathematics.

"Try it this way," Jules prodded in a whisper, showing me step-by-step how to arrive logically at an answer. I tried the equation one more time as he suggested and light began to pierce the fog. If only my math teacher would be so patient!

I was *so* glad I had ended up at Jen's class a few nights previous. During the break, I had been recounting to Jules my difficulties with math. He casually mentioned, without the least show of bragging, that he had been a math whiz in high school. Would I like some help? he asked.

I eagerly accepted. Not only was I failing math and thus jeopardizing my graduation, but secretly I had a crush on Jules. Tall and lanky, he wasn't as good-looking as Carlos—or even Kenny. Yet he had a disarming smile and treated everyone with the utmost thoughtfulness. Until that evening at RCIA, I figured he would be interested in my older sister. During the break, though, he had talked only with me.

I was truly grateful for his help and told him so as we left the library. He insisted on seeing me safely home.

"Did you like the talk at RCIA the other night?" he asked as we walked.

"Yeah, I did. I never knew all that stuff about Mary before."

He smiled. "What sticks most in your mind?"

143

I thought a minute. "Well, it got my attention when the priest talked about the same thing that's on this medal I'm wearing."

I tugged on the ribbon around my neck. The medal from Frank and Beatrice, which I had been wearing regularly for some time, popped out from under my shirt.

Squinting at the tiny letters, I read out loud, "*O, Mary, conceived without sin, pray for us who have recourse to thee.* See, that's what it says."

"I know!" He laughed. "I wear a Miraculous Medal, too."

"So," I went on, "I finally found out what 'conceived without sin' means. That God saved Mary from sin from the very first moment of her existence. But I wonder—why was Mary treated different than the rest of us? Was it because she was to be the mother of Jesus?"

"You got it," he said. "God created her 'full of grace,' as the Gospel of Luke says, so she'd be worthy to be the mother of God's own Son. That's why she was redeemed from the very moment of her conception."

We stopped on the sidewalk outside my building and I pulled my coat more tightly around me. Although the wind had picked up and I was shivering, I was reluctant to end our discussion.

"But the man behind me said Mary needed a savior, too," I said. "I don't get it."

Jules answered, "He was talking about what Mary said to her cousin Elizabeth—from Luke, chapter one—'My spirit rejoices in God, my Savior.' He wanted to know how we can say Mary had no sin on her soul, when she herself declared she needed a savior."

"And what was the answer again?"

He took off his scarf and put it around my neck. As I snuggled my frozen nose into its warmth, I wondered if maybe Jules, too, was enjoying our conversation and didn't want it to end.

He said, "Look at it this way, Tony. What if you were taking a walk along an unfamiliar path in the woods, and suddenly the path ends and you fall over a cliff, and you manage to grab a root sticking out and are dangling there—"

My eyes, peering over the scarf, must have looked bewildered because he chuckled.

"Wait, I'm getting to the point! So…if you're hanging there, and some guy comes along and throws you a rope and pulls you up, wouldn't you call him your savior?"

"Uh, yeah, I guess so."

"What about if the guy was to catch you just *before* you fell over the cliff? Wouldn't he still be your savior?"

I nodded.

"In the same way, Mary was saved from falling over the 'cliff' of sin—only it was at the moment of her conception instead of later like the rest of us. That was a special gift from God because she was to bear the Son of God. Does that help at all?"

I would have to think about it some more, but it did sort of make sense. I was trying to think of another question to ask in order to delay his departure, when I saw Jen hurrying along the slush-covered sidewalk towards us. She had her arms wrapped around her like she was freezing. It was no wonder, since she didn't have her coat on.

"Hi, Tony. Hi, Jules." Jen exhaled a cloud of vapor as she trotted past, unlocked the front door with stiff fingers and left it open for me. Puzzled, I tossed the scarf back to Jules and ran up the inside stairs after my sister. I caught up with her at the door of our apartment.

"Jen! Are you out of your mind? Where's your coat?"

She didn't say anything until she had entered the apartment, wrapped a blanket around herself and toppled like a mummy onto the sofa.

"Whew! That's better. Hey, make me some hot coffee, would you?"

By the time I brought it to her she had stopped shivering, but she gratefully sipped the steaming beverage.

I looked at her crossly. "Jen, did you have another coat stolen?"

"Nope. I gave it away."

"You what? To who?"

"To a girl I saw. She only had a sweater on and was cold."

"Well, that's all *you* have on now, too," I pointed out.

"But I do have another coat. You know, the one I made?"

"That's not warm enough for winter!"

Jen shrugged. "Oh, well, winter's almost over. I can always get another one. The poor thing was freezing."

"And where'd you see this girl?"

"She was standing on the corner of Port Street and Sixth."

My mouth dropped open. I knew that corner was notorious for its "activities." Was my sister out of her mind? She gave her coat away to a *prostitute!* I was about to scold Jen for her naïveté when something out of the ordinary caught my eye.

I looked down to see the sewing box, its top wide open, on the floor beside the overstuffed chair. Jen a*lways* stashed it away on the other side of the chair, next to the wall, when it wasn't being used.

"Did you leave your sewing box here?" I asked Jen.

"I don't know." She walked over with the blanket trailing behind her. "I was doing some sewing before I left for work today, but I thought I put it away." She began straightening the spools and other things.

"That's strange," she said, "I'm not usually so messy."

That was true. Jen tended to be picky about how everything was placed in the sewing box. And she never left the top open to gather dust.

The same awful thought hit both of us at the same time. Jen scrambled to look around the bedroom while I ran to the kitchen and began yanking pans out of the bottom corner cupboard. Hidden way in the back was my jewelry box. I pulled it out and opened it with trembling hands.

I heaved a sigh of relief. My necklace was still there! I put the box away and threw back the pans, then noticed Jen checking the back door.

"It's not locked," she said. "Did we leave it that way or did someone else get in?"

We retrieved the coffee can, still used for bus fare, which was stashed in the pantry. It was empty. Neither of us could remember if we had taken the last of the change.

"Do you think we should call the police?" I asked.

"We're not sure anything is missing. Tony, we have to remember to double-check that back door from now on!"

Even though it took us awhile to get over our jitters, before long we convinced ourselves we were just being paranoid.

Jen and Dolores had plenty of items between them to sell at the "Springtime Fling" in March. Jen made enough from the craft show to cover the remainder of her hospital bills, and our neighbor had a little extra cash to buy necessities for the new baby coming. Only a week later, Dolores delivered a healthy baby boy. When she brought her new son home, we went down to see him.

Jen handed Dolores a present. "This is for the *bambino*."

The children helped unwrap the handmade baby blanket and their mother smiled her thanks. Jen's eyes never left the tiny face with dark eyes peering out from the bundle on Dolores's lap.

"Would you like to hold him?" Dolores asked.

Before my sister realized what was happening, the baby was deposited in her arms. Startled for a moment, Jen juggled him awkwardly before lifting him to her shoulder. There she nestled the baby close to her cheek while she rocked back and forth, patting him gently on the back. No one else but me noticed, but tears welled in her eyes.

She felt a tug on her arm and looked down to see Nina.

"That's *our* baby," said the child. "Do you have a baby?"

Jen shook her head. "No," she said with a small, sad smile. "I wish I did."

She handed the newborn back to his mother, bid *adios* to the family and hastily left.

That was the last time my sister ever made any mention of the baby she had lost. She must have worked through her grief by immersing herself in other things. Like her newest project—to make blankets for the homeless shelter. She figured it would be a great way to use up the fabric scraps which were accumulating at an alarming rate.

The next weekend, I came home from work to find people in our living room busily quilting squares of material. Leona smiled at me.

"Hey, Antonia," she said. "Come and join us."

Mama Lucy explained, "We're making kilts."

I laughed. "No, thanks. I'd probably stitch my thumb to the blanket. Sewing is Jen's thing, not mine."

I saw Bobby—you know, of the Flying Fantini Brothers?—plying a needle along with the women. He must have noticed my look of surprise.

He explained, "Had to learn to sew to keep my costumes in repair. No wife to do it. Come on, we'll teach you how. It's easy."

I got out of it by saying I had a date, which was absolutely true. Ever since the math homework night, Jules and I had been hanging out together. I loved every minute I spent with him. He was nothing like Kenny. Jules was more caring than any guy I had ever known. He didn't get upset over every little thing and he really listened to me. He never asked for anything beyond simply holding my hand. With him, I felt...well...*cherished.* I was crazy about him.

Speaking of boyfriends, my sister seemed to have sworn off them once Killer was out of her life. One day I was teasing her about Carlos, who was going to be her sponsor when she became Catholic.

"The two of you will make a very handsome couple," I said with a wicked grin, "when you're standing together at the ceremony."

She barely glanced up from the sewing machine where she was making a satiny blue dress to wear for the big day.

"The two of who?"

"You and Carlos. I think he likes you."

"Knock it off, Antonia!" she exclaimed, shoving a pin into a seam. "Carlos and I are just friends. He's not interested in me."

"Oh, sure." I was smugly certain she was wrong. "What makes you think that?"

"Because Carlos is going to be a priest, and priests don't get married."

"A priest!" I was astounded. The thought had never crossed my mind.

"Oh," I said, feeling quite stupid. Except for the clacking of the sewing machine, there was silence in the room while I digested the new information. I finally came to the conclusion that I should give up matchmaking. Anyway, Jen seemed so much happier than before, even without a boyfriend. I changed the subject.

"Jen, you said you'll be received into the Church the night before Easter. At the, uh... Easter vigil? Well, what exactly is going to happen? I mean, are you going to be baptized?" I had a mental image of water cascading all over her nice new dress.

She stopped working and thought for a moment. "Well, I'm not really sure at this point. I understand that baptism puts an indelible, or irremovable, mark on your soul. It makes you a member of Christ's family forever. So once you're baptized—even as a baby—you can't get baptized again. I sort of remember going to church when I was little. So maybe I *was* baptized."

148

"Is there any way to find out for sure?"

She shrugged. "I've thought long and hard and just can't remember what church we went to. I don't even know where we lived at the time! I just wish Mom had told us more about our background."

She frowned in frustration and went back to her sewing.

"Well, Jen, have you prayed about it?"

Her eyes, wide in surprise, flew up to my face.

"I mean, you're the one always talking about prayer and how much good it does. So...put your money where your mouth is!"

She didn't respond. Considering, though, the way things turned out, she must have taken my excellent advice.

Before long, Jen launched herself into yet another endeavor.

One day I found her picking up empty liquor bottles and other garbage in our hallway. I tried to find any excuse not to help but, next thing I knew, we were both working our way down the stairs and through the second floor. When we reached the ground floor, Mona poked her head out of her apartment, snarled something at us and disappeared again.

Guilty conscience, I figured. Cleaning up should have been *her* job.

During the following week, Jen picked up more trash *and* swept the floors. She even tried washing the graffiti and grunge off the peeling wall paint. That didn't work out so well. Still, just the little bit of difference in the building's appearance began to make a difference in the residents. Bobby offered to keep the first floor picked up and he pestered several of the jobless men on the second floor to keep their hallway clean. A few of the people even began greeting each other when they'd pass in the halls. Of course, there were those who went out of their way to make rude comments or even drop additional litter, but Jen ignored them all and kept at it.

Apparently, that wasn't enough to keep her busy. As the nicer weather of April rolled in, she picked up trash outside, too, cheerfully keeping the sidewalk and alley in respectable shape. It wasn't long until she had children from the neighborhood, who initially stood around making fun of her, joining the clean-up crew. She made the work more interesting by making a contest out of it. When she realized there really wasn't much for kids to do around there, she began organizing games for them.

With everything else she was doing, and only a little more than a week left before Easter, Jen was still trying to finish her new dress. One evening while she worked on it, I heard a small shriek from her. The tension on the sewing machine had gotten messed up and the stitches were forming little loops instead of nice straight lines.

We tried fiddling with the various knobs, but only ended up making the problem worse.

"Dang!" she said. "I guess I'll have to take it back to that shop to get it adjusted!"

"Hold on," I said. "What about those old instructions at the bottom of your sewing box? Let's see if there's any information in there which might help."

Jen splayed open all the tiers of her grandmother's sewing box. She pushed aside the balls of yarn in the bottom tray and slid out the dog-eared instruction booklet. As she paged through it, a sheet of paper fluttered to the floor.

27

The following day, Jen and I headed out to a salon where I was treating her to a real haircut for her big day. On the way, we stopped at St. Therese's. While waiting at the office window, we heard a familiar voice greet us. We turned and saw Frank, and Jen gave him an exuberant hug.

"Can you believe it?" she asked him. "I found out I was baptized when I was a baby! My mother put my baptismal certificate in a strange place, but I found it yesterday."

"That's wonderful!" Frank replied. "So I guess you'll be confirmed and receive your First Communion at the Easter vigil. Am I invited?"

He was teasing her. Jen laughed.

"Of course! And so is Beatrice! Carlos, of course, is my sponsor. Without all of you, I wouldn't be here right now!" Jen was babbling, but she was too excited to care. "I'm just waiting for the secretary to make a copy."

If only Jen had had her baptismal certificate in hand at that moment to show him, we could have saved ourselves a whole lot of time and trouble. But Frank was in a hurry that day, saying he had just finished his Holy Hour and someone was waiting to take him home. He waved goodbye to us and left.

"What's a Holy Hour?" I asked Jen, after the secretary had given back the original certificate and the two of us headed to the hair salon.

"It's when you spend an hour in front of the Blessed Sacrament." I had no clue what she was talking about, so she explained, "Remember when I told you about that youth group when Milo asked everyone to go to church and pray for an hour? Well, that's a 'Holy Hour.'"

She shook her head, smiling. "Every day there's more information to absorb, more new words—but I'm learning fast! 'The Blessed Sacrament' means pretty much the same thing as the Holy Eucharist, or Holy Communion, or the bread and wine after it's consecrated to become the Body and Blood of Jesus. I told you that before. Remember?"

I nodded. I also remembered Jen saying she would receive the Sacrament of Reconciliation in a few days—what she called "going to Confession." She said her sins would be forgiven and she could receive her First Communion in a state of grace. Or, as she put it, with a "squeaky clean soul."

I was happy for her. She needed a way to put her past behind her. If Confession helped her know she was truly forgiven, maybe she could find peace of mind at last.

The evening of the Easter vigil arrived. Although I lacked full understanding of its significance, I still felt a shiver of excitement as I slid into the church pew with Jules, Frank and Beatrice. In the darkened church, everyone was handed an unlit taper. Jules whispered to me that the darkness represented the suffering and death of Jesus. Outside the church, he said, the priest was lighting an *Easter fire* which would dispel the darkness of night just as the light of the risen Christ dispelled the darkness of death. Then a very large candle—the Easter candle—would have grains of incense inserted into it, representing the wounds of Christ, and the Easter candle would be lit from the Easter fire.

Jen was right, I thought. There *was* a lot to learn.

I watched as a deacon came through the back doors carrying the lighted Easter candle. He chanted, "Christ, our Light!" The congregation sang in response, "Thanks be to God!"

Jen and Carlos, along with the others being received into the Church and their sponsors, followed the deacon with their own smaller lighted candles. Processing up the aisle, they lit tapers as they passed.

"Christ, our Light!"

"Thanks be to God!"

Jen's candle touched my taper. The flame caught and she winked at me before she and Carlos continued with the others to their pew up front. I touched my taper to Jules's, and watched as the lighting progressed down our pew, from Jules to Frank to

152

Beatrice and on to others. It occurred to me that that was the only way candles could be lit—or hearts could be touched. One to one, on and on, continuing to the ends of the earth.

"Christ, our Light!"

"Thanks be to God!"

Little bright flames leapt to each person along every pew and soon all faces in the church glowed. Yes, the darkness was truly dispelled.

We sang the first hymn, blew out our candles and, in the dark once more, sat for the reading of Scripture. There were a number of passages from the Old Testament, telling the story of God's love and providence for his people from the creation of the world through the time of the prophets. I had never heard that before. It was pretty amazing.

After the readings and Psalms, we blinked in the sudden brightness as all the lights came on. Trumpets blared, bells rang out and the choir intoned, "Glory to God in the highest, and peace to his people on earth!" There was a ripple of anticipation in the church as we listened to the Gospel story of Christ's resurrection.

Then the priest walked partway down the aisle and thundered, "Jesus Christ has conquered death! It is fitting that we sing with great joy, as we are celebrating a great wonder—His resurrection! His rising from the dead assures us that death is not the end of the story. Alleluia!"

With one voice, the congregation echoed, "Alleluia!"

"Because of Christ's passion, death and resurrection," he proclaimed in his strong voice, "everyone who believes in him and does the will of the Father will also rise from the dead and live with him forever in heaven! Do I hear alleluia?"

"Alleluia!"

"Our life on earth is short. Eternity, on the other hand, is a very long time. Where am I going to spend it? Where are *you* going to spend it? In heaven there is no more death, no more sickness, no more sadness. Only joy and peace and the fullness of God's presence. No matter where we find ourselves right now, no matter what we've done or how far we have strayed, God offers us his mercy and forgiveness so we can start over, start fresh. If you have been away, come back to God! Come back to the one who created you and loves you beyond all telling. You need have no fear. God is a God of love. His love for us never ends, never changes. We are a people of great hope in God's promises. Christ has conquered death! Alleluia!"

As I listened to the final "Alleluia" die away, I didn't realize what those words about resurrection and hope would come to mean to me in the not-so-distant future. At the time, my attention was focused solely on those who were being baptized. After the baptisms were done, Jen and the others walked forward to stand on the altar steps. Waiting there next to Carlos, my sister radiated happiness. I had never seen her look so beautiful.

Carlos put a hand on her shoulder as the priest, ready to trace the Sign of the Cross with oil on her forehead, inquired what name she had chosen for Confirmation. I still didn't know that myself. All along, Jen had been undecided about which saint to pick as her special patron for her continuing walk with Christ.

"All those Christian brothers and sisters in heaven—and I never knew about them!" she said to me one day. "Tony, do you realize that being part of the Church means I'm discovering not only a mother, but a whole family?"

However, she never mentioned what name she had finally decided on. In a soft voice, Jen responded to the priest's question.

"Mary."

Tears ran down her cheeks, but there must have been great elation in her heart as she placed herself forever under the patronage of her heavenly Mother.

When it came time for Communion, even though I couldn't see Jen's face as she went forward to receive, I realized it was, for her, the culmination of all the long months of study and prayer. At last she was receiving her Lord—his precious Body and Blood—in Holy Communion. I'm sure nothing else mattered for her at that moment.

As I waited in my pew while Frank, Beatrice and Jules went up for Communion, a powerful longing hit me. More than anything else, I suddenly desired to be part of that same family— Christ's family—to which Jen and our new-found friends belonged. I wanted the peace of heart, the joy, the all-encompassing *love*, which they seemed to have.

At that very moment, I made up my mind to join my sister on her journey of faith.

28

"Today's another sizzler," I moaned one day early in the summer. "Can't we find a better place to live?"

Depressed at the thought of enduring another season of stifling temperatures in our third-floor apartment, I looked imploringly at my sister as she chopped vegetables for supper. Sighing, she mopped the perspiration off her forehead.

"You're the one good at finances. Can we afford it?"

I pulled out the spiral notebook where I had come up with a system for keeping track of our money. I ran my finger down the columns of figures.

"I have six hundred dollars saved—"

"We're not touching that!" Jen was adamant. "Now that you're out of school, you'll be able to work more hours and build up your savings to go to college someday."

I grinned, feeling so relieved to be done with high school. With Jules's help, I had managed to pull my math grade up to a "C" and would officially graduate in two weeks. I couldn't wait.

"Look out, world, here I come! I'm gonna make a big cake for my party—" Jen's eyebrows shot up. "Okay, okay," I said, "*you* take care of the cake!"

I turned back to the notebook. Our common fund was growing, so maybe we *could* think about looking for a new place soon. Then I took a closer look at my sister's portion.

"Jen, you've taken out money again."

"Yeah, well…Dolores didn't have enough for diapers last week, and Nina had that ear infection and needed medicine."

"A couple of weeks ago, you bought Melvin's blood pressure pills for him!"

She shrugged. "What was I supposed to do? His daughter's in the hospital and couldn't send money this month. He would have gone without his medication or used up his food budget."

Jen put navy beans in a pot and added water. Not soup again! Maybe she should be worrying more about our own food budget and not so much about others.

"Are you buying things for Mona, too? I've seen you going into her apartment. Jen, how can you stand her? I'd stay away from that old grouch if I was you. She might bite."

"You don't know Mona at all. She's not that bad. She's under a lot of stress."

"What kind of stress?"

"It's her husband. He's bedridden. Has been for years."

Mona had a husband? That was news to me.

Jen was still talking. "He needs almost constant care and there's no family to help out. So I've been stopping by once in awhile just to give her a break."

That made me think of something else. "You're also stopping by the church after work a lot, too. How come?"

She shrugged. "I like to pray in front of the Blessed Sacrament whenever I have a few minutes. You know, it's strange—but once the conviction settles into your soul that Jesus is really there, you just have to be with him as much as you can!"

Besides Leona and Lucy, I wanted to invite all our friends from St. Therese's to my graduation party. I called the church office and asked for Frank's number.

"Um...you know," I said, "the thin, white-haired man in the Legion of Mary?"

"That would be Frank Hollander," the secretary replied.

Hollander. The name rang a bell, but I didn't have time to dwell on it as she was saying, "I can't give out his number. But if you want to leave yours, I'll have him call you."

By the time I was finished with the phone calls, I completely forgot about the conversation. There was so much to do in the following weeks that graduation day was upon me before I realized it. The ceremony itself was a blur. The only thing I remember clearly was the party afterwards.

It was fortunate the weather was unseasonably cool that June afternoon, as we never before had so many people packed into our apartment. Jen set out the fruit salad and sandwiches we had made and Leona brought a tray with crudités, or what Mama called "an apartment of vegetables." After we finished eating, Jen trotted out a beautifully decorated cake with "Congratulations Tony!" written on the top. And there were no scraped-off letters.

"Wait! Before cake, it's picture time!" Jules called out. Chaos reigned as he peered through the viewfinder, arranged and rearranged the guests while motioning for everyone to squeeze more tightly together.

From where I was putting away leftover sandwiches in the kitchen, I looked on the scene with amusement, wondering when my absence would be noticed. Suddenly Carlos hollered, "Hold on, Jules! The star of the show isn't here!"

They all laughed and Jen sputtered, "Hurry on, Tony! For crying out loud! Hurry on, would you?"

From where he stood in the back row, Frank reached through the line of shoulders and tapped Jen. "What did you say?"

"I was just telling Tony to get a move on. Let's get these pictures done so we can have dessert!" Impatiently, Jen grabbed my arm and pulled me into the pack.

"No," said Frank. "You said 'hurry on' instead of 'hurry up.' Why did you say that?"

"I don't know. That's the way I always say it. Why?"

"I used to know—" Frank's voice trailed off when he realized the others were waiting for him. He stood up straighter for the picture.

"Say 'cheese'!" said Jules.

"Say 'please,'" said Mama.

The shutter clicked and then Carlos commandeered the camera. Jules sidled in next to me and furtively grasped my fingers. I smiled widely for the shot.

We finally got our cake and I opened my gifts. At the time, however, I didn't realize it would be my sister who would end up receiving the best gift of all.

"I'd like to talk to you about something," Jen said to Frank as our guests began to leave. "Can you stay a little longer?"

Carlos stayed, too, to drive Frank home. At the kitchen table, the four of us polished off the last of the sandwiches. I wasn't really listening to the casual conversation buzzing around me. I only came to attention when I heard Jen address Frank.

"I want to join the Legion of Mary. How do I go about it?"

"Good grief, Jen," I said, "you're always jumping into something. Why don't you think about it a little longer?"

She shook her head. "I *have* thought about it. Tony, you're grown up now and I don't exactly have to take care of you any longer. I only have my job and there's not much housework to do around here. I have some free time. I've been thinking it would be nice to give back, the same way I was given to." She turned again to Frank. "So, can I join up?"

Frank's blue eyes twinkled. "Actually, you can't." He chuckled when he saw her crestfallen look. "*Nobody* can. What you need to do is come to meetings for three months. At the end of that time, if you still want to, *then* you join. But even during the probationary period, you can take part in the visitation we do. Would you like to do that?"

Jen's countenance brightened as he talked. She eagerly nodded.

Carlos said, "We'll be happy to have an extra pair of hands to help with the work, since we'll be losing one soon."

"Oh, no! Who?"

Frank smiled again, a sad but resigned smile. "It's me," he said. "I'm going to be leaving St. Therese's."

"What?" Jen and I cried out at the same time. The church wouldn't be the same without Frank around.

He explained, "My eyesight is steadily getting worse and my legs aren't what they used to be. Jill's been after me to get out of the house before I do something stupid like fall and break something. So I guess it's time—" His gentle smile continued, yet I could imagine the heartache of leaving the home and parish where he'd been for a lifetime.

When everyone remained silent, he went on, "But I figure that God has something else he wants me to do, and I'll do it from Jill's. It'll also give me more time to spend with my grandsons. And of course, my house will be put to good use by the Legion of Mary."

He sighed. "It's getting hard for me to do the work, anyway. So instead of being an active member, I'll become an auxiliary, or praying, member. I'll be supporting the work of the Legion with my prayers." He reached over and squeezed Jen's hand, smiling encouragingly at her, while tears formed in the rest of our eyes.

"You'll do a great job in my place, Jennifer," he said.

"No one can take your place, Frank," said Carlos. "But it'll be good to have Jen."

"When are you leaving?" I asked.

"Well, I move pretty slow these days, so it will take me at least a month to sort and pack my things. After I leave, Legion members will spend time getting the house ready for its new life. Redoing the kitchen, new paint and the like."

Jen didn't say anything more, but I knew she was distressed about Frank leaving. She had grown quite fond of him. She retrieved her sewing box and set it on the floor by her chair. Whenever my sister was upset about anything, she sewed. Pulling out her latest project, she stabbed needle and thread through the fabric.

Small talk continued for a few more minutes before Frank said, "Well, Carlos, my boy, these ladies have had a long day. We should get going."

He stood up and his foot struck the sewing box, sending spools of thread flying across the floor.

"Oh, so sorry," he apologized.

Jen scrambled after the spools. "Don't worry about it. No harm done." She set the sewing box on the table and began replacing the thread.

Immediately, Frank bent down to peer more closely at the box. He ran a finger over the smooth wooden sides.

"For heaven's sakes!" he exclaimed. "Where did you get this sewing box?"

"It was my grandmother's," Jen said, lining up the spools.

I was watching Frank's face. He looked bewildered.

"It's Alice's," he said softly. "This is Alice's sewing box!" He turned to look at Jen.

"You're Jennifer Hollander!" he cried, his voice breaking. "My little Jenny!"

Still holding spools of thread, Jen froze with her hand in mid-air.

"Hollander?" she said slowly, like she didn't really know what she was saying. "Hollander," she repeated, a look of disbelief on her face. "Yes, I *was* Jennifer Hollander. I'm Jennifer O'Day now."

She stared wide-eyed at Frank. "You're...you're my grandfather?"

He reached out his long arms and pulled her close to him. He was crying openly—and the rest of us cried, too.

"My grandfather?" Jen asked once more, her voice muffled against his chest. She looked up into his face. "My Poppa?"

Frank chuckled through his tears. "Poppa! That's right! That's what you used to call me when you were a little girl! Poppa."

All of a sudden, he released her and sat down heavily in the chair. His hands trembled and his face looked chalky as he took several deep, shaky breaths. We hovered anxiously over him, asking if he was all right.

He nodded, brushing away our concern. "I'm fine! Better than I've been in years."

With tears still running down his cheeks, he looked up at Jen who was standing beside him and tightly holding his hand.

"God has answered my prayers! I have my Jenny back!"

29

Needless to say, we didn't get to bed until late that night. Carlos patiently stuck around for hours while Jen and her grandfather tried to figure out how things turned out the way they had.

"But why did Mom take me away?" Jen asked.

Frank sighed. "Oh, Jenny, your mom was so young when she married Steven—your father. When he died in that skiing accident, she didn't know what to do, especially with a child to raise. Even though your grandmother and I tried to help take care of you, it didn't surprise us when she married again within a short time. That Brian O'Day, with his curly hair and charming smile, was a dashing fellow!"

I grinned. That was my father he was talking about.

He continued, "Your mom and Brian lived in this area for a short while, but I guess the young man wasn't cut out for settling down."

"He was a salesman," Jen said. "He drove all over the Midwest, selling advertising to radio stations."

Frank nodded. "I didn't hold it against him for leaving. But it was hard losing you, especially since your grandmother had recently passed away." His voice caught, but he cleared his throat and went on. "I was just hoping your mother would keep in touch."

There was silence for a few moments before Jen said, "Maybe she would have, if it hadn't been for the cancer."

Frank whispered, "Oh, no," as she went on to explain.

"Breast cancer. She beat it for awhile, but it was hard for her with my stepfather gone so much. By then she had another child—" she glanced at me, "—and I think she felt overwhelmed.

161

She didn't talk much about the past, so somehow I got the impression that you, too, had passed away." Jen looked nonplussed, but plunged on. "That's why it never occurred to me to look you up.

"Then Dad...I mean, Brian—I always called him Dad since he adopted me and I don't remember much about my real father—"

Frank looked sad but didn't say anything.

"—was killed while changing a flat tire on the side of the road. So our mother had to raise us by herself, and eventually the cancer came back."

"I'm so sorry. It must have been so hard for you girls."

In the silence that followed, I reflected that I couldn't imagine it being any harder. But Jen had had to bear the worst of it because of taking me under her wing. I made up my mind to tell her sometime how much I appreciated it.

Jen suddenly exclaimed, "Oh, yeah! It's no wonder you asked why I said, 'hurry on!' You must have remembered my mother saying that."

"Yes," said Frank. "It was unusual enough that I remembered it after all these years. Yet I still didn't put two and two together. All these months of knowing you, and it never even occurred to me you were my own granddaughter. How could I have been so blind?" His tears began again.

Jen squeezed his hand. "I was so little when we moved away, I'm sure it was hard to picture me grown up. Besides, even my own mother wouldn't have recognized what I had become—" She stopped and sighed before continuing, "—and if you were blind, so was I. How could I not have noticed your eyes are exactly the same shade of blue as what I see in the mirror every day?"

I nodded. It was all so obvious. Now.

Carlos, quiet up to that time, finally spoke. "Frank, what are the chances you'd be the one to knock on your long-lost granddaughter's door? Couldn't we call that a miracle?"

It certainly was a miracle for Jen and Frank, or "Poppa Frank" as we began to call him. He and Jen began to reconnect. She went to his house to see him often, helping him pack up his belongings while they caught up on their missing years. Neither seemed to mind that the work slowed to a crawl as her grandfather told old family stories and packed up some of her grandmother's things for Jen to have.

It didn't occur to me to be jealous over my sister's good fortune, since there were many wonderful things which had begun to happen in my own life. Jen had found a family and, in a different way, so had I. Jules had been taking me to his home where I found myself practically adopted into his large Italian family. His warm, wonderful mother treated me like one of her own children. His many brothers and sisters, always involved in one activity or another, pulled me along with their enthusiasm as if I had always been part of their lives. It was during the impromptu ball games, late night sing-alongs and never-ending games of Monopoly that I fell in love with his family. That was good, since I had already fallen hopelessly in love with Jules.

Through many long hours of conversation, I was given insight into the heart of a godly man who lived life, and his faith, with conviction and passion. He told me his mother had dedicated him to the Blessed Virgin Mary when he was born. He took that dedication seriously, entrusting all his cares and problems to Mary, believing she held the key to her Son's heart. He even said he had asked her to bring him a good wife. When I heard that, my heart leaped. I sure hoped he was talking about me!

Jen had a chance to get better acquainted with the rest of her family when we were invited to her Aunt Jill and Uncle Harold's home for a Fourth of July picnic. We arrived toting a large watermelon and were greeted like the long-lost family we were. Of course, it was really Jen who was "family." I was simply swept along in the happy tide.

At the picnic, I overheard Frank and Jill talking. I hadn't meant to eavesdrop. I was looking for the bathroom and took a wrong turn in the spacious house. Hearing their voices in a bedroom, I paused outside the door. They were discussing how to set up the room for Frank's moving in when I heard Jen's name mentioned.

"I don't know how I'll be able to see Jenny," Frank said, "when she's in the city with no car and I'm way out here in the suburbs."

There was a short silence. Then Jill said, "Well, why don't you give her *your* car? It's still in good shape and you don't use it any more."

"That's a great idea! I hadn't thought of that. I doubt if she has a license, though, as the girls take the bus everywhere."

I heard Jill laugh. "Believe me, Dad, she'll get a license! The bigger problem might be how to keep the car from getting stolen, or stripped for parts, in that part of the city."

"True. Maybe she can keep it in my garage under lock and key. She can always take the bus to my house to get it. Darn it, Jill! I almost wish I hadn't given the house away! Jenny and Tony need a better place to live. But I can't do anything about it now."

"Harold and I are able to help them out financially. But I get the feeling that Jenny wouldn't hear of it."

I nodded. She was right about that.

Jill continued, "Dad, what about that trust fund you set up years ago for Jenny?"

Trust fund? Now, that was exciting news! I listened more closely.

"But she can't access it till she's thirty-five," Frank answered. "Meanwhile…"

My heart sank. As I tiptoed past the door to finish my bathroom search, I heard Jill say, "Well, Dad, we'll think of something."

One Sunday after the Rosary at Dolores's place, my sister arrived home followed by her grandfather and Beatrice. Jen immediately headed to the kitchen for cold drinks.

"Just like old times!" I laughed, gesturing at the pile of laundry on the sofa. I moved it to the table so our visitors could sit.

With a smile, Beatrice replied, "No, Tony, things *aren't* the same as they used to be, are they?"

"I guess that's true enough. But this place is still every bit as hot!" As I repositioned the overworked fan, I noticed a secret smile pass between them. Something's up, I thought.

Jen returned with the drinks. She hadn't said a word since she came in, which was highly unusual for her. I chalked it up to the oppressive heat. It had a way of sapping a person's energy.

"Jenny," Poppa Frank said, "you mentioned at Dolores's you wanted to talk to us."

The downhearted manner in which Jen nodded made me realize the problem wasn't the heat.

"I'm getting so frustrated every time I try to pray," she said, swirling the ice cubes in her glass. "I used to feel so close to God." She looked up at them with tears sparkling on her eyelashes. "*Especially* after I was able to receive the Eucharist. Knowing Jesus would come to me in Communion—*to me!*— because he loved me and wanted to be with me! That was such a wonderful feeling! I was praying all the time and it was exciting to read the Bible. I just couldn't get enough of God." She crunched an ice cube between her teeth and fell silent.

Our visitors waited for her to continue. Finally, Beatrice prodded, "And?"

Jen looked troubled. "Now I feel like I'm floundering. My prayer seems so dry and pointless, and anything I come across is way more interesting than reading the Bible. I feel like I've dropped into a black hole. I thought God was close to me and I loved him so much. But maybe I was wrong."

Jeesh! Jen seemed to have no qualms about letting all her feelings hang out. I was uncomfortable sitting in on her soul-baring, so I slipped into the kitchen to start supper. I went about it quietly, though, so I wouldn't miss a word.

"Jenny, you're experiencing what every person who's serious about prayer goes through sooner or later," her grandfather said.

"I am? What do you mean?"

Frank thought for a moment. "Let me explain it this way. When I married your grandmother, I was so much in love. I couldn't wait to see her and talk to her and just *be* with her. She was all I thought about, even while I was at work."

Jen smiled at the word picture he was painting.

"But those initial feelings of being in love don't last forever. They're not supposed to. They're what propel us to get married, but no marriage will last very long on just warm, fuzzy feelings. A married couple's love needs to grow and become stronger, based on their *decision* to go on loving each other, even when it's hard and those feelings aren't present. But it's that very decision to love which ends up bringing about deep, lasting joy in a marriage. Do you see how that relates to God and us?"

"I think so. God gives us those beautiful feelings about him to draw us into a relationship with him. But we can't run forever on those feelings."

Beatrice nodded. "God knows exactly what we need at every moment to find real happiness in this life and the next. Even if he's withdrawn the *awareness* of his presence from you, he's always close to you, Jennifer, even when you don't feel him there. What usually happens is the closer you get to God, the further away he seems."

"How come?"

"Because," said Frank, "when we persevere at prayer, our eyes are opened to see ourselves more honestly. You might say prayer shines a spotlight on all those places in our soul which have been dark for so long. We start to realize there's much in us that isn't exactly conformed to God's plan for us. So we begin to feel distant from God."

"That's for sure. Lately all I can think about is the awful things I've done in my life."

"Jenny, if you're sorry for those sins and have gone to Confession, you can be certain God has forgiven you. That's just the devil dredging up those things to throw in your face."

Jen sighed. "Yeah, I guess I know that. But it's so hard. How can I tell if I'm really on the right path when praying? It's so confusing sometimes."

"Whenever you're troubled in prayer," suggested Beatrice, "first examine your conscience to see if there really is a sin separating you from God. And since we're all so good at fooling ourselves, ask the Holy Spirit to enlighten you. If there *is* something that needs clearing up, go to confession. But having said that, there are a few things that can help you in prayer."

"Like what?"

"For one thing, you can ask the Blessed Mother to help. Who knows Jesus better than his own mother? Rest assured, she can help you. And another thing—Mother Teresa said if you want to pray better, you should pray more."

"More!" Jen groaned. "I'm so distracted now, I can't imagine trying to pray more!"

"I know what you mean!" said Poppa Frank, laughing a little. "But you can make *everything* you do a prayer, by doing it out of love for God. Anyway, struggling in prayer is part of the journey. I, myself, have always had trouble praying the Rosary—"

"You?" Jen was amazed. I was, too. Whenever we saw Frank, he had rosary beads in his hands.

"Oh, yes," he said. "Distractions are a way of life when you pray, *especially* a meditative prayer like the Rosary. There was once a woman who told Pope John XXIII that she was going to give up praying the Rosary because she was so distracted. He told her, 'My dear woman—never, never, never give up saying the Rosary. The only bad Rosary is a Rosary left unsaid!'"

"It's the same with any prayer," Beatrice added. "Distractions happen, but you just have to keep bringing your attention back. One time, I remember being so frustrated about all the things that kept running through my mind. But suddenly this thought came to me—which do you think touches a mother's heart more? A bouquet of dandelions given to her by her little child, or a perfect flower arrangement sent by someone who can't be bothered to come see her?"

"Probably the dandelions," answered Jen.

"Why?"

"Because the child has picked the dandelions out of love for her."

"In the same manner, just keep giving your own poor distracted prayers to the Lord with great love."

If my sister kept asking questions, we would have to invite our guests for supper. I added bread to the hamburger to stretch it.

"That's a lot to think about," Jen said with a sigh. "But how do I know I'm on the right track?"

"Keep on doing what you're doing and trust God to guide you," said her grandfather. "I'll bet you're seeing answers to prayer even in the midst of your struggles."

"That's true, I am," Jen answered. "It's weird. Sometimes I seem to say the right words or do exactly the right thing, or something unexpected happens and it turns out to be just what's needed. Is that what you mean?"

Beatrice smiled widely. "It seems to me, through your prayer and openness to God's working in your life, you're starting to see the fruits of the Holy Spirit!"

Fruits. That sounded like a good idea. I began to cut up apples for a fruit salad. I thought our visitors might leave then, but Frank said, "Jenny, now we have something we want to talk to *you* about." I grabbed a few bananas to add to the salad.

Frank was beaming at his granddaughter. "We were wondering if you and Tony would be willing to move into my house and oversee it for the Legion of Mary."

Move into his house? I dropped the knife with a loud clatter.

"Really?" Jen squealed. "You want us to do that?"

Frank chuckled at her excitement. "Of course! We can't think of anyone better to be in charge. And, as managers, you wouldn't have to pay rent."

Yes! I could *really* save money for college! Like me, Jen was thrilled.

"That would be wonderful! What exactly would we have to do?"

"Just run it on a day-to-day basis, make sure any repairs are taken care of, welcome the Legion members who will come for meetings and other things, decide who rents the rooms—"

Leona! The thought popped into my mind so abruptly that the words immediately popped out of my mouth.

"Can we ask Leona and Lucy to move in, too?"

Frank smiled. "I can't think of anyone better to have as your first tenants! The apartment upstairs might be perfect for them."

"Oh, Poppa Frank!" Jen started to cry. "It'll be like coming home for me! I can't wait! When can we move in?"

"I'll be moving soon, and then a few things need to be done to get it ready. It should be finished in early November. Do you think that will be okay?"

Okay? It was more than either of us could have hoped for! Jen would have her home, complete with a front porch and trees in the yard. As for me, I couldn't wait to bid "good riddance" to that horrible apartment building.

I should have known it wouldn't let us go so easily.

30

On a warm day at the end of summer, I sat on a patch of parched grass with my back leaning against the ailanthus tree in the alley. While swatting the annoying black flies, I watched Joachin, Miguel and several kids from the neighborhood playing ball in the empty lot behind our building. Jen had talked them into helping her clear out the bottles, old tires and other trash which had littered the area ever since I could remember. She even managed to badger some men from our building into hauling away a broken sofa and the old car parts dumped there. Then she called the city to cut down the weeds and the lot became a halfway decent baseball field.

In the shade near me, Nina played with her dolly while I watched Miguel take a hefty swing at the ball.

"Way to go!" Coach Jen yelled. "Good cut! Keep your eyes on the ball and hold the bat straight as you swing. I know you can do it!"

Joachin lobbed another wobbly pitch to his brother and Miguel connected bat with ball.

"Run!" shouted Jen. The boy took off for first base. When the lone outfielder bobbled the ball, Miguel ran to second.

"You're safe! All right!" Jen cheered.

She tossed the bat to Miguel at second base and instructed him to bat from there. That way he could have the thrill of running to home plate and scoring a "run." Since there weren't enough children to form two teams, Jen simply made up her own rules. With each child batting from whatever base he found himself on, you really didn't need teams.

"Tony!" Nina called out from behind me. "Look what I found!"

I went to look and she pointed at a small bird flailing its wings in the dust.

"It's a sparrow," I said. "Wonder if it's hurt?"

Nina called to the others to come and see as I picked up the bird. It nestled unafraid in my palm. I carefully examined it by stretching out its wings. Other than missing a few feathers, it didn't seem to have anything wrong. After much discussion on what to do with it, we all decided it would be best to put it back up in the tree.

"That way," Jen said, "it won't be killed by the alley cats around here. If it rests and grows stronger, maybe by tomorrow it can fly away."

I tucked the little thing into my shirt pocket and shimmied up the trunk of the ailanthus. It was easy to do because the tree grew at quite an angle, with its large, lopsided crown leaning toward our building. As I set the bird in a juncture between trunk and limb, I heard my sister tell the kids it was lucky it wasn't a baby bird which had fallen from its nest.

"They say once a human touches a baby bird," Jen said, "the mother bird can smell it and will reject the baby."

"What are you telling them?" I called down. "Do you really think birds can smell?"

"Of course!" she answered. "If they don't take a bath."

The kids giggled. I realized I had been set up.

The next day when I went to toss the garbage, I found the bird on the ground again. I brought it back up to the apartment with me and Jen decided we would keep it in a box until it was able to be on its own again.

"Okay," I said, "but you're digging the worms!"

She grimaced, but gamely took on the care of the little bird, even moving its box out onto our balcony during the day for fresh air.

A few days later, Jen was getting ready for another blanket-making party. As usual, she invited any of the other residents who might be interested in helping. I wasn't too happy when the first to show up that afternoon was Wanda. She was such an odd sort, with her unwashed hair and mismatched clothing. She acted so strangely at times I wondered if she was on drugs.

"The other lady who lived with her must have moved out," Jen had said to me earlier. "Or died."

I shrugged. "Who knows? But I don't like her."

My sister said she was probably lonely, and continued to invite her to the get-togethers. Usually Wanda didn't come. It was too bad she did that day.

Jen invited her to have a seat on the sofa, and Wanda sat there like a bug on a rug while my sister attempted to make conversation. Jen talked about the weather. There was no response. She showed Wanda some new material she had bought. The woman looked at it but said nothing. Jen asked her if she'd like something to drink, and Wanda silently shook her head. My sister cast around for some way to break through the stone wall.

"Hey, Wanda!" she said brightly. "Come and see what we have on the balcony!"

I followed her out to the bird's box and Wanda trailed behind. Jen picked up her little feathered friend.

"Here," she said to Wanda, "put out your hands and I'll let you hold him."

I'm sure Jen thought that holding such a tiny, helpless creature would have the effect of drawing Wanda out of her shell. But nothing of the sort happened. For a long moment, Wanda stared unblinkingly at the bird nestled trustingly in her palm. Then, without any warning, she stepped closer to the railing and hurled the poor thing onto the concrete below.

In utter shock, Jen and I stared down at the ground, looking for any sign of movement from the bird. But it lay still.

Jen flushed crimson and fired an angry look at Wanda.

"What did you do that for?"

Wanda shrugged and gazed back without emotion. "I felt like it," she said in flat voice.

"How could you do such a thing to a poor, defenseless creature?" My sister's jaw tightened as she fought to keep control of herself.

When the woman didn't answer, Jen took a steadying breath. "Please leave our apartment! Now!" She took firm hold of Wanda's arm, showed her out and slammed the door. Jen's eyes filled with tears.

"How could anyone be so cruel?!"

She managed to pull herself together before the others showed up that day, but she never again invited Wanda up to our place. That's not to say she totally ignored the strange woman. She was always polite to Wanda whenever we saw her in the halls, and one time even took her a plate of cookies. But friends? Not by any stretch of the imagination.

By the following week my sister was busier than ever as she helped her grandfather with the final details of moving. She didn't neglect her work with the Legion of Mary, either, visiting homes in the neighborhood with the same drive she brought to everything else.

If she was, as she claimed, going through a dry period in her prayer life, it wasn't obvious to me or anyone else. It seemed to bring her great joy doing things for others. When I asked her once how she managed to accomplish so many good things, she told me it had turned out to be true what she learned at that very first youth meeting.

"It *is* possible to experience the power of God—through prayer, Scripture reading and receiving the sacraments of Reconciliation and the Eucharist. There's no way, Tony, I could do these things by my own power."

And she certainly did a lot. I wonder if she sensed she didn't have much time.

31

In October we lost Poppa Frank.

For weeks, he had been in the hospital with heart problems. Jen and I went to see him as often as we could. It was difficult seeing him lie pale and still in the hospital bed, but his whole demeanor brightened as soon as his "little Jenny" walked in. For her part, she put on a brave face for him, saving her tears for when she was at home with no one but me around. At the hospital she would sit by his side, telling him about everything going on in her life.

One time she teased him that he was just trying to get out of doing his work.

"Ah, well," he answered with a tired smile. "If I can't work, I can suffer, and that's just as good when it comes to doing the will of God."

He told us we should have boundless trust in God's love, that God will surely respond to our faith in him. Jen clung tightly to his hand and to every word he uttered, struggling mightily with the harsh reality of her grandfather's rapidly declining health.

His funeral took place on a Saturday morning. Everyone said how appropriate it was that he passed away during October—the month dedicated to the Rosary. Frank always talked about Mary. He said Mary's only vocation was, and still is, to lead others to her Son. That Jesus came to us through his mother, so we shouldn't be afraid to go to him through her. That Mary had spent thirty years in the company of her Son, so Jesus must have taught her things about God the rest of us could never imagine.

Like her grandfather, Jen came to depend on her heavenly mother Mary, especially when Frank's passing left a big hole in her heart. Jen still had the rest of her family—her aunt and uncle and cousins—and me, of course. But no one could replace her Poppa.

"We found each other so late," she lamented to Beatrice at the funeral home. "Why would God take him home just when we were getting to know each other again?"

Beatrice brushed away tears from her own eyes. "I guess we'll never know the answer to that till we get to heaven. Frank had complete trust in God, and simply went about doing the work he felt God calling him to do. It sure seems his prayers were answered when it came to finding you. You have no idea how much joy you gave him these past few months. Your grandfather was so proud of you."

Jen wept openly. "I think he cared about me even before he knew who I was, when I was sunk in the depths of sin. I don't know where I'd be now if it wasn't for him coming to my door in the first place. What I will do without him?"

Somehow, Jen managed to keep going after her grievous loss. Every so often, though, she would pause for a moment, thinking of something her grandfather had said.

"Remember, Tony, when he claimed the best thing about dying is that suddenly everyone's saying nice things about you?"

We would laugh—and it helped ease the pain just a bit.

Although it was difficult, life went on. By the end of the month we began to pack our things in preparation for the move. Almost every day, Jen brought empty boxes home from work. We used what we needed and took the extras down to Leona's.

"Antonia!" Lee exclaimed one day when I showed up with yet another box. "You've brought me so many, I think you want me to pack Mama!"

"Packrat Mama," said Lucy.

Leona chuckled. "She sure is! I've been complainin' about how much stuff she has. How much we *both* have. I think we need to do some parin' down!"

"Don't forget to save any old clothes you don't want for Jen. She's going to use her spare time, once we're settled in, to get ready for another show."

"What spare time? That girl's right busy!" Leona laughed, cutting a slice of apple pie for me. "Now you jes' set yourself down and eat this while I look through my clothes."

That was an offer too good to refuse. It was getting late when I ran back upstairs to start our supper, completely forgetting the clothing Leona wanted to send with me. I unlocked our door and rushed in. Then, sucking in my breath sharply, I stopped dead. There was a man pawing through our packed boxes.

Weasel! I knew we hadn't seen the last of that loser.

"What are you doing in our apartment?" I demanded.

The guy spun around and I got the shock of my life. It wasn't Weasel.

"Well, hiya, Tony," Kenny said. The familiar smile spread slowly across his face but I no longer found it attractive.

"What are you doing here?" Then I noticed his left hand had something shiny dangling from it. "Hey! That's my grandmother's necklace! Give it to me!"

"Well, isn't that nice? Your grandmother's necklace, huh? It ought to be worth something, don't you think?"

"Kenny, please! It means a lot to me." I tried to speak more calmly. "Please give it to me."

He began to walk toward me and I noticed his eyes glittered strangely. I took a nervous step backward.

"Aren't you glad to see me?" he asked. "It's been quite a while."

He stopped a few feet away and his gaze wandered over me. I shifted uneasily.

"Well, now." There was a smirk on his face. "I was just thinking how much I used to like those kisses you gave me."

Ugh. That was something I didn't want to remember. Kenny had always expected a show of affection for any little thing he did, or thought he did, for me. Quite a contrast to Jules, who never pressured me for anything.

As Kenny came closer, I took another step back. The late-afternoon light streaming through the open back door cast a menacing yellow gleam to his smile. He held the necklace high in the air and let it swing from his fingers.

"So, whatcha gonna give me for it?"

I pretended I didn't know what he was talking about.

"It's really not worth very much, Kenny. It only has sentimental value."

"Oh, really? Looks like a diamond to me. That ought to be worth a *little* something!"

Suddenly his right hand snaked out and grabbed my wrist.

"Ouch! You're hurting me!" I tried twisting from his grip and pushing against him with my free hand. But Kenny was too strong for me. He held on tightly and leaned closer, intending to kiss me, but I turned my head and his lips landed on my ear. He angrily hauled me away from the wall.

"So now you think you're too good for me?" His breath was hot in my face. "You sure *used* to like those kissing games!"

Abruptly, he changed the subject. "You got any money?"

My wrist throbbed in his grasp. Trembling, I pointed to the bedroom with my other hand. "My purse is in there. If you let me go, I'll give you everything I've got."

I knew that was the wrong thing to say as soon as the words were out of my mouth. How stupid of me! My money *and* me in the bedroom. He would have what he wanted no matter what I did. I began crying as he pulled me towards the bedroom.

At that very moment, the apartment door opened wide and I heard Leona's voice. "Yoo-hoo, Antonia! You forgot the...Hey! What's goin' on here?"

With Lee's build, she could pass for a linebacker. When she drew herself up to her full height and charged Kenny, he made the wise decision to beat a hasty retreat. I wasn't about to let him get away so easily. As he dodged behind a pile of boxes to keep them between himself and what he must have seen as a crazed Amazon, I toppled the pile.

It caught him off balance, and only with great difficulty did he get his feet back under him. He lost his grasp on the necklace and it fell to the floor as he vaulted over the tumbled boxes. Kenny vanished out the door and we could hear his footsteps clattering down the stairs.

Leona brought me tissues and glasses of water, and fussed over me until I calmed down.

"You oughta call the police!" she said.

I shook my head and showed her the necklace clenched in my sweaty hand.

"He didn't get what he wanted." I didn't tell her the rest of the sordid tale, only adding, "Not much longer, Lee, and we'll be out of here. I can't wait!"

She nodded. "I know. It's not a good place for a young gal like you. I'm glad to be leavin' too."

"If only he hadn't been able to climb up the balconies so easily! I hate this place!" I shivered. At that moment, our building seemed almost diabolical.

Of course, I told myself after Lee had gone home, I was just upset.

32

I guess most days which end in tragedy start out normally enough, and that day was no exception. My sister and I spent the afternoon of Wednesday, the eighth of November, running errands—like returning library books and filling out change-of-address cards—in preparation for the big move on the weekend. Throughout the day the thermometer barely nudged above freezing and there were periods of torrential rain.

Jen complained about being thoroughly chilled by the time we returned to the apartment.

"Sure hope the weather is better than this on Saturday. Who would think it would be so cold this early in November? And how come we don't have an umbrella?" Jen toweled off her hair.

I shook water droplets from my coat. "Wasn't it you who asked why we should pay good money for a new umbrella? Didn't you tell me you'd pick one up at the Salvation Army?"

Jen looked a little sheepish. "Guess I never did. Sorry."

She chopped onions, broccoli and red pepper as I packed the last of my books and set the table. After that I leaned against the kitchen counter to watch her sauté the vegetables. When she began to grate potatoes, I groaned.

"Not potatoes again!"

"This is a new recipe from Irene. It's called *rosti*. She said it's really pretty good."

Jen removed the vegetables from the skillet, poured in more oil and patted in a layer of shredded potatoes. She spread the vegetable mixture over it, added cheddar cheese, and topped the whole thing with more potatoes. A short time later, I noticed her laying a plate upside-down over the skillet.

"What are you doing?"

"The recipe says to flip over the pan so the rosti will fall onto the plate. Then you slide it back into the pan to cook the other side."

With potholdered hands she turned the skillet upside down, shook it and lifted it off. We stared at the plateful of jumbled vegetables and cheese. Where were the potatoes? She peered into the skillet.

"Shoot! The bottom layer's stuck good. Take that spatula there and loosen it while I hold it over the plate."

It missed. The crusty potato layer fell with a *splat* onto the counter. As we stared at the steaming, gooey mess, I heard a snicker from Jen. Then came a chortle and, before I knew it, she was laughing uproariously. She set the pan down and laughed and laughed. Her shoulders shook so much she had trouble scraping everything back into the pan. Even as she plopped the scrambled rosti back on the stove to finish cooking, she was still giggling and trying to get hold of herself.

Yes, I'll always remember how much we laughed. It really brought home to me how much my sister had changed. In the not-so-distant past, she would have hurled a cooking disaster like that one against the wall in a fit of rage. But in recent days, a sense of peace seemed to have taken hold of her, and along with it came a carefree joy which found delight in the most ridiculous of things.

Our eyes still damp with tears of laughter, we somehow managed get the rest of our supper on the table. The rosti turned out to be tastier than it looked. Jen and I talked companionably together and lingered a long time that night over the inelegant entrée.

"What do you think you'll miss least about this place?" I asked her.

"Probably the cockroaches!" she exclaimed. "Did you see them run last night when I turned on the lamp? They were everywhere! How come there's more now than when this place was a mess?"

"You know, I discovered why you can't get rid of them. Remember when you set out boric acid to kill them?" Boric acid was one of those helpful hints she had picked up in the *'It Pays To Be Frugal'* Guidebook. "I was watching a cockroach one day...and as it died, it was laying an egg! No wonder they're the longest-lived insects on earth!"

"We'll have to remember to keep taping those boxes closed as we pack them. Don't want to take any roaches along to Poppa's house." She sighed. "I guess I'll have to stop calling it 'Poppa's house.' But it'll always seem that way to me."

She looked across the table at me. "I hope you know that Aunt Jill thinks of you, too, as part of the family. I may be her niece, but you're my sister."

"I know," I said. "She's really nice. And her family, too. But I kind of have a family of my own now." I felt my face grow warm as Jen scrutinized me closely.

"What's this?" She flashed a big grin. "Have you and Jules been talking about your future together?"

"Maybe." I smiled back, keeping my voice light. "His mother already treats me like part of the family."

"Well, you're lucky. Jules is a terrific guy. He's going with you to your RCIA classes, isn't he? Is he going to be your sponsor?"

I nodded and started to say something else, when all of a sudden there was a deafening *crash!* The whole apartment shook, and Jen and I jumped up at the same time. A tangle of dark, dripping branches was protruding through a gaping hole in the back wall and ceiling. Wet leaves, pieces of brick and chunks of plaster kept dropping to the floor.

I tried to calm my racing heart and rushed to help Jen pull packed boxes away from the damaged wall.

"I'd better call Mona." Jen straightened and took a deep breath. "Though she probably heard the crash from down there."

It didn't take long for Mona to arrive.

"All the rain musta loosened the roots of that blasted tree!" Mona fumed, a look of utter disgust on her pinched face. "Long time ago, I told the city they should cut it down. Now look! Well, blast it all, ya can't stay here! It's gonna get cold real fast in this place. Not to mention wet."

"I already called Leona," said Jen. "We're going to bunk down there tonight."

As Mona strode out, we heard her grumble, "Hope this doesn't cost me my job."

Jen and I looked at each other.

"Her job?" I said in surprise. "Do you think the owners will blame her for what's obviously not her fault?"

"They just might," muttered Jen as she began selecting what she wanted to take to Leona's.

I made several trips up and down the stairs. I wasn't about to leave my books behind, and I took many of my clothes and, of course, my jewelry box. Jen took only her sewing box and a few other things. Late that evening, the four of us sat around Leona's kitchen table, eating banana cream pie and discussing the disaster.

All of a sudden I remembered something.

"Oh, no! I forgot my makeup!"

They all laughed. "Now, that *is* a disaster!" Jen said.

"A young, pretty girl like you doesn't need no makeup," Lee declared, but I was already out the door.

I could hear Mama calling after me, "Just wait till you have time zones on your face like me!"

I took the steps two at a time until I got to the first landing. There I stopped and sniffed the air. Something smelled funny. I flew up the second flight of stairs and immediately turned and flew back down again.

"Jen!" I screamed. "Smoke! There's smoke upstairs!"

Jen rushed out of Leona's apartment into the hallway. Already the acrid smell was stronger.

Jen shouted, "Lee! Call 9-1-1 and get Mama out!" She was already heading down the first-floor hallway, pounding on doors. I ran to help her.

Bobby threw open his door.

"Fire!" I yelled. "Go help Mona get her husband out!" Jen sprinted past me to the stairs.

"Where are you going?" I shrieked.

"The kids! Gotta get the kids out!"

I ran up the steps after her to the second floor which was already hazy with smoke. We burst through Dolores's partly-open door. The desperate mother was holding a wailing baby in her arms and trying to shuffle along with two howling boys clinging to her legs.

Jen yelled, "Get out! Now!"

Dolores was panicky. "*Dios mio!* I can't find my Nina!"

"I'll find her! Tony, help her with the kids!"

"Jen!" I began to cough as the smoke thickened. "You gotta get out!"

"Go!" she hollered, throwing around blankets and pillows in her search for the child. "Get down to the floor where you can breathe! Dolores—go! I'll find Nina! I promise!"

I grabbed the boys' hands and Dolores reluctantly followed. Crouching low, we made our way to the staircase and quickly ran down. Out on the front sidewalk a crowd was gathering.

I spied Leona and Lucy and shouted at them to follow me around to the back. In the dark alley next to the upended tree roots, we huddled miserably together in the cold and drizzle. Leona took the baby from Dolores and rocked him until he quieted. The little boys kept shrieking. Numbly, we all stared at the smoke billowing from Melvin's windows and the hole in the roof.

Suddenly we saw a shadowy figure emerge, coughing, onto Dolores's balcony. Dolores screamed, *"Mi bebe! Nina!"*

The child had a stranglehold on Jen's neck. We raced over to the building as Jen pried Nina's arms loose and dangled the child over the balcony railing. At that moment, Bobby appeared beside me and yelled up at Jen, "Go ahead! I'll catch her!"

The little girl dropped safely into his arms. I heard sirens wailing in the distance as Dolores, rain mingled with tears on her face, grabbed her little one from Bobby and hugged her tightly.

"Jen!" I called up to her. "Climb down the balconies!"

"Where's Wanda?" she hollered back.

I spun around and searched desperately through the throng of faces for Wanda. She wasn't there.

"Jen, come on! It's getting worse! Climb down!" I sounded hoarse against the roar of the fire.

Jen coughed and yelled again. *"Where is Wanda?!"*

Her voice was muted amidst the crackling flames, like it came from the depths of a cavern.

"She wasn't in front," Bobby said to me. "I just came from there."

"Have you seen Wanda?" I shouted to Leona. She shook her head.

I looked up again at Jen. She had pulled off her sweater and tied it over her nose and mouth. A thick cloud of smoke hid her for a moment and then cleared enough for us to see her once more.

In a muffled voice, she called down, "I'm going back to get her!"

"Jen! No!" I hurled the terrified words into the black night.

Pulsing blue lights stabbed through the dark as police cars careened into the alley. Frenzied shouting came from the crowd, and over the commotion I heard Lee's strong voice begging me to come away from the building. But I didn't budge from where I stood staring upwards in anguished horror. Sobbing, I screamed at the empty balcony.

"Jen! No! NO! JEN! JENNNNN!"

33

If that was where Jen's story had ended, it would have been almost too much to bear. Though years have passed since the tragedy, the pain of it remains seared like a scar on my soul. In the last few months of her life, my sister had found her greatest joy in the giving of herself to others. Yet after that terrible night, the small spark of faith she had helped enkindle in my heart was nearly extinguished.

I was to find out, however, that Jen still had one last gift to give me.

Of the days following the fire, I have little memory. Time itself seemed to be out of order. Every second lasted an eternity— yet hours would pass in a flash. In my stupor, others had to push and prod and guide me along.

The funeral was held, of course, at St. Therese's. As Jill gently took my hand and led me into the front pew, my head ached in muddled confusion. I found it impossible to keep focused as the funeral Mass began. My mind went reeling back to the previous evening's wake service. There, an elderly man had approached me.

"Are you Jennifer's sister?" he asked.

I had never seen the man before. I stared dully at him as he continued, "I wanted you to know how sorry I am. I thought the world of your sister. She and a young fellow came to my door one day and invited me to church. I put them off that first time, but they came again. Their persistence was why I came back to the sacraments. I hadn't set foot in church for over fifty years."

Tears flowed down over his white beard but he didn't seem to notice. "Your sister told me there was nothing I'd done that God couldn't forgive me for. She talked about God's love and mercy and said that if God could forgive her, he could forgive anyone. I'm so grateful I was able to put myself right with God again. I just wanted you to know that." He shook my hand awkwardly and stepped away.

After he left, a young couple came over. The woman smiled shyly, saying, "We heard what that man said. Your sister came to our door, too. It was because of her we got our marriage blessed and our children baptized. Every time Jennifer would see us in church, she'd greet us like old friends." Her face crumpled and she gripped her husband's hand. "We're so sorry about what happened. Please know we'll be praying for you."

Others with similar stories came by. I didn't recognize any of them. How did Jen know so many people?

At last, Leona arrived at the funeral home and I sagged against her.

"You okay, hon?" she asked. I shook my head and my tears spilled over. She put her arms around me.

"Antonia, Jennifer's in a better place."

I really wished I could believe that. "But, Lee...why? Why Jen? And for someone like Wanda?"

She shook her head sadly. "I can't imagine any greater love than layin' down one's life for another. *Especially* for someone like Wanda. I don't know the reason why. Nobody does. I only know we have two choices when something awful like this happens. We can be mad at God and turn away from him, or we can hold onto hope and go on trustin' him in spite of everything."

"I don't know," I sobbed. "How can I do that? First my father, then my mother. And now Jen. How can I go on without Jen?"

"You can—and you will. You can get through anything with the grace of God and the help of others. Jes' look at all the people he's put into your life to help you!"

I thought of her words again as I sat in the pew with Jill's family. When I had first arrived at the church that morning, I was amazed to see all the people who came for the funeral. Beatrice, Carlos, Rosalie and a score of Legion of Mary members filled the section reserved for them. Jules and his family took up an entire pew and Milo was there with the youth group. There were many others I didn't recognize. Where had they all come from? A year ago we didn't know anyone.

Those from our building—Bobby, Dolores, Leona and Lucy—were sitting together. Melvin had not survived. Inspectors found it was not the falling tree which had started the fire, but faulty wiring in Melvin's apartment. With no fire stops in the old walls, the flames spread rapidly through the third floor and much of the second before being extinguished. Jen's body had been found near Wanda's.

During the homily, Jill passed me a tissue and I tried again to concentrate on the priest's words.

"The Jennifer I came to know," he was saying, "was a young woman who fell in love with God. I was her teacher and confessor, and I saw her grow in her faith by leaps and bounds over the past year. I've never met anyone who threw herself so totally into the hands of Our Lord like she did."

Yes, I nodded desolately. That was Jen. Once she began something, she held nothing back.

"At the moment Jennifer encountered the person of Jesus Christ and made the decision to follow him," the priest said, "she died to herself and began to live for him. She seemed to grasp in a short time what some people never learn in a lifetime. That our lives are meant to be filled with God's love and with good deeds done for others. That we are the hands and feet of Christ in this world. That there is nothing more important, more needed, than to bestow the same gracious love and mercy on others that God bestows on us."

I thought of the candles at the Easter vigil, each one lighting another until all the darkness was driven away.

The priest continued, "Jennifer came to believe in the power of prayer in her life. I think these words, addressed to young people by Pope John Paul II, describe her experience."

From a paper he held in his hand, he read, "*Prayer can truly change your life. For it turns your attention away from yourself and directs your mind and your heart toward the Lord. If we look only at ourselves, with our own limitations and sins, we quickly give way to sadness and discouragement. But if we keep our eyes fixed on the Lord, then our minds are filled with hope, our minds are washed in the light of truth and we come to know the fullness of the Gospel with all its promise and life.*'"

He looked up again at us. "It was through prayer, Scripture and the sacraments that Jennifer began to experience a hunger for God, a desire to put him at the very center of her life—

and that transformed everything else for her. She believed what St. Paul wrote in his letter to the Galatians. He said, 'It is no longer I who live, but it is Christ who lives in me.'

"Every day she could, Jennifer came to Mass during the week—"

She did? She had never said a word about it to me.

"—because, she told me once, she couldn't live without the Eucharist, that the strength she drew from the Bread of Life was what enabled her to reach out to others the way she did."

I remembered a conversation I had had with Jen shortly after her grandfather's death.

"Tony," she told me, "I know now that *everything* I have comes from God. And anything worthwhile I may accomplish in my life has been entirely by his grace. When it's time for me to go home to him, I go with empty hands."

Perhaps others thought it strange, but I had insisted Jen be buried with her hands empty, palms facing up towards heaven. That's what she would have wanted.

"We shouldn't be surprised," the priest said, "that, in the end, Jennifer gave her life to try to save another. For her, it was a natural outgrowth of the radiant charity the Holy Spirit infused into her heart. It is certainly a double tragedy for us, burying Jennifer so soon after her grandfather. But God doesn't promise to shelter us from the crosses, toils and disappointments of life. He only gives us his power to overcome our trials and never lose hope—a hope that's grounded in the resurrection of Jesus Christ, in his triumph over death.

"Surely, Our Lord has greeted our beloved Jennifer at the gates of heaven with, 'Well done, my good and faithful servant! Enter into the joy of the Lord.'"

On the way out of church after the funeral, a boy from the youth group stopped me.

"Tony, I wanted to tell you how much Jenny helped me when my parents divorced," he said. "She spent tons of time just listening to me talk. And if I needed extra cheering up, she brought me chocolate-chip cookies!" He pressed a cassette into my hand. "Here. I thought you might like a copy of Father's homily today."

After the interment, a luncheon was provided in the church hall, so it was late in the afternoon before I could escape.

Jules offered to give me a ride, as did Jill, but I told them both I needed to be alone. Before long, I found myself riding a bus aimlessly around and around the city streets. Huddled into my coat to ward off any intrusion by other passengers, I spent hours staring out the grimy windows. The overcast skies and gray-tinged snow matched my mood exactly. Only as darkness was descending did I finally force myself to get off and walk the final blocks to Frank's house—my new home.

I held my collar close around my neck while the snow, early for the season, gusted against me from all directions. I concentrated solely on putting one foot in front of the other, steeling myself against any unnecessary thoughts. Desolation hovered over and around me, and I was afraid if I tried to think, it would swoop in and carry me off. To where, I didn't know—but I was sure if that happened I'd *never* find my way back.

I dragged my feet around the final corner and raised my head to look for the house. It was difficult to see anything in the blustery snow. Maybe, I thought, the house also had been suddenly snatched from me. But it didn't really matter. Nothing seemed to matter any more. Perhaps my sister had found a faith which was firm and unmovable as a rock, but I no longer knew what to believe.

I lifted a heavy hand to shield my eyes from the snow. There, halfway down the block, I saw the house. A brightness came from the front porch light being on. I stopped, squinting my eyes in the gathering dusk.

Was someone on the porch? I could almost swear I saw someone standing in the glow from the light. It sort of looked like…

It looked like Jen! It did look like Jen, but it couldn't be! I blinked hard and brushed my hair back out of my eyes, trying to figure out what I was seeing.

How could Jen be standing on the front porch? I shook my head. I must be imagining things. Yet…

"Tony!"

I could have sworn I heard my name whipping off the tail of the wind. I strained to see, but it was impossible to make anything out clearly in the swirling snow. Was that really a person, veiled in white flurries—and could it possibly be Jen? I began to run.

"Jen!" I screamed.

"Tony, hurry on—" The words seemed to echo from an unfathomable distance.

"—it's beautiful here…"

I cried out as my feet pounded the wet sidewalk. Tears blinded me, and my breathing rasped so loudly in my ears I couldn't be certain what I was seeing or hearing. Just as I reached the house, my shoe caught in a crack in the concrete and I pitched forward onto my knees. For an instant, everything reeled as pain shot through me. I sucked in a quick, agonized breath and looked upwards at the porch.

There was, in the brightness of the light, only a spiraling whirlwind of snowflakes.

I really did know she wouldn't be there. My sister was gone. All the time my overwrought imagination had been trying to undo everything which had been done, deep inside I had known Jen could not be standing on that porch.

Down, down onto the hard, snow-dusted ground I sank, feeling hollowed out by a horrible aloneness. My fingers clawed at stiff blades of grass while torrents of grief began to pour from me. I thought I had already wept every tear which could possibly be wept, yet more kept coming. Wave after wave washed over me, crashing against the seawall of my resistance, my "No!" to what life had handed me.

Before long it became a flood, and it turned out to be just what I needed—a cleansing flood, washing away whatever had constricted itself around my heart. It was at that very moment the cloud of anguish began, just a little, to lift.

I don't know how much time passed before I was able to move. Eventually I noticed I was getting wetter and colder by the minute. Ignoring my aching knees, I hauled myself stiffly onto my feet and stumbled up the steps onto the porch.

Next to the front door I saw a newly-installed plaque. I paused a moment to look at it.

"*Mary's House,*" it read. "*In loving memory of the Hollander Family.*"

Even in my pain, I had to admire how appropriate it was. Mother Mary's house, for sure. Wasn't it just like a mother to see to it that both Jen and her grandfather made it safely to their eternal home?

Inside, I could hear Leona upstairs conversing with her mother. Still feeling raw emotionally and not up to talking to anyone yet, I began wandering the first floor. Drop cloths, ladders and paint cans were everywhere. In the kitchen I saw new, gleaming cabinetry with spacious counters. When Rosalie cooked there now, she would have nothing to complain about. On the floor, the steel sink lay on its side. The dishwasher, also, was waiting to be installed.

Like a bolt of lightning from the blue, the thought of Mona came into my mind.

I had heard that the burned-out apartment building was slated to be torn down, and that she and her husband were staying at the city shelter. But Mona was handier with a pipe wrench than most men I knew. Wouldn't it be good to have a repairman—excuse me, a repair*woman*—around Mary's House when the need arose? I poked my head into the bedroom off the kitchen. It had its own bath. Perfect!

Another idea reeled out like thread from a spool. I knew Dolores and her family had gone to live with relatives, but what about Bobby? Wouldn't the basement ceiling be high enough to hang a trapeze?

Little by little, a spark was being rekindled in me. I began wondering if there really *was* a plan for my life—something that only I could do. Maybe I, too, like the house, was a work in progress. Maybe both of us had been given a new direction in life.

With a new, tiny feeling of hope breaking in around the edges of my grief, I wandered into the dining room. The chairs and the long table, draped in plastic, looked ghostly. The memory of Thanksgiving dinner in that room with my sister brought a fresh sting of pain. Yet I was beginning to believe that I could, in fact, accomplish the task given to me. I could run Mary's House—with the help of God, of course. And his mother. Not to mention Leona and Mona and Bobby...

One last room was still waiting to be visited. Pulling aside the plastic sheet strung across the doorway, I stepped into the living room. When I flipped on the switch, floor lamps bathed everything in a warm glow. Everything was exactly as I remembered. Frank had left not only the furniture but all his books for the new residents. I could almost feel his gentle presence there.

And then, on one of the end tables, I saw the sewing box.

Leona, I knew, must have brought it with her. I shook my head, marvelling. Unlikely as it seemed, Jen's grandmother's sewing box had come full circle.

I walked slowly over to the fireplace. On the hearth sat Frank's lovely statue of the Blessed Mother, her hands downwards in a gesture of dispensing God's graces for the world. A veritable storehouse of graces—and maybe miracles, too.

My attention was caught by something around the statue's neck. I reached out, lifted off a worn ribbon and stared at a Miraculous Medal gleaming golden in my hand. It looked like Jen's. The ribbon had a knot in it at the exact place she had tied it one day when it broke. Jen never took the medal off. Hadn't I had seen it on her just before the casket was closed?

I tried my best to remember but, in the end, just couldn't be certain. I had to smile when I considered what Mama Lucy would say about the whole business.

"That's quite a conflubberance, isn't it?"

I found myself thinking back to the very first time Frank and Beatrice had knocked at our door. With their knock, Jen began a journey which changed not only her life, but mine and others as well. It became for her a magnificent adventure—that of discovering God and his plan for her life. By the end of the journey she had found not only peace of heart, but more joy than either of us had ever imagined.

Hers had been an ordinary life, yet it had been made extraordinary by the power of God.

This, then, is my tribute to an extraordinary sister.

Thank you, Jen.

Endnotes

For further reading about God's unending love for us:
Deus Caritas Est (God is Love), encyclical of Pope Benedict XVI, 2005.
From the introduction of encyclical: *"We have come to believe in God's love:* In these words the Christian can express the fundamental decision of his life. Being Christian is not the result of an ethical choice or a lofty idea, but the encounter with an event, a person, which gives life a new horizon and a decisive direction." Pope Benedict XVI

For further reading about prayer:
Opening to God: A Guide to Prayer, Thomas H. Green, Ave Maria Press, Notre Dame, Indiana, 1977.

Living Prayer, Mother Angelica, Servant Books, Ann Arbor, MI, 1985.

The Ways of Prayer: An Introduction, Michael Francis Pennock, Ave Maria Press, Indiana, 1987.

Page 21
"God heals the broken-headed."
Referring to Psalm 147:3: "He heals the brokenhearted, and binds up their wounds."

"Ask and you shall perceive, knock and the store shall be opened unto you." Referring to Matt 7:7: "Ask and you shall receive, knock and the door shall be opened unto you."

Page 23
"...twelve stars are mentioned in the book of Revelation..."
Revelation 12:1: "A great portent appeared in heaven: a woman clothed with the sun, with the moon under her feet, and on her head a crown of twelve stars."
For more information about the Miraculous Medal, go to www.amm.org

Page 26
"The Bible says that we are all children of God..."

1John 3:1: "See what love the Father has given us, that we should be called children of God; and that is what we are."

Page 30
"If you pray, God will listen. Period."

Jeremiah 29:12: "When you call upon me and come to pray to me, I will hear you."

"Prayer is talking in a personal way with God. If you don't have an intimate relationship with him, it wouldn't matter if you said dozens of prayers. They'd just be empty words."

"If our hearts are far from God, the words of prayer are in vain." [Catechism of the Catholic Church: paragraph #2562]

Page 30
"...St. Therese of Lisieux..."

St. Therese was a cloistered Carmelite nun who died in France in 1897 at the age of 24. Known as the "Little Flower," she is one of the most widely admired saints of contemporary times. Her "little way" of holiness can inspire us to do everything, even the smallest things, out of love for God. For more information, go to www.littleflower.org

Page 31
"Scripture tells us 'we don't know how to pray as we ought.'"

Romans 8:26: "Likewise the Spirit helps us in our weakness; for we do not know how to pray as we ought..."

"Prayer is a gift..."

"Only when we humbly acknowledge that 'we do not know how to pray as we ought,' are we ready to receive freely the gift of prayer." [Catechism of the Catholic Church: paragraph 2559]

Page 33
"He told us that ignorance of Scripture is ignorance of Christ."

Taken from the words of St. Jerome, 342-420 A.D., who knew the Scriptures better than most, having translated most of the books of the Old Testament from the Hebrew language

Page 38
"Scripture says that nothing unworthy shall enter heaven!"

Ephesians 5:5: "Be sure of this, that no fornicator or impure person, or one who is greedy (that is, an idolater), has any inheritance in the kingdom of Christ and of God."

194

Pages 40-41

"You know, the part about Christ loving us while we were still sinners?"

Romans 5:8: "But God proves his love for us in that while we were still sinners Christ died for us."

"...I would have noticed the speck in my own eye resembled an awfully large log."

Matthew 7:3: "Why do you see the speck in your neighbor's eye, but do not notice the log in your own eye?"

Page 62

"They're called guardian angels. And we can ask them to protect us."

Matthew 18:10: "Take care that you do not despise one of these little ones; for, I tell you, in heaven their angels continually see the face of my Father in heaven."

Psalm 91:11: "For he will command his angels concerning you to guard you in all your ways."

"Beside each believer stands an angel as protector and shepherd leading him to life."   St. Basil (329-379 A.D.)

"There's even a prayer that goes..."

> "Angel of God, my guardian dear,
> To whom God's love commits me here,
> Ever this day be at my side,
> To light, to guard, to rule, to guide. Amen."
> [Traditional guardian angel prayer]

Page 70

"I had such a feeling of peace by the time we got done."

John 14:27: "Peace I leave with you, my peace I give to you. I do not give to you as the world gives."

Page 71

"Our only need is for God. When that need takes over our life, all other things fall into place."

Matthew 6:33: "But strive first for the kingdom of God and his righteousness, and all these things will be given to you as well."

Page 73

"The priest talks about God and how we can know he exists..."

"When he listens to the message of creation and to the voice of conscience, man can arrive at certainty about the existence of God, the cause and the end of everything."
[Catechism of the Catholic Church: paragraph #46]

Page 88

"Carlos told me the Mass is at the center of their faith as Catholics..."

"The Eucharist is the heart and the summit of the Church's life, for in it Christ associates his Church and all her members with his sacrifice of praise and thanksgiving offered once for all on the cross to his Father..."

[Catechism of the Catholic Church: paragraph #1407]

Page 91

"The Legion of Mary..."

Founded in Ireland in 1921 by Frank Duff, the Legion of Mary is the Catholic Church's largest lay apostolate, with over two million active members and 20 million auxiliary, or praying, members in more than 160 countries. The object of the Legion of Mary is the greater glory of God through the spiritual development of its members by prayer, instruction in the Faith and active apostolic work. For more information about the Legion, go to www.legionofmary.org.

To find the nearest Legion of Mary group, call your local diocese.

Page 103

"On the night before he died, he took bread and said, 'This is my body.' And he took wine and said, 'This is my blood.'"

Mark 14:22-24: "While they were eating, he took a loaf of bread, and after blessing it he broke it, gave it to them, and said, 'Take, this is my body.' Then he took a cup, and after giving thanks he gave it to them, and all of them drank from it. He said to them, 'This is my blood of the covenant, which is poured out for many...'"

"...He's the Way, the Truth, the Life..."

John 14:6: "[Jesus said,] 'I am the way, and the truth, and the life. No one comes to the Father except through me.'"

Page 118

"...if you're going to pray, you should first forgive those who've done you wrong."

Mark 11:25: "Whenever you stand praying, forgive, if you have anything against anyone; so that your Father in heaven may also forgive you your trespasses."

Page 119

"And that's what forgiveness is really about, isn't it? Loving others as God loves them..."

"One pardons to the degree that one loves."

Francis de la Rochefoucauld, bishop of Beauvais, France, martyred during the French Revolution

Page 119

"And therein lies the battle, doesn't it?"

"Prayer presupposes an effort, a fight against ourselves and the wiles of the Tempter. The battle of prayer is inseparable from the necessary 'spiritual battle' to act habitually according to the Spirit of Christ: we pray as we live, because we live as we pray."

[Catechism of the Catholic Church: paragraph #2752]

Page 120

"Just pray as you can, and don't pray as you can't."

Words of Frank Duff, founder of the Legion of Mary

Page 127

"Faith don't fall on you out of the sky. You have to live like you do have faith..."

"Faith is never there automatically; it must be lived."

Pope Benedict XVI

Page 131

"... the Sign of the Cross..."

"The sign of the cross...marks with the imprint of Christ the one who is going to belong to him and signifies the redemption Christ won for us by his cross."

[Catechism of the Catholic Church: paragraph 1235]

For further information, see *Sign of the Cross: Recovering the Power of the Ancient Prayer* by Bert Ghezzi, Loyola Press, Chicago IL, 2004.

Page 132

"Prayer enlarges the heart until it is capable of containing God's gift of himself."

Quote from Mother Teresa, founder of the Missionaries of Charities religious order. Mother Teresa was known all over the world for her passionate commitment to the poor and unloved. She saw prayer as the most important thing we do, because from it comes the grace to know God's love and respond to it by loving others. She died in 1997 at the age of 87 in Calcutta, India.

Page 132
"The Bible sez to pray all the time."
>1Thessalonians 5:15: "...pray without ceasing..."

Page 144
"God created her 'full of grace,' as the gospel of Luke tells us..."
>Luke 1:28

"...the words that Mary said to her cousin Elizabeth..."
>Luke 1:47: "...and my spirit rejoices in God my Savior..."

For more about the role of Mary in God's plan of salvation:
Hail, Holy Queen by Scott Hahn, Doubleday Books, New York, 2001.

See also *True Devotion to Mary* by St. Louis Marie de Montfort., Tan Books and Publishers, Rockford, IL, 1941.

Pope John Paul II said of this book, "The reading of this book was a decisive turning point in my life. I say 'turning-point,' but in fact it was a long inner journey...This 'perfect devotion' is indispensable to anyone who means to give himself without reserve to Christ and to the work of redemption."

Page 173
"If I can't work, I can suffer..."

Taken from the words of Edel Quinn, a young Irish woman who spent more than seven years establishing the Legion of Mary across East Africa. Although suffering from tuberculosis, she drew her strength from the Holy Eucharist and a deep prayer life. Depending entirely upon the help of the Blessed Mother, she exemplified the missionary spirit of the Legion until her death in Kenya at the age of 33.

He told us we should have boundless trust in God's love, that God will surely respond to our faith in him.

Quote from Edel Quinn (see above)

That Jesus came to us through his mother, so we shouldn't be afraid to go to him through her.

"This devotion is a secure means of going to Jesus Christ, because it is the very characteristic of our Blessed Lady to conduct us surely to Jesus, just as it is the very characteristic of Jesus to conduct us surely to the Eternal Father...It is a path trodden by Jesus Christ, the Incarnate Wisdom, our sole Head. One of His members cannot make a mistake in passing by the same road."

St. Louis de Montfort, *True Devotion to Mary*, pp. 104, 106-7

Page 185

"I can't imagine any greater love than laying down one's life for another person..."

1John 3:16: "We know love by this, that he [Jesus] laid down his life for us – and we ought to lay down our lives for one another."

Page 186

"...our lives are meant to be filled with God's love, and with good deeds done for others."

1John 3:18: "Little children, let us love, not in word or speech, but in truth and action."

Page 187

"Well done, my good and faithful servant. Enter into the joy of the Lord."

Referring to Matthew 25:21

For further information about the Catholic Faith:
Catechism of the Catholic Church, 1997, Libreria Editrice Vaticana.
(available in bookstores or online at
www.nccbuscc.org/catechism/text/index.htm)

www.jimmyakin.com

Reflection/Discussion Questions

1. Leona told Jen that when you give God time, he himself will teach you how to pray. Do you think that statement is true? Does praying more help you to pray better? Or is *quality* prayer possible without *quantity* prayer?

2. Jen quoted the youth minister as saying, "The only way to bring order into our world is to love properly. And the only way to love properly is to understand how much God loves us, and the only way to understand how much God loves us is to pray." What do these words mean to you?

3. Jen said, "I don't think I really know *how* to pray. I never feel like I'm doing it right." Leona responded, "Oh, I can't imagine there's a wrong way to pray! God's lookin' at your heart and he's jes' happy you're talkin' to 'im!" Do you ever feel like you don't know how to pray? What do you think would happen if you asked God to help you pray?

4. "Prayer can change things—instantly, if God wills it. But usually prayer changes us, and then *we* have the strength to change things. Sometimes, though, prayer simply helps us see things differently, accordin' to God's plan instead of our own. Even if we don't quite understand it all, we have that hope deep inside us which don't quit." Do Leona's words give you more hope in your own prayer life?

5. "And therein lies the battle, doesn't it?" Frank's words, taken from the *Catechism of the Catholic Church*, demonstrate that no one, even a person well-versed in prayer, always finds it easy. What difficulties do you have in prayer, and will any of the suggestions in this story help you to persevere?

**The following prayer is by Frank Duff,
founder of the Legion of Mary.
It is not just for Legion members, but for all
who aspire to holiness in their everyday life.**

Oh, my God, I do not ask for the big things—
the life of the missionary or the monk, or those others
I see around me so full of accomplishment.
I do not ask for any of these; but simply set my face
to follow out unswervingly, untiringly, the common life
which day by day stretches out before me,
satisfied if in it I love You,
and try to make You loved.

Nature rebels against life with its never-ending round
of trivial tasks
and full of the temptation to take relief
in amusement or change.
It seems so hard to be great in small things,
to be heroic in the doing of the commonplace;
but still this is Your will for me.
There must be great destiny in it. And so I am content.

And then to crown the rest, dear Jesus,
I beg you to give me this fidelity to the end,
to be at my post when the final call comes,
and to take my last, weary breath in your embrace.
A valiant life and faithful to the end.
A short wish, dearest Jesus, but it covers all.

From the author of *Grandmother's Sewing Box*— a Divine Mercy story

Windmill Gardens

Looking out the kitchen window at her beautiful garden, the woman is startled to see a teenager emerge from the woods and slip into the old work shed. She tries to help the runaway, yet the girl's past remains a mystery.

The gardener has a few secrets of her own, which may explain why she acts a bit eccentric at times. But she intercedes for her young guest with a heart which has come to know God's love and forgiveness, and so is able to extend mercy to another.

**Finding hope amid the challenges—
the much-anticipated sequel to *Windmill Gardens***

The Christmas Baby

Irrepressible Del is back! In this second novel in the Windmill Gardens series, everyone's favorite gardener has marriage on her mind. As she joins the choir at St. Bernard's parish and makes preparations for Christmas, the question arises again and again, "Just what *is* God's plan for Christian marriage?"

In the midst of all the activity, a young woman finds herself in troublesome circumstances. Before long she will need to make a decision which will change her life forever.

$14.95 plus shipping and handling. Available at
www.BuyBooksOnTheWeb.com
or call 877-BUY BOOK